THE WHISPERERS OF EVERNOW

BOOK ONE - THE KINGDOMS OF EVERNOW

HEIDI CATHERINE

SEQUEL HOUSE

For my mother - a true master of the spoken word

BEFORE THE EVERNOW

" *he Whisperers are whispering. The Whisperers are whispering. The Whisperers are whispering.*"

A thousand hushed voices rose from the arena and swirled in the air, floating down the grassy hill and into the ears of the people in the Valley of the Blessed. They raised their heads at the familiar hum, straining to catch the words. But the whispering was too quiet, sounding more like an ocean than a wave crashing on the shore.

What did King Virtus desire this time? More riches? Another wife? Or perhaps more Whisperers to add to his army of voices?

Never did he whisper for more food for the people. More beds for the hospital. More schools for the children. The King's Whisperers granted his wishes alone.

"*The Whisperers are whispering. The Whisperers are whispering. The Whisperers are whispering.*"

The Conductor swept his sword across the arena, satisfied his army's voices were warm.

The first row of Whisperers fell into silence and knelt on their mats with their heads bowed, the hoods of their robes shading their faces. Once in place, the second row followed, then the third. This continued until the final row were on their knees. One thousand

Whisperers, men and women alike, all waiting to hear the King's deepest wish.

The Conductor raised his sword above his head, his eyes scanning his army, looking for anyone out of place. The Whisperers kept their heads down, perfectly still, barely blinking, scarcely breathing. That sword could remove a head with one swoop. Or two if the Conductor's aim was off.

Satisfied once more, the Conductor brought the sword down slowly, holding it in front of him and resting the tip at his feet. He looked to the balcony at the rear of the arena and nodded at the waiting King. The Whisperers were ready.

King Virtus tilted his head, a subtle movement, yet it was enough.

"The Queen has birthed a son," the Conductor whispered.

The first row of Whisperers lifted their heads and removed their hoods, eyes and ears glued to their leader.

"The Queen has birthed a son," the Conductor repeated.

No noise could be heard as the first row of Whisperers rose to stand on their bare feet.

"The Queen has birthed a son," they whispered.

The second row lifted their heads and removed their hoods. The Conductor nodded and they stood.

"The Queen has birthed a son," the first two rows whispered together.

With each row that joined, the chant became louder, the arena filling with hushed voices, whispering in unison, over and over, as they brought the King's wish to life.

It didn't matter what the Whisperers wanted. It didn't even matter what the Queen wanted. They all knew that soon she would birth a son.

The Whisperers accepted this would happen, just as they accepted their role in life. Their purpose was to whisper. Their power was in their voices. They were no longer individuals, with hopes and dreams and names. They were part of an army, granting wishes for their King.

Except for one Whisperer. He didn't accept any of this.

His name was Jeremiah.

JEREMIAH

THE BEFORE

"*S*urprise!"

Jeremiah opened his eyes and squinted at Micah, who was waving an orange in his face.

"Surprise!" she said again, jiggling her skinny legs in some kind of happy dance. There was nothing she loved more than surprising him, and she'd shout this word like it had magic powers.

"Surprise, yourself!" He snatched the orange from her and brought it to his nose. "Mmm."

"Give it back!" She leaped on top of him, knocking the air from his lungs. The orange rolled to the floor and she pounced after it.

"Where did you get that?" He sat up and rubbed the sleep from his eyes. It'd been years since he'd seen an orange. Micah was only eleven. He doubted she'd ever seen one before now.

"Da gave it to me. Isn't it the most beautiful thing you ever saw in your life? Just look at the color of it! It matches my hair." She held it up next to her head, as if to prove her point, and grinned.

Jeremiah liked his sister's hair, although he didn't see anything particularly special about this color on a piece of fruit. His memory of the taste, on the other hand. *That* was beauty in its finest form.

"Where did Da get it?" He swung his legs out of bed and yawned loudly. "Is there one for me?"

Micah shook her head. "You have to go get yours. There's one for every person over sixteen."

He frowned, forgetting he'd recently had a birthday. His frown deepened when he realized Micah was right, certain that his coming of age couldn't be a good thing.

"It's a special gift from the King," Micah continued. "Ma and Da got one each. They shared Ma's, even though Da didn't want to. He said this one's all for me."

Jeremiah didn't understand. King Virtus never gave out gifts, special or otherwise. He was the sort of king who liked to keep his gifts all to himself, sitting in his palace on the top of Mount Allegro, looking down on all his people.

Micah rolled the orange around in her hand. "Hello, my pretty. Would you like me to eat you now?"

"Where are Ma and Da?" Jeremiah wasn't likely to get much sense out of Micah. Better to speak directly to their parents.

"In the square, eating an orange." She rolled her eyes, far more dramatically than the situation required.

Jeremiah reached for his shoes, put them on, then slipped on the leather cord he liked to wear around his neck. The shell from a walnut dangled from the cord like it was some kind of jewel. To him it was. It was his lucky charm, reminding him of the time he'd found a tree loaded with walnuts and had taken off his shirt and filled it with as many as he could, running home, then returning for more. Feeding his family like that was the warmest feeling he could remember. From that day on, he'd made it his duty to fend for his family, carting goods for market stallholders in exchange for vegetables, tending chickens for farmers for a payment of eggs, or cleaning out chimneys to put a few coins in his pocket.

"You stay here and eat your orange." He ruffled Micah's matted hair. It'd only just grown back since Ma cut it during the most recent lice outbreak. "I'll be back soon."

She grinned, still holding the orange like it was made from gold. Perhaps to her, it was.

"Wash your face and hands before you eat," he said. "You're covered in mud. Your freckles are starting to join up."

She wrinkled her freckly nose and poked out her tongue. He was surprised even that wasn't coated in dirt.

Micah's problem was that she liked to dive headfirst into any experience, more than she liked to worry about cleaning its evidence off her hands or face. She climbed trees, made slingshots, did somersaults off chairs and taught herself to sing the alphabet backward. He once even caught her fast-asleep standing on her head. Her enthusiasm sometimes inspired him, but mostly it just broke his heart. One day she'd grow up enough to realize the life she cherished had nothing to offer her. There was no hope for people in the Valley of the Blessed. It was a ridiculous name. The only thing they'd been blessed with in life was an abundant supply of air.

Jeremiah closed the front door behind him and made his way to the town square, almost tasting the orange already, as he wondered what the catch could be. What could the King possibly want from his people that he hadn't taken already?

He meandered through the crowd looking for the familiar shape of his parents. Perhaps they'd already made their way home. Maybe he wouldn't bother with the orange and would head back too. His stomach growled as if hearing his thoughts.

"Jeremiah! Over here."

It was Tallis, his best friend. He wasn't holding an orange, but he had the same excited look in his eyes that'd shone from Micah's earlier.

The square was teeming with people, all looking far happier than they had on Giving Day when their stockings had been even emptier than their groaning stomachs. That day, which was supposed to be a celebration of the miracle of life, was becoming a little less colorful each year as the enthusiasm of the people waned. There wasn't a lot of joy in giving your child a doll made from straw or your mother a flower that was actually a noxious weed picked from the meadow. Giving Day was becoming a day to dread. It was hard to celebrate the miracle of life when your days were filled with misery.

Jeremiah wondered where all these oranges had come from. And if the King had so many to hand out today, what did he normally do with them when he wasn't in such a generous mood?

"Where have you been?" asked Tallis, slapping him on the back.

"Just at home," he said, not wanting to admit he'd been asleep at this late hour. Sleep was his favorite thing to do after eating. And unlike food, sleep was in plentiful supply around here.

Tallis shook his head, not fooled. "You really should be better looking than this, with all the beauty sleep you get. Although the girls have always found you pretty, I suppose."

Jeremiah punched him playfully on the arm, keen to steer the subject away from girls. He was interested in them, just not in any one of them in particular. He saw this as a good thing. If there was no girl, then there'd be no children. And he couldn't bear the thought of having children only to have to watch them starve.

"So, what's going on?" he asked Tallis. "Micah woke me up making even less sense than usual."

"Ah, so you *were* asleep!" Tallis laughed, bending his wiry frame forward as he clutched at his ribs. "I knew it."

"So, what's going on?" Jeremiah asked again, ignoring his friend's amusement at his expense.

Tallis pulled himself together and cleared his throat. "Everyone over sixteen is getting an orange. It's been going all morning. I thought you were never going to turn up. Nearly came to drag you out of bed myself in case the oranges ran out. All we have to do is complete a simple test."

Right. So, there was a catch. One *simple* catch, which worried him more than if it were a complicated one. Nothing in life was simple.

"What's the test?" He tugged on the walnut shell hanging from his neck, not trusting King Virtus for a moment. His name might have roots in honor and integrity, but his nature most certainly did not.

Never had there been a more selfish king, leaving his people to starve, while his own girth expanded by the hour. He was the fattest king Forte Cadence had ever had. He looked like a kingdom himself.

"Dunno." Tallis shrugged. "You have to look at a couple of paintings and tell them what you see."

Jeremiah raised his eyebrows. "I don't know anything about art, unless you count the drawings Micah does in the dirt with a stick. None of us know anything about art. You sure?"

"That's what everyone's saying." Tallis took a step toward the queue.

"So, what's the test for?" Jeremiah's feet remained planted to the ground.

"Dunno." Tallis shrugged again.

"You don't know much, do you?"

Tallis rolled his eyes. "It's got something to do with something called Whisperers."

"Whisperers?" Jeremiah had never heard of such a thing. It didn't sound like that could be good.

"Come on, let's go line up." Tallis pulled on his arm.

"You go. I might sit this one out."

"You are *not* serious!" Tallis grabbed him this time, practically dragging him to the end of the line. "How can you say no to a sweet, juicy orange?"

"It's not the orange I'm worried about." Jeremiah rubbed his arm as Tallis let go. "It's the test."

"It's just looking at a couple of paintings. What's the harm in that?"

"You mean, what's the point in that?" Jeremiah ran his hands through the mass of dark curls that sprouted relentlessly from his head. "How could that possibly be helpful to the King?"

"Who cares? Maybe he's arguing with the Queen over what painting to hang above their bed." Tallis waved his hand in front of Jeremiah's face. "Are you even listening to me?"

"Sorry." Jeremiah pointed at his parents who were approaching. "I was looking for them earlier."

His parents smiled as they made their way over.

"Where were you, Ma?" he asked, kissing his mother's cheek and tasting orange. She was pregnant, her swollen belly looking like it'd expanded by more than the size of half an orange since he'd last seen her. Life would get even harder once the baby was born. They didn't even have enough for the four of them. How would they cope when they were five? He just hoped it wasn't twins.

"We were taking a rest while we ate our orange," his mother said.

"You gave yours to Micah," he said to his father, who was leaning heavily on Ma's arm for support. Despite her current state, she was far stronger than he was. He looked well today, better than Jeremiah had seen him in days.

"Micah's a growing girl," his father said. "And your mother's orange was a big one, so we shared."

Jeremiah doubted that. His parents were always going without, so he and Micah could have more.

"We'll see you back at home?" His mother squeezed his hand and stepped away. "Enjoy your orange, darling."

Jeremiah nodded. "Micah's at home. I'll join you when I'm done."

As they reached the front of the queue, the sweet smell of oranges hit them and saliva flooded Jeremiah's mouth. He was hungry. *So* hungry. Maybe Tallis was right. What harm could come from looking at a few paintings? His parents certainly looked better for having shared their reward.

Sensing he might still change his mind, Tallis pushed him forward, and Jeremiah stumbled toward a palace worker, sitting behind a table. She was around his mother's age and wore a crisp white gown that would stay that shade for approximately five minutes if she lived in the Valley of the Blessed. Clean clothes were yet another luxury they'd failed to be blessed with.

"Name." The worker didn't even look up from the list in front of her, scanning for a name she'd not yet heard.

He gave his name and she found it, crossing it off with the tip of a feather.

"Left hand." Once again, she didn't look up, instead dipping her feather in an ink pot and grasping his hand firmly to draw an X on the center of his palm. That was one way of making sure nobody cheated the King out of an extra orange. Ink like this took days to rub off.

"There," she said, granting him the privilege of eye contact for the first time, as she pointed to a curtained-off stage that'd been set up behind her.

Jeremiah glanced over at Tallis who was giving his name to another worker at the table beside him.

Tallis looked across at him and mimed eating an orange, an enraptured look plastered to his face.

Jeremiah shook his head and laughed. Sometimes his friend was just like an older, male version of his sister. It was no wonder Tallis and Micah got along so well. Ignoring his instincts screaming at him to turn around and run, he went to the stage.

"Next candidate," he heard someone call from behind the curtain.

A guard nodded at him and he stepped through the curtain with no thought other than the taste of an orange.

The stage area was only small with temporary walls set up on its sides and rear. There was a door in the far wall and he couldn't help wondering what was behind it. The roof was open and sunlight streamed in.

A dark shape to the side of the stage caught his eye and he turned to see a large bowl of oranges on a table. His reward for all this nonsense. In the center of the room was a chair.

"Sit," a palace worker instructed. This one was female too and seemed to have been to the same school of manners as the worker at the desk. She was wearing an identical white gown, only she'd managed to get a large gray mark smudged on it.

Jeremiah smirked as he took his seat, glad that her perfection had been ruined.

"What do you see?" she asked, holding up a painting.

Not being able to find a trick in her question, Jeremiah looked at the artwork.

"I see a circle made up of colored dots." He tilted his head to study it closer.

"What do you see in the dots?" she asked from behind the painting.

A shape emerged as the colors grouped together in his mind.

"A triangle," he said.

The worker put down the painting and picked up another one. She couldn't look more disinterested if she tried. How many of these tests had she done today?

"And what do you see in this one?" she asked in such a monotone that Jeremiah was surprised she wasn't actually asleep.

He looked at it, trying to find a shape or pattern hidden within. This must be where the trickery began, for there was no shape swirling together inside his mind.

"There's nothing. Just dots."

The worker shook her head slightly, seeming to wake herself up, and coughed as she stepped closer to him. "Are you certain? Look again."

"I'm certain." He should've let Tallis go first, so he could tell him what he was meant to see.

"You realize that to lie to the King is a crime punishable by death?" She tapped her foot as she waited for him to try again.

Jeremiah searched the painting, looking for something. Anything! But all he saw was dots.

He shook his head, ignoring the churning in his gut.

The worker picked up a third painting and held it in front of him instead, her eyes wide as she awaited his response. He let out a deep breath, certain he'd see something in this new set of dots.

"And this one?" she asked.

His eyes began to water, he was staring so hard. There had to be a shape in there. Somewhere. Yet no swirling took place. He rubbed his eyes and tried again. Maybe he should've waited until he woke up a little more.

"A star," he said, taking a guess. It could hardly be a triangle again and there was no way it would be a circle made up of circles. A star seemed the next best choice. Or maybe he should've said square…

"You see a star?" The worker looked him directly in the eye. "Are you sure you see a star?"

"No." He shifted in his seat. "A square. I see a square!"

"A square now? Are you sure this time?" Her stare was so intense he felt as if she was burning holes in his retinas.

"No," he said, unable to continue the lie. "I don't see anything again."

"I have one more test for you." The worker studied his face with far greater interest than she had when he'd arrived. He didn't want to be interesting to her! He wanted her to be just as bored as she'd been when he'd arrived.

She put down the painting and picked up a fourth one, holding it for him to see. This one was different from the others. It was still painted with a series of dots, except this one had more detail, seeming more like something to hang on a wall, instead of being used for a test.

"What do you see?" the worker asked.

Jeremiah leaped to his feet and smiled, pleased to be shown a picture that finally made sense.

"Sit down." The worker frowned to show she was serious.

"I see this one!" Jeremiah sat down and tried to stop his leg from jiggling. "It's a painting of a bowl of oranges, just like the bowl over there."

"Are there any differences between them?" the worker asked.

He looked between the two. The same blue bowl with the same floral pattern. The same oranges, piled high.

He shook his head. "It's the same. There are a few less oranges in the real one. Otherwise, everything's exactly the same."

The worker put down the painting and pointed to a door at the back of the stage. For just the smallest flicker of time, he thought he saw sadness brush her eyes.

"That way," she said.

Jeremiah had seen other people leaving from the same curtain they'd arrived through. He didn't want to leave via any back exit.

"Do I get my orange?" he asked, heading for the bowl.

"That way," the worker said again, this time louder as her finger pointed directly to the door at the back of the stage.

"It's okay," he said, plucking an orange from the bowl. "My friend's out this way. I'll just take my orange and leave."

The worker blew a whistle and two guards stepped through the curtain, blocking his path. His orange dropped to the floor as they took hold of his arms.

"Let me sit the test again," he said, his feet planting themselves to the timber stage. "I wasn't looking properly. I'll pass it this time."

"You already passed," said the worker, as the guards dragged him to the door at the back of the stage.

"Tallis!" he cried, not sure what he expected his friend could do for him. The palace guards were known to be brutal. There was very little use in fighting against them.

The worker opened the door and the guards tossed him through it roughly and he landed heavily in the dark. He sat up and rubbed his rear end, aware the sharp pain he was feeling was the least of his problems.

"You passed the test," said a voice.

"Passed?" he asked, looking around for the owner of the voice. "I couldn't see half the paintings."

"What do you see now?"

A light flickered to life and a soft glow filled the small room, revealing the owner of the voice. It was a tall, well-built man, the lines on his face suggesting he was middle-aged. He held a lantern in one hand. In his other, was a sword, which he was leaning on like a walking stick.

"I see you," said Jeremiah, trying not to let his voice quaver.

"And what am I wearing?" The man held the lantern in front of his torso and flashed his yellow teeth in what he seemed to think was a reassuring smile.

Another trick question, obviously. How to answer it correctly this time? Jeremiah decided to stick to the truth. Making guesses had gotten him nowhere earlier.

"A gray robe with a hood," he said, scrambling to his feet.

The man nodded. "Interesting observation, Whisperer."

"Whisperer?" There was that word again. The same one that'd filled him with dread. "What's a Whisperer?"

"You're a Whisperer."

"What do you want from me?" Jeremiah crossed his arms. This man was playing games with him! "When will you release me?"

"I'm not holding you prisoner, Whisperer." The man smiled again.

"Why do you keep calling me that?" Jeremiah took a step toward the door, not the one he'd been thrown through, but another, leading away from the testing room and the guards.

"Because I told you. That's what you are. And you may call me Conductor ... for now."

Jeremiah didn't want to call him anything. He wanted to be far away from here and back at home in bed, wrestling an orange from Micah's hands, not breathing stale air inside this wooden cell.

He tried the door handle, not at all surprised to find it locked.

"If I'm not a prisoner, then why can't I leave?" He tried to steady his breathing, not wanting his fear to creep into his voice.

The Conductor smiled. "Because I haven't made you my offer yet."

There was nothing this awful man could offer him that he would want. Not all the riches in the palace. Jeremiah crossed his arms and waited.

"King Virtus is looking for Whisperers for his new army to protect Forte Cadence. You, I believe, have the necessary skills." The Conductor tapped his sword on the floor, marking the timber with its tip.

The King was very selective about who joined his army. Only the strongest and fastest bothered to apply. A life of fighting and risking your life in exchange for a full belly and a bed. It didn't seem like such a fair deal to Jeremiah, who was neither strong nor fast enough to entertain it as a serious option. Until now.

"How does looking at paintings make me worthy of joining the King's army?" he asked.

"This is a special army, Whisperer."

Jeremiah recoiled. "No, thank you. I'd like to return to my family now. You said I wasn't a pris—"

"Hush!" the Conductor hissed. "You don't understand. It's your family we need to talk about."

Jeremiah's stomach dropped. Not his family. If this vile man dared to threaten his family, he was going to lose it. He eyed off the sword, wondering how to wrestle it from the Conductor's grasp.

The Conductor came closer and reached for him with his index finger, looping it in the leather cord around his neck, which suddenly felt more like a garrote than a lucky charm.

"Your family is hungry. And there's great hunger yet to come. How do you plan to feed them when the winter's here? Walnuts don't grow in winter." He glanced at the walnut shell hanging from the cord. "Many people won't survive. But others … will."

The Conductor dropped his hand and Jeremiah tucked the walnut into his shirt. "My family's fine. We do our best."

He thought of his father and the struggle he'd been having with his lungs. He could barely breathe the spring air without his medicine, which they could no longer afford. And once his mother had the baby, things were only going to get worse. This awful Conductor was right. They'd be lucky to survive the winter. Maybe he shouldn't be so quick to dismiss this offer. Although, how did he know what the Conductor said was the truth? If he left his family and the promise of food was a lie, then they'd have no hope at all without him there to protect them. No, he couldn't leave them.

"I can make sure your family is well-fed, not just this winter, but every winter of their lives. Enough food and medicine for every one of them. Except you have to come with me, Whisperer."

Jeremiah shook his head. "How do I even know that you'd keep your promise?"

"You don't. I'm giving you the King's word. It's up to you if you decide to trust him. Sometimes in life, you have to take a chance. Because a chance is better than no chance at all."

"My family needs me." He crossed his arms. Why should he trust the King? He'd never done a single thing to earn that trust.

"Let me be clear," said the Conductor. "The King is requesting your service and making you a very generous offer in exchange. Are you certain that you wish to turn him down?"

Jeremiah opened his mouth, then hesitated. Was he actually being given a choice here? "My family needs me," he said again, hoping that this was enough.

"Very well." The Conductor set down his lantern and fished a key from the pocket of his robe. "Think about it the next time your stomach is begging you for food."

Jeremiah blinked. His stomach was begging him for food right now. It always was. "I have enough to eat," he lied.

"Come to the palace when you change your mind," said the Conductor, inserting the key in the door.

"I won't be changing my mind." Jeremiah crossed his arms and waited for the door to be unlocked.

The Conductor paused before he turned the key, and looked deep into his eyes, his pale blue irises pooling with a hatred that Jeremiah had trouble understanding.

"It wouldn't be wise to tell anybody about what you saw in here," he hissed. "Understand me, Whisperer?"

Jeremiah nodded furiously, happy to agree to anything, as long as that door opened, and he was allowed to walk through it.

The Conductor turned the key and light poured in as he opened the door.

Jeremiah didn't pause to shield his eyes as he made a break for freedom. At the pace he moved, perhaps he was fast enough to join the regular army after all.

"Tallis!" he called, as he went around the stage to the crowd of people in the square, hoping his friend was okay. "Tallis!"

"Jeremiah! What's wrong?" Tallis was behind him, taking hold of his arms to pin him to the spot. "Where the devil have you been?"

"It's not *where the devil*, it's *who the devil* because I think I just met him myself."

"What—"

"Surprise!" Micah jumped out at him from behind Tallis and giggled.

"Enough of the surprises," said Jeremiah, not in the mood for his sister's favorite game.

"Are you okay, Jeremiah?" asked Tallis, putting an arm around Micah to take the sting out of her brother's harsh tone.

"Come with me and I'll explain." Jeremiah was already walking backward away from the square. He turned and ran, hearing the footsteps of Tallis and Micah kicking up the dirt behind him. He didn't care if they followed or not. He just needed to get as far away as possible from the square and that horrible Conductor.

He led them to a copse of trees beside a field. The same place he'd once found the walnuts. In the distance he could see Mount Allegro, with the King's arena perched on top, its golden oval-domed roof catching the sun and sending colorful rays of light bouncing in all directions. The arena was the jewel of Forte Cadence. This was where the King's army trained and when the wind blew in the right direction, grunts and yelps could be heard floating down the grassy hills to the Valley of the Blessed.

The kingdom of Forte Cadence extended far beyond here, with villages and valleys dotting the many rolling hills. The Valley of the Blessed was the closest to the palace, which had turned out to be more of a curse than a blessing. If the King were to extend his cruelty beyond watching them starve, then surely they'd be the first he'd target. So, they lived in fear as well as hunger. Forte Cadence was the largest of the world's five kingdoms, which made King Virtus the most powerful man alive. Jeremiah often wondered what life was like in other kingdoms. Were the people as hungry as they were? He dreamed of one day escaping Forte Cadence to find out.

Jeremiah ran beyond the first line of trees and collapsed onto the ground, lying on his back as he heaved for breath.

Micah did a tumble-turn and landed next to him, resting her cheek on his chest, which was rising and falling at such a rate her head looked as if she were bobbing on a stormy sea. She giggled.

Tallis sat on his other side, far more serious than Micah.

"What happened?" Tallis asked again, rolling his orange in his hands. "Where's your orange?"

"Forget the bloody orange!" Jeremiah pulled himself up to rest on his elbows, pushing Micah away. "I've got bigger problems than a piece of fruit. I told you it was a trick!"

"Jeremiah?" Micah sat up. Her eyes were wide as she registered this wasn't a time for laughing. "Didn't you pass the test?"

"That's just it, I did pass the test. Turns out it wasn't a test you want to pass."

"Hold on," said Tallis. "They showed you two paintings, right? First a triangle, then a letter B. Or some people saw a letter K."

"No." Jeremiah slapped his own forehead. The letter B or K! That was all he'd had to say to get his orange and avoid suspicion. "I saw the triangle first, then nothing in the second painting. And nothing in the third."

"They showed you a third? Nobody got shown a third!" Tallis ran a hand through his hair as his eyes darted around.

"And a fourth. Although in that one I saw nothing except a bowl of ora—" He stopped himself from saying more by biting his tongue. "Damn it! I wasn't supposed to tell you what I saw. The Conductor told me not to."

"We won't tell anyone," said Micah, drawing her fingers across her grubby lips.

"Who's the Conductor? Jeremiah! Tell us. Are you in danger?" Tallis got up and kicked at the dirt, his arms swinging wildly as he turned in a circle and sat back down.

Jeremiah had never seen his friend like this. It was as if he was a mirror of exactly how he himself was feeling, with too much frustration building inside and no way to let it all out.

"The guards took me to a room and there was a man there. He said to call him Conductor." Jeremiah shivered. "He told me the King is forming a new army of something called Whisperers."

"And he wants you?" Micah put an arm around him and buried her face in his hair. "You can't go, Jeremiah. I need you. We all need you!"

"What if you didn't need me?" Jeremiah lifted her face, so he could look into her eyes. "What if you had everything you needed in life and didn't need me at all. Would that be good?"

"No! It wouldn't be good." Fat tears erupted from the corners of her eyes, sending muddy trails down her cheeks. "Don't go. Please!"

"You're not seriously considering this, are you?" asked Tallis. "We'd never see you again. Ever."

"I told him no," said Jeremiah. "It's okay, Micah. I told him no. I'm not joining any army."

He pulled his sister to his chest once more and looked at his friend over the top of her mess of hair. They locked their gaze and spoke without words, both understanding that he may not have a choice here. The King wanted him. And the King was known for getting what he wanted.

"I'm sorry," said Tallis. "This is my fault. I should never have made you do it. You didn't even want to! Here, take my orange. You have it."

Jeremiah shook his head, pushing the orange away. "Share that with your brothers. You didn't force me. Nobody forced me. I didn't have to do it. I can make decisions for myself."

"I hope so," Tallis said, shaking his head. "I really, really hope so."

"Da is getting sicker," said Jeremiah. "And Ma will have the baby soon and that'll be another mouth to feed."

"Which is exactly why you can't leave us," wailed Micah. "Winter is coming and I hate winter."

"The Conductor promised to feed you every winter for the rest of your life. And get Da the medicine he needs." Jeremiah felt his heart breaking. There was no way to convince Micah this was a good thing. Mainly because it wasn't.

Tallis rested his arm on Jeremiah's shoulder. He was shaking. "Don't do it."

"I won't." Each time he spoke of refusing the Conductor's offer, his words became emptier, hollowing out like a fallen tree under the snow.

"Good," said Micah, tapping her fingers on his chest. "Don't go."

"I won't," he said again, catching Tallis's eye, just as a tear escaped down his friend's face and landed on the ground.

Tallis knew it, just as he knew it, too.

The choice that wasn't a choice at all, had been placed in the palm of his hand and was burning his skin like a coal from the fire. He could continue to hold it, while he and his family turned to ash, or he could throw it into the air and see where it landed.

Maybe the Conductor was right. A chance had to be better than no chance at all. Didn't it?

JEREMIAH

THE AFTER

"Thank you, Whisperer," said the Princess.

Jeremiah nodded. So slight was the movement, it was barely there at all. Long ago, the impulse to speak had gone. Many days had passed since he'd had to bite his tongue to stop the words from escaping his lips.

His words belonged to King Virtus now, purchased for a fee far less than he now knew they were worth. Although, how could he put a price on his family's lives? That fee had guaranteed food in their stomachs for as long as they lived. It would see Micah grow into the woman she was born to be—wild, free, beautiful and brave. He'd had five summers stolen from him since arriving at the palace, which meant his mother's baby would not only have been born, it would no longer be a baby. He wondered if he had the brother he'd sometimes imagined? Or another sister to compete with Micah? It was hard to imagine a small child that he'd never met, living in his house. Did he or she sleep in his bed and sit at his place at the table? It felt strange to think of being replaced like that.

Although, more than he wondered about this mysterious sibling, he wondered if the medicine had cured his father? Da had been sick for so long. It didn't seem fair for a man who was still so far from being old. Hopefully, he'd been cured and was now able to live life as he was supposed to. That alone would make Jeremiah's decision worthwhile.

Whatever had happened to his family since he'd been gone, he'd never know. Not with his body locked inside the palace and his words locked inside his head.

He set down the Princess's breakfast tray, avoiding her eye, despite feeling her gaze upon him. She was watching him closely, as was her habit. He longed to be able to stare back at her and take in the full force of her beauty, rather than the glimpses he caught as he avoided looking at her. The Princess had taken after her mother in looks, which was lucky for her. King Virtus had a face as ugly as his heart. The Queen, on the other hand, was widely known as the most beautiful woman in the kingdom. Although that was only because most people in the kingdom had never seen her daughter.

The Princess wasn't much older than Micah, or perhaps the same age—it was hard to think of Micah as a teenager now—yet life had dealt two very different hands. He wondered how this was decided and by whom. Two females born at roughly the same time, and one gets to wear silk slippers and comb her golden hair like a mane down her back, and the other has to wear the dirt of the village on the soles of her feet and cut her hair for fear of lice. Not that this was the Princess's fault of course. She was no more responsible for the life she'd been born into than Micah was.

"I said, thank you, Whisperer," the Princess repeated. Her voice was gentle, yet insistent, as she tried her best to draw some words out of him.

Jeremiah nodded once more, looking out the window to her left as he waited for her to empty her tray. If the Conductor or one of his guards caught him looking at the Princess, her face would be the last thing he ever saw. Even the small nods he'd begun to give her, were a risk. It just felt so wrong to give her nothing when she insisted on giving him so much.

"Do you like orange juice?" she asked, taking her glass from the tray. He hated oranges and anything to do with them ever since *that day*. But the Princess didn't know that. She seemed to love them almost as much as Micah had.

"It really is delicious." She took a long sip of her juice. "Would you like some?"

She held out the glass to him and he took a step away, wishing she wouldn't do that. His hand went to his throat, as it sometimes did, looking for his lucky walnut shell, even though he hadn't worn it for years.

The Princess wasn't allowed to speak to him, however, that didn't stop her. It never had. She'd been speaking to him for years now, trying to get him to say something back. He wondered if she played this game with the other Whisperers. He'd never seen her try it with any of them. For some reason, he seemed to be her favorite. An unenviable position when he was supposed to have no name.

"I think your name might be Thomas." Once again, he could feel her eyes upon him.

Each day she tried to guess his name, searching for the smallest reaction. He was preparing himself for the day she got it right. For if she learned his name, he'd certainly face the sword. Surely, she must know the danger her games put him in? She just didn't seem to be able to resist talking to him, even if she knew he'd never be able to speak back. Perhaps she was just as frustrated and bored with the monotony of her existence as he was.

Whatever Micah was doing right at that moment, he'd bet anything she wasn't bored. Not that he owned anything to bet. He'd given all of that up the day the Conductor had knocked on his door, asking if he'd reconsidered the King's offer. He'd even given up his lucky walnut shell, looping it around Micah's neck and telling her it was her turn to bring the family good fortune. The Conductor had sniggered from the door and smiled with his lips, his eyes remaining cold and distant.

To think it was the Angel of Death his mother had been worried might pay their family a visit. The Conductor was like the devil himself. You sold him your soul, only instead of sending you to the depths of hell, he took you to a place far worse... the King's palace.

Jeremiah moved the rest of the breakfast items from the tray, careful that they didn't make the smallest noise as they touched the table.

"I won't tell anyone if you talk to me, Thomas." She brushed her hand against his own, the sudden warmth causing him to withdraw from her abruptly. Human touch was even rarer for a Whisperer than speaking. "You can trust me."

This was something else the Princess did each day. She begged him to speak, promising he could trust her. And he did trust her, which was yet another reason he couldn't speak to her. For if he did and someone were to overhear, then she could be punished as well, and that wasn't something he could live with. He wasn't able to protect Micah anymore, but he could do his best to protect Princess Rose.

He'd known her name was Rose long before he met her. Everyone did. It was the right name for her. He thought he'd guess it straight away if he hadn't already known it. She was beautiful and delicate. And also very sharp. Nothing got past her. Just like a real rose, you'd be a fool to admire her for her looks and forget about the sting that could be left if you didn't pay attention. Not that her stings were intentional of course, for her heart was as soft as the center of the sweetest smelling rose. It was her position in the palace that was dangerous, not the person herself.

"My mother's pregnant," she said. "It will be the boy you whispered for."

Jeremiah tried not to listen, not wanting to know any more secrets than he already did. Although as much as he tried, the Princess seemed to want to tell him everything that happened in her life, filling his ears each day with information as if he were some sort of diary. Perhaps it unburdened her to do this. Maybe she assumed his ears were deaf to her words, just as his tongue was mute when not whispering for her father. No, he was certain she knew he was listening.

"I've told you before how surprised I was that Father took so long to whisper for a boy." He heard her set down her glass and he knew she'd be looking at him.

She *had* told him this before. And Jeremiah had been surprised about it as well. The Queen had given the King four daughters, including Rose. Why not whisper for a boy and be done with it? It was widely known that was what the King wanted. There'd been a line of kings named Virtus, stretching back in history as far as anyone could remember. Forte Cadence had never been without one. This was a problem for the current King, given that as the law stood, the throne would be passed to his children in birth order, which made Princess Rose his heir, whether he had a son or not. His son would be fifth in line, no matter what anatomy sat between his legs. Although this didn't seem to stop the King wanting a son.

"I did hear Mother begging him once to let nature take its course," the Princess said to his back. "Not that Father ever pays attention to begging, so I don't know why he listened to her that time."

Jeremiah wanted to point out that he hadn't listened. He'd obviously had enough of waiting and had decided to take matters into his own hands when he'd had them whisper for his precious son.

"My mother's frightened, Thomas," the Princess continued. "I asked her if she's scared she'll have another girl and she said she's scared of having a boy. Honestly, does that make any sense to you?"

It did make sense to him and the sense weighed heavily on his mind. He may not be allowed to speak, but he could see plenty of things the Princess was blind to. Without a change in the current law —which must be impossible or surely the King would already have changed it—there was only one way this baby boy could end up as heir to the throne. Was King Virtus brutal enough to dispense of his own daughters? Jeremiah hoped with all his heart that he wasn't.

The idea of Rose as Queen one day was the only thing that gave him hope. He was certain she'd change the way they lived. Although even if she managed to stay alive, what hope did she have of ever becoming Queen, with a father who could whisper for life until the end of time?

He turned to leave, unable to delay his departure any longer and needing some space from his depressing thoughts.

"Thank you, Thomas." The Princess leaped from her chair and stood behind him. If he were to turn around, he'd feel her soft breath on his face. "I think you have very kind eyes. Next time maybe you'll look at me."

He was glad he'd already turned away, for his face held the reaction she'd been searching for.

The Princess's words made him feel like a person, not a Whisperer. And more than he missed speaking, more than he missed Micah or Tallis or his mother or father, he really did miss being a person. It was for this reason that as much as he wished the Princess wouldn't endanger him by speaking to him, he was so very glad she did. If he hadn't had her words to look forward to each day, he'd have lost his mind long ago. She was the one thing that kept him sane in all this madness. His Rose in a garden of thorns.

"Goodbye Thomas," she called in a hush, as he closed the door behind him.

He paused for a moment, silently calling goodbye to her in return, despondent that it would be another full day before he saw her again, which meant another full day of not being spoken to by another living soul. Unless the Conductor chose to speak to him, of course, and that was never a good thing. Did he count as a living soul? Perhaps not. His soul was far too cold to be considered living.

Jeremiah made his way down one of the many corridors, his bare feet padding silently on the carpet.

A female Whisperer approached from the other direction. They both looked the other way as they passed. With a thousand Whisperers in the palace, dressed in the same gray robes, all with cleanly shaven heads and not one of them with a name, it was hard to keep track of who was who. But Jeremiah made a point of it, giving them all names inside his head.

The one who passed him just now, was *Mean Mouth,* who wore a permanent scowl on her face. She looked very similar to *Long Nose* and a little like *Dancing Feet,* except he knew the difference. This was his private gift to the Whisperers. They may have let go of who they were themselves, but he refused to let this happen. There was more about them that was different than the same. You just had to try a little harder to see it.

He wound his way through the passageways to the dining hall. Whisperers sat in lines, carefully holding their wooden spoons so as not to make a noise, as they scooped their porridge from their bowls.

Taking his place in the queue behind *Sharp Teeth*, he waited his turn, willing the groans in his stomach to keep silent. When the Princess had asked him if he liked orange juice, he couldn't have answered her even if he'd been allowed. He didn't know. Whisperers weren't fed such luxuries, and on the rare occasion his family had chanced upon a piece of fruit, they'd eat it, skin and all, just as they'd done *that day*. Juicing was an extravagance out of reach to people like him. It seemed like such a waste.

Sharp Teeth shuffled forward, head bent, hands clasped in front of him and no sign of anything going on inside his mind, other than patiently waiting for breakfast. Just the way the Conductor had trained them. A model Whisperer.

To the rest of them, Jeremiah must also seem a model Whisperer. From the outside, he did everything he was supposed to. Thankfully the Conductor couldn't see inside his head or it would no longer be attached to his neck. Did the others dream of a life that held more than this, yearn for their families, and name each other so they could tell them apart? What name had they given him? *Tall Guy? Blue Eyes? Sleeps-a-lot?* It wouldn't be *Curly Hair* as none of them would know that's how his hair chose to sprout. And it wouldn't be *Hungry One* as they couldn't know how much his stomach ached for food day and night.

When he'd first come to the palace, *Darting Eyes* had still been a Whisperer. His body had done everything the Conductor had taught him, but his eyes had betrayed him. He'd watched every movement, caught too many glances and ultimately suffered the fate of the sword. People with darting eyes can't be trusted with the King's secrets.

Jeremiah had learned from that, determined not to suffer the same demise. His family would only continue to be fed if he remained a faithful Whisperer. If he were to lose his head, then the Conductor may as well take the heads of his family too. They were as good as dead without the food they received from the King in exchange for his Whispers.

The line moved forward and *Sharp Teeth* was handed a bowl of porridge. Jeremiah could see black dots in the bowl from where he stood and hoped they were raisins. He knew better than to seem interested, keeping his gaze to the floor. Occasionally, when the King was feeling generous, they'd get a small treat, like raisins in their porridge. Either that or the King had noticed their pale complexions and threw in some raisins to ward off disease. He wouldn't want anything to happen to his precious army.

Most of the real soldiers had left the palace when the Whisperers arrived. Only a few remained behind as guards. Jeremiah wondered where they'd all gone. Hopefully, back to the families they'd left behind. The thought of that gave him hope that maybe one day he'd be able to do the same.

The Princess had told him once in her morning chatter that the soldiers had been bartered to other kingdoms in exchange for Whisperers. One Whisperer for ten soldiers. The other Kings and Queens had laughed at her father, more than happy to hand over what appeared to be ordinary, useless citizens for skilled fighters.

Jeremiah wondered if this could be true. Had King Virtus really sent out his workers with their paintings and their oranges, visiting kingdom upon kingdom until he had one thousand Whisperers in his command? It seemed like quite a process.

The Princess had been worried about this at first. Who bartered away their army like that? What would happen if they were attacked, with no army to protect them? Jeremiah had been worried too, not for himself, but for his family. With no army, what hope did they have if they were invaded? Thankfully there'd been no attacks since the Whisperers had arrived.

The other Kings and Queens would certainly not be laughing now. King Virtus was untouchable. Attempted invasions of Forte Cadence mysteriously failed each and every time. The Princess told him stories of hailstorms blinding their enemies' armies as they crossed the border, or hideous diseases that ran rife among their soldiers as they prepared for battle, or fires that ravaged their villages, forcing their attention elsewhere. Forte Cadence had never been safer since the Whisperers moved into the palace.

Jeremiah had no idea how King Virtus had known to set up the strange army that they formed. Either someone was advising him or he had special powers far greater than the world had ever seen. He shuddered at the thought of that. If the universe had to give one man such power, why did it have to be someone so vile and selfish?

Sharp Teeth stepped aside and Jeremiah took his place at the servery to fill his bowl. There were definitely raisins in the porridge. Loads of them! He could almost taste their sweetness already. He fought the urge to smile, before remembering the last time they were served a treat like this. It was the day before a Whispering had taken place. Did that mean another was imminent? He looked toward the door to see if the Whispering flags had been raised, and saw they were absent. There was no Whispering planned just yet.

He despised Whisperings, not for the act itself, as that was quite a pleasant change to the monotony of his daily life, but because granting the King's wishes was the last thing he wanted to do. He wasn't a man who deserved his wishes granted.

It wouldn't be so bad if all the wishes were to keep the kingdom safe. There were those Whisperings, of course, and at those particular ones Jeremiah was certain the Whisperings took on a new energy, for they were whispering words from their hearts as well as their fear of the sword.

It was the Whisperings for the King's foolish desires that bothered Jeremiah. Whisperings for a trimmer royal waistline, Whisperings for a new golden carriage, Whisperings for a fresh strawberry pie when there was snow on the hills.

Or more recently, the Whispering for the Queen to birth a son. A son that was certain to bring about the death of the one good thing in this whole palace.

Jeremiah took his place at the table next to *Short Man*, careful to set down his bowl gently and not scrape the leg of the chair on the floor.

The first spoonful of porridge was so sweet it made his eyes water. He blinked and cast down his gaze, hoping nobody had noticed. It was incredible how much pleasure one small change could bring. Would it be too much to hope these raisins would become a regular treat? Most definitely.

There were no regular treats in his life. Except for Princess Rose. He sometimes wondered if his task of bringing her breakfast each day was a test. Had the Princess been challenged to get him to speak so the Conductor could draw his sword across his neck? Or was the palace waiting for his admiration for her to reach such a point that they could take away his job and injure his heart even more than they already had? No matter how likely either of these options were, he couldn't help dismissing them each time they entered his mind. The Princess wasn't testing him. She wouldn't know how. She was too innocent. Too pure. And if the palace was waiting for his admiration to grow, then they need not wait any longer. He loved her, in a way that was neither innocent nor pure. She'd become his everything, in place of all the things in his life that'd been taken away. She filled the empty spaces in his heart with golden light.

Still, was he a fool to trust her? Because no matter how he felt about her, she was still the King's daughter. Perhaps her kindness was a trap?

He finished his porridge, far more slowly than he would've liked, resisting the urge to lick the bowl clean. There'd be no food now until nightfall when the soup would be served. If those watery bowls of liquid could be called soup.

As he stood to return his bowl, he let his glance sweep the room as subtly as he could manage. Soon there'd be a new Whisperer to replace *Slight Limp* who'd been taken to the dungeon when a coughing fit had taken hold of him during breakfast a few days earlier. It was doubtful he'd ever return. A trip to the dungeon was usually a one-way ticket.

His gaze caught on an unfamiliar head bent forward at the table. A female, he thought by the shape of her shoulders, although he hadn't been able to look for long enough to tell. With their shapeless gray robes and hoods, gender was sometimes hard to pick immediately.

He took his bowl to the cleaning room and handed it to the Whisperers assigned to the dishes, grateful today as he was every day, that this hadn't been his assignment. Washing one thousand bowls and spoons without making a sound must be one of the most difficult jobs in the palace.

He wove his way slowly between the tables, waiting for the right moment to shift his gaze to the new Whisperer, hoping this one would last longer than the previous few had. More often than not, they'd only last a few days, before they broke. If they lasted longer than that, then usually they were here to stay. For this reason, he waited a week until he named them. It was even more heart-breaking to lose a comrade when they had a name.

A guard stood at each of the doors, observing them eat. The Conductor was at the rear of the room, tapping his sword on the floor as a warning, each time he saw or heard something he didn't like. It was the only noise in the room. Occasionally the sword would be used without the warning.

Chancing a glance, Jeremiah lifted his head, disappointed to see the new Whisperer had her head turned away. His glance was enough to make him sure it was a female. It was also enough to unsettle him. Her shape wasn't the shape of a stranger at all. There was something hauntingly familiar about her. Was she an old Whisperer returned from the dungeon? Was *Wide Nostrils* back at last?

His head snapped back down at the sound of the tapping of the sword. The Conductor had noticed his gaze. He must be more careful. There was plenty of time to study this new Whisperer later.

A spoon clattered to the floor on the other side of the room and a clear gasp rang out. The room froze, even more silent than the silence that'd come before it, as each Whisperer held their breath. Please, let the Conductor show mercy. The clumsy Whisperer held still, half standing with a bowl clutched in his hand. The shaking of the bowl gave away the fear of the man who held it. It was *Nine Fingers*. Jeremiah had dreaded this day he knew would come, having witnessed his clumsiness before, when it'd gone unnoticed by the Conductor.

The other Whisperers continued to eat in silence, outwardly denying what they knew was about to happen. A noise like that wouldn't go unpunished.

Jeremiah took the opportunity to turn his head to see the new female Whisperer, knowing this was his only chance. The Conductor had bigger crimes to punish. He scanned the tables, searching for her, only to find her looking straight back at him.

Their eyes locked and held. Jeremiah's knees weakened, as his porridge threatened to make another appearance. It couldn't be. It couldn't possibly be.

No!

Silent tears spilled from his eyes and he wiped them away, helpless to stop them. He shook his head, his feet glued to the carpet.

The new Whisperer mouthed the words *I'm okay.*

But she wasn't okay. Nothing was okay. And it would never be okay again.

As the sound of *Nine Fingers* being dragged away rang out across the dining hall, Jeremiah was unable to stop a name from escaping his lips. It was a name he never wanted to say in here. The name of a person he never wanted to see sitting before him like this.

"Micah!" he gasped, walking slowly from the room so he could find somewhere private where he could weep.

MICAH

THE BEFORE

"Come back, Jeremi-ah!" Micah's voice broke with the pain of her words. She was sitting on the branch of a tree, looking toward the arena, as she swung her short legs in front of her.

The arena looked so innocent on top of Mount Allegro. If Micah didn't know what it was, she might even think this long, rectangular building was beautiful with its oval dome made from gold. Although she knew that to take one step on Mount Allegro, would be certain to land her in the King's dungeon. She could see the King's palace looming behind the arena, its stone walls a stark contrast to the golden roof of the arena, as it stretched its way into the sky. It had to be five levels high at least, unlike the homes in the Valley of the Blessed, every one of which was a single level high. Even the wealthiest people in the valley couldn't afford to construct anything that required something as elaborate as stairs.

It was hard to think that somewhere on top of that mountain was her brother. He belonged in the valley, not up in the clouds.

"Come back, Jeremiah!" Micah cried out again. He'd been gone for almost three moons now and she missed him in a way that made her heart feel like it had a piece missing.

"He's not coming back." She looked down to see Tallis standing at the base of the tree, staring up at her. She liked Tallis. He was tall and wiry and reminded her of a stork. She told him that once and he'd stood on one leg and flapped his arms and squawked.

"Tallis!" She wasn't expecting to see him here. He'd been behaving as if he were an old man ever since Jeremiah left. What happened wasn't his fault. Well, no more than it was hers. She'd also encouraged Jeremiah to go and get his orange *that day*.

"Surprise!" he said, using her favorite word, except the way he said it, it sounded more like a death sentence than the magical word she'd always believed it to be.

Micah patted the space next to her on the branch and motioned for him to join her.

"I can't climb up there." He shook his head.

"Can so," she said, wondering what the problem was.

Realizing he wasn't going to join her, she swung herself out of the tree and landed at Tallis's feet.

"I want him to come back," she said, sitting down on the grass, pleased that Tallis hadn't become such an old man that he couldn't sit beside her.

"He's never coming back." He wrapped his arm around her and she snuggled closer, pretending for a moment that he was Jeremiah.

"He has to come back! If he knew what's happened since he left, he'd be running home, straight down that mountain."

"They'd kill him before he reached the bottom. You know that. And besides, he doesn't know. He never will. Face it, Micah. He's gone."

She wrenched her body away from him at these words. She didn't want to hear it, despite knowing it was true. She would never see her brother again.

Or her father, whose body was still fresh in his grave. She wasn't sure of it—nobody could be—but she strongly suspected it'd been the medicine that'd killed him. The Conductor had promised the King would feed them for the rest of their lives. Except he never said how long he was going to let them live. Da had been doing all right at first, improving every day with food in his belly, until he'd been given the medicine. That was what had killed him. There could be no other explanation.

And now Ma wasn't looking well either. People said it was just the baby getting closer, but Micah didn't believe them. It was more than that. Babies didn't make your skin turn gray or your hair fall out. She was being poisoned just like Da was. Micah had begged her to stop taking the vitamins the palace was supplying her with, but Ma wouldn't listen. She'd even accused Micah of being jealous of the gift Jeremiah's sacrifice had provided.

"I think the vitamins are making my mother's head go crazy," she said, feeling all her fight slip from her body.

"What vitamins?" Tallis plucked a blade of grass from the ground and twirled it between his fingers.

"The King gives her vitamins for the baby. They're killing her. Just like they killed my father."

"Tip them out then!" Tallis threw the grass aside and looked at her, his eyes wide and his mouth dropping open.

"Tried that." Micah shrugged. "She just goes and gets more."

"Then tip those out too."

She didn't like the way he was looking at her. She was hoping he'd tell her she was being foolish. Instead, he believed her every word. She didn't want to be right about this.

"Can I live with you if—"

"Micah! Don't. She'll be okay," he soothed.

"The food's getting less, you know. Each week, things are missing. Soon there'll be nothing. And we don't even have Jeremiah to help us now."

"You've got me." Tallis wrapped his arm around her again.

"You have your own family to worry about." She reached for Jeremiah's lucky walnut shell that she'd worn around her neck since the day he'd left. She didn't even take it off to sleep. So far it hadn't brought her any luck, but it did make her feel close to Jeremiah. It was the only small part of him she had left, if you didn't count the memories she was holding onto.

"We'll figure something out." Tallis gave her shoulder a squeeze.

"Like what?"

"I dunno. Like something."

She looked at her brother's best friend. He was kind. He was fun—well, he used to be—although he wasn't being very smart. If something was going to be figured out, it was going to have to be by her. She was going to get Jeremiah out of the palace. Somehow.

"What do you think he's doing right at this moment?" she asked.

"Eating a roast chicken." Tallis patted his stomach. "With potatoes and gravy and juicy green peas."

Micah blinked back some tears. This didn't seem likely, however, she hoped it was true. Jeremiah loved to eat and they'd never had enough food to fill his belly.

"What do you think that test was all about?" she asked. "Why did they care what he saw in those paintings? Tell me again what they looked like."

"Just dots with a shape inside. Nothing special."

"I don't get it. Jeremiah said he couldn't see them, except for the first one."

"Shh." He put his finger to his lips. "He also said he wasn't supposed to tell us that. Be careful who you say that to. We don't want him getting into any trouble."

"Any more than he's already in."

"We don't know that."

She did. She could feel it. As bad as things were for them, she was certain her brother was suffering even more.

"It just doesn't make sense to me," she said. "Why would they want people who *can't* see the shapes? Wouldn't they want the people who can see them?"

Tallis shrugged. "Who knows. Have you ever known King Virtus to do anything that makes sense? One day, when Princess Rose becomes Queen, things will change."

That was the hope the people clung to. The Princess didn't go out in public, however, a few villagers who'd been to the palace had claimed to have seen her. The general consensus was that she had a kind face. Micah wasn't sure about this. Jeremiah had a kind face too and look how far that'd gotten him.

"I hate the King." Micah picked up a stone and threw it toward Mount Allegro. "He stole my brother and my father. And now he's trying to steal my mother and the baby. He's not going to get me, though. He's not."

"Maybe I'll get you instead." Tallis bared his teeth and held up his hands like claws. Thrilled to see a glimpse of the old Tallis return, Micah scrambled to her feet and squealed.

Tallis roared and Micah took off in the direction of the valley, her laughter slowing down her steps, until Tallis caught her and scooped her into the air, lifting her onto his shoulders and galloping forward.

"Faster, donkey, faster," she cried, pretending to whip him.

"I'm not a donkey! I'm a scary beast!"

She laughed louder this time, turning her troubles to a small moment of joy and keeping it warm inside. That was what she missed most about Jeremiah. Laughing with him. She could still hear his laugh inside her ears.

"Where to, Princess Micah?" asked Tallis, when they reached the edge of town.

"Princesses don't ride on the shoulders of scary beasts." Micah grabbed at Tallis's hair to steady herself.

"Ouch! Then I'm a dragon. Princesses always ride on the backs of dragons."

"Fly me home, dragon! Back to my palace at once!"

She laughed, glad she wasn't a princess for real. The Princess and her sisters must have a dreadful life being locked inside the palace. She'd bet the Princess didn't know how to do cartwheels or juggle five stones in the air. She just sat in the palace all day brushing her hair and asking her maid to do up her frilly dress. How boring!

"Hey Tallis," she said, wriggling free from his shoulders, to walk beside him. "Do you think Jeremiah's met Princess Rose?"

"I don't know." The expression on his face changed and the old man in him returned, as his shoulders hunched over. "You ask strange questions sometimes."

"Because I think she'll fall in love with him and let him go."

"Oh, Micah. Princesses don't fall in love with people like Jeremiah."

"Why not? He's handsome. Better looking than her fat, ugly father." She pulled a face to show her disgust.

"Micah! Hush! Don't be saying these things in the street. I told you before, you never know who can hear you." He bent down to get eye level with her. "Jeremiah gave up lots of things to keep you safe. Don't you go getting yourself into any trouble. You have to live two lives now. One for him and one for you."

Micah wondered exactly how she was going to do that. The one life she lived now already seemed pretty full up.

"Bye, Dragon," she said, when they reached her front door.

"Bye, Princess."

She curtsied, holding out her dress as she dipped and noticing how dirty her fingernails were. Jeremiah would've told her to clean them. Maybe it was time to take that bath she'd been avoiding all week.

She went inside and closed the door.

"I'm hooooome." She hopped on her left leg, deciding maybe she'd give that a go for the rest of the day, instead of walking, to see how many hops it would take for her leg to get tired.

"Micah!" The tone of her mother's voice made her forget instantly about hopping. Or walking. She ran through their small house, looking for her.

She stopped when she found her, grinding to a halt so fast she got a splinter in her bare foot.

Her mother was lying on the floor of the kitchen with blood soaking through her clothes and pooling around her.

"Ma!" she gasped.

"Micah, you're here." She smiled at Micah and reached out her hand.

Micah wanted to go to her, hold her hand and make everything okay, except she couldn't get her feet to move forward. She was eleven years old. Too young to be a mother to her own mother. She still needed her mother for herself.

"Please." Ma's voice was croaky. It seemed a miracle she was actually alive. Micah had no idea that much blood could fit inside a person.

Forcing herself to step forward, she crouched next to her mother and took her hand, watching blood mingle with dirt as their fingers entwined.

"You were right," Ma said. "The vitamins..."

"It's okay," she said, knowing it wasn't. There was nothing okay about this.

"You must save Jeremiah." Her mother's words seemed as much of a struggle to get out as they were for Micah to hear.

"I'm so afraid." Now her own words were a whisper. Admitting she was scared was difficult. People with lives like theirs didn't speak of being afraid. They kept themselves brave. It was the only way to face the challenges of every moment of every day.

"You can do it," her mother said, her words now barely audible. "You can do anything. You're the most amazing girl in the whole wide world."

"Tallis called me a princess." She wasn't sure why she said this. It just seemed right to fill the air with words.

"You're not a princess. You're so much better than a princess. You're Micah. You're my girl." Her mother's squeeze of her hand was so weak it was barely there, yet she felt it. Just as she felt the love pouring between their hearts.

"I'll get the doctor," said Micah, knowing it was far too late for that. "And I'll get you a blanket. Your teeth are chattering."

She left her mother's side and ran to her bed, knowing there was a risk she wouldn't make it back to her in time. For a selfish moment, she wondered if that would be so bad. She was afraid to be there at the moment she slipped away.

She'd been there when her father had closed his eyes and that image had haunted her dreams every night. Losing her mother was even worse. Not just because this was the woman who'd carried her in her womb, but because the moment her heart stopped beating, then so would that of the baby. Her brother or sister who would never have a chance. Did any of them ever really have a chance? There had to be a better way to live than this. Maybe being a princess wouldn't be so bad after all.

She hurried back to her mother and spread the blanket over her, covering her up to her chin, not wanting to cover her face, even though she was certain her selfish wish had come true. She shouldn't have bothered with the blanket. Her mother was dead. Why hadn't she just stayed here and held her hand in her final moments?

"I love you, Ma," she said, wishing she'd thought to say this before she got the blanket, not after. Her mother had believed in heaven and angels, so if any of that were true then she'd have heard her anyway.

To think that only months ago, they'd been preparing for their family of four to become five. Now there was only one. Her.

She sniffed, realizing that she wasn't crying. She was certain she should be crying at a time like this. Perhaps she'd already used up all her tears. When Jeremiah had left, she'd cried for a week. That'd felt better than this, like somehow the tears were taking some of the pain out of her body.

She squinted, trying to squeeze out some tears, but nothing happened. Why? She'd loved her mother. Maybe this kind of pain was too great to find its way out through her tears? It was going to stay trapped inside her until she figured out how to pound it into little pieces, small enough to find an escape.

Perhaps it was her brother's escape she should be thinking about instead. How was she going to honor her mother's wish and get him out of the palace?

She looked at Ma, the smell of blood filling her nostrils. Instead of pushing her pain out, she seemed to be only drawing more in.

That was when she realized. Maybe she was thinking about this whole thing the wrong way. She was never going to get Jeremiah out of the palace. Maybe it would be easier to get herself in there instead.

MICAH

THE AFTER

*M*icah wasn't sure what was worse—finding Jeremiah, or how she'd have felt if he'd been lost forever.

It was definitely him she'd seen in the dining hall. It was his eyes. Still just as kind as they were blue. Although she wasn't used to seeing tears spilling from them. She'd never seen him cry before.

This wasn't the only thing that was different about him. He was older, as you'd expect with five years having passed, which meant he was taller. But also thinner. Stooped. He just looked … broken somehow. King Virtus had broken her brother.

She took her bowl to the cleaning room, grateful she hadn't been assigned to this room as one of her tasks. Cleanliness had never been one of her strong suits. She hadn't worked out what Jeremiah's jobs in the palace were yet, however now that she'd seen him, that shouldn't take too long.

Jeremiah was still her favorite person in the world. She loved him even more than she'd loved her parents. He was smart, funny and caring, having looked after her in a way most big brothers never did.

When Da first got sick, Jeremiah had worked so hard to make sure they didn't starve. Not once did she hear him complain about it either. It was the opposite. He'd joke about it, walking in the door at night, bent over, pretending his back was too sore to stand up straight. She'd laugh and climb on top of him, sitting on his shoulders, until he had enough and would tip her onto the bed and tickle her.

It wasn't until years later, when she was working hard herself, that she began to wonder if it'd been a joke at all. Survival was hard work. He was probably just as sore as he'd said he was, if not worse. She knew she'd ached in places she hadn't previously known it was possible to hurt. Even her fingernails had felt sore.

She glanced down at her nails now, noticing how clean they were, possibly the only positive thing to happen to her since coming to the palace.

Tucking her hands back under the long sleeves of her robe, she made her way slowly to the arena for rest time. She was used to running or skipping everywhere she went. Walking at this pace was difficult. It reminded her of the hunched way Tallis had walked around the village when Jeremiah first left.

She tried not to smile as she thought of Tallis.

She'd gone to live with his family for a while after Ma died. It'd been a shock to find herself homeless. Females in Forte Cadence weren't allowed to own property, so Micah and her mother had assumed their house would pass to Jeremiah when her father died. Except not long after her mother joined their father in the ground, palace guards had seized the house, ejecting Micah onto the street. It was only luck that they hadn't caught up with her before her mother died. That would have been one final shock in her life that she hadn't needed. Micah tried to explain that she was living in her brother's house, but the guards said Jeremiah belonged to the King now.

Tallis had found her crying in the gutter, watching as the guards set fire to the only home she'd ever known. It felt like another death and the impact left her feeling hollow. Without saying a word, Tallis had wrapped an arm around her and taken her back to his house.

His family never said anything about not wanting her there, but she could feel it in the way his mother glanced at her when she shared out the evening meal, trying not to make it obvious she was giving her sons a larger share. Tallis tried to even it up when he thought his mother wasn't watching and Micah would push his spoon away. It didn't sit well with her to take from a family who had so little themselves.

When Micah turned thirteen, she went to Tallis's mother and told her she was leaving. She explained that she was old enough to fend for herself, and despite the sadness in Tallis's mother's eyes, she didn't argue with her. Instead, she pulled Micah into her arms and wished her good fortune. Micah had felt the walnut shell pressing against her chest as if taunting her with its inability to bring her any luck.

She didn't say goodbye to Tallis, purely because she knew he wouldn't let her leave. Or he'd insist on coming with her and she'd already taken enough from his family—she couldn't possibly take their eldest son too.

She'd walked from farm to farm until she found someone prepared to let her sleep in their barn, tending animals in exchange for food and water.

However, she knew nothing about animals and when three pigs were found dead one morning after she forgot to fill their water during a particularly hot spell, she'd been asked to leave. She'd felt awful, having accidentally denied those poor animals the one thing she herself had come to the farm seeking, and vowed to do a better job next time.

She found work at a neighboring farm, although when it became obvious that the farmer would rather she tend his personal needs than those of the animals, she'd left there too.

After walking west for three days, she'd eventually found work at an orchard bursting with berries being grown for the palace. She was given board in an old farmhouse alongside a dozen other workers and they picked berries that whole summer, until their hands turned purple, from both the fruit and their blisters.

When the picking was done and it was time to move on, she went with the workers to beg for a job in the markets. It was easier for the men, who were strong and could carry loads of produce with ease, just like Jeremiah had once done. Nobody wanted to employ a skinny girl with a dirty face and purple hands.

But those days felt like so long ago now. She was in another lifetime now, here in the palace.

Micah adjusted her hood and entered the arena, making her way past the first rows of mats, unable to stop her eyes from searching for Jeremiah. He was there with his head buried under his blanket. She noticed his body shaking and knew the tears that'd fallen from his eyes in the dining hall were continuing to rain down.

She walked past him and continued down the rows of mats, fighting the urge to turn around and throw herself on her brother to tell him she was okay. Hopefully, once he got used to the idea of her being here, his tears would dry up. He only knew her as a helpless child. He had no idea how she'd learned to fend for herself.

She'd proven that when she'd been unable to find work at the markets and had decided to try something different where she could use the unique skills that she'd developed over the years. She couldn't lift heavy objects or cook a decent meal, but she could do tumble turns and handstands and juggle and dance. She developed complex routines that she'd perform at the markets, before holding out an empty cup to the people who stopped to watch. Often the cup remained empty, although every now and then somebody would give her a coin or two. It was enough for her to scrape by. Sometimes she camped with the workers from the orchard, although mostly she preferred to keep to herself. She slept under bridges and in doorways and occasionally in a warm bed if someone felt sorry enough for her. She bathed in the river and wore clothes discarded by other villagers. In the summer months, she'd return to the orchard to pick berries.

Once, Tallis had seen her at the markets and begged her to return home with him, saying that his family missed her. She knew that was a lie. It was possible he missed her, but his family didn't, especially at dinnertime. The only person in the world who she knew for sure missed her, was Jeremiah. That was why she'd had to bide her time until she was sixteen and could sit the test of the Whisperers. Then she could join him. She'd thought life in the palace couldn't be any more difficult than the life she was already living. At least there she'd have her brother. How little she'd known back then.

Tallis had returned to the market to look for her as often as he could and they'd spend time together, like they had when they were young. She'd looked forward to his visits and how they reminded her of her childhood. He was the next best thing to Jeremiah, even if he wasn't the same.

But that was in the Before. This was how she'd come to think of the first sixteen years of her life. The Before. And as hard as they'd been, they were nothing compared to the After. For just as much as Jeremiah was now broken, so was she. His heart may have had more time to break into even more pieces than hers, but that was the only difference now.

The Conductor had stripped her of her clothes, her name, her tangled red hair, and her voice. He'd taken everything that made her Micah and left a body in a hooded robe in her place. A body whose job was to whisper on command and stay alive with minimal fuss at all other times. No, not minimal. No fuss. Zero. Fuss equaled death. And she couldn't save Jeremiah if she were dead.

Until she'd seen him in the dining hall, she hadn't even known he was still alive. Her training had taught her that continuation of life wasn't something a Whisperer could count on, no matter how careful they were. It'd been years since Jeremiah had left, with a thousand opportunities in every day of those years for him to lose his head.

So, it was with relief when she first saw him walking slowly into the dining hall. His eyes had been cast downward, but she saw his secret glances at the servery. He'd always loved his food. By the size of his frame, clearly, he was getting even less of it in the palace than he'd been getting at home. Except his hunger still existed. She could see it in the way he moved, certain that the Conductor couldn't. Because the Conductor knew the After Jeremiah and she knew the Before. And the Before was the only version of him that counted. That was his true self.

She settled down on her mat and pulled her blanket over her head in the same way Jeremiah had. At least she didn't have to control the expression on her face from under there.

She wondered if Jeremiah would get his true self back one day when they began life in the Evernow—a life when they no longer pined for the Before or the After. A life when they were happy to live forever more in the Now.

The Evernow was something she'd heard people in the valley talking about when she was young and had never really understood it. She'd been perfectly happy, despite the grumbling in her stomach, not realizing there was any other way to live. But her parents had known. Times hadn't been so tough when they were young and they yearned for happier times once more. Their Evernow.

Micah understood this with brutal clarity now.

Once she and Jeremiah were out of this place, never would they return. The Evernow was the life she longed for. A time when she was happy to be exactly where she was at that moment. The thought of this was the only thing that'd stopped her collapsing when she saw her brother after so long apart.

He was alive. And that made all her efforts worth it. She'd live through a thousand versions of the hell she'd just survived if she knew this was waiting for her at the end.

Seeing Jeremiah once more was the greatest victory of her life. Until he'd seen her too and his face had broken apart, revealing all the cracks in his soul. Thank the stars that Whisperer had dropped his spoon and diverted the Conductor's attention. She felt bad for feeling this way—that Whisperer had been robbed of his chance of an Ever-now. However, if it were a choice between a nameless man and her brother, she'd save Jeremiah every time. She would've dropped her spoon herself if it meant it would keep him safe.

His face told her that he felt the same. She was the last person he wanted to see in the palace. And he must surely know that he'd helped her get here. If he hadn't told her how to pass the test, then she would never have known what to say. He probably still didn't even know what it was about him that made him able to pass the test.

She rolled over, trying to get comfortable, doing it slowly so that the blanket didn't rustle. She had to be twice as careful as any of the other Whisperers. Because she wasn't like them. She was an imposter, which not only put her in danger, it also made her dangerous. The Conductor really had no idea what he'd let into the King's palace.

It was time to bring it down.

ROSE

THE BEFORE

*W*hen Rose was young, her mother told her a story about a girl locked up by an evil witch in a high tower in the middle of a lonely forest. The girl's hair grows so long that the witch is able to climb up her braid and visit her, feeding off her beauty to retain her youth. One day, a handsome Prince comes upon the girl and she holds out her hair for him to climb. They fall in love and he visits her every day, until the girl accidentally mentions him to the witch, who flies into a rage, cuts off the girl's hair and banishes her into the wilderness. The next time the Prince visits, the witch fools him by holding the girl's severed braid from the window. The Prince climbs the braid and when he reaches the top, the witch lets go and he falls into the thorns below and is blinded. He stumbles through the forest until he finds the girl and her tears fall into his eyes and once again he can see. And of course, they live happily ever after.

Rose had heard her mother talk of something called the Evernow, and this "happily ever after" sounded a bit like that. When the prince and the girl were together, at last, they wouldn't be wishing for their days before or their days after. They'd just be enjoying every minute they had with each other right in that moment.

Rose stretched out in her bed as she thought about this. The palace was quiet and she'd only just woken from a dream about the girl in the tower. She often dreamed of her. The story haunted her like it was trying to tell her something.

It was a strange story and Rose had searched it for hidden messages, wondering why her mother had chosen to tell it to her. Was she warning her of dangers inside their own palace? It was hard to tell. Perhaps it was just a story with no meaning at all. But the Princess felt so much like the girl in the tower. She was certain it must've been a story made up just for her.

Although, the witch wasn't a bit like her own mother. Her mother was far from evil and had been beautiful long before Rose was born. She didn't need to harness her beauty from anyone. Her father made no secret of the fact that was the reason he'd married her.

As she grew older, Rose started to see there were more similarities between the witch and her mother than she'd first thought, for both of them were responsible for keeping a girl locked inside a tower, hidden from the world. However, the witch had kept the girl hidden, afraid of her running away. The Queen kept her hidden, afraid that she would never get the opportunity to escape.

"One day you must leave," her mother would tell her, when she was sure nobody was listening. "There's no happiness to be found here, my darling girl. When I tell you to run, you must listen. Do you understand?"

Rose wondered where she'd go and who she'd meet. Would she find her true love like the girl in the story? Or would he come to her? Would she meet an evil witch? And why did her mother want her to run anyway?

She had no idea what evil lay outside the palace. The only evil she knew, lived within. The evil even had a name. A few names actually. His Royal Highness, His Majesty, His Grace, King Virtus, Ruler of Forte Cadence. Or to her ... Father.

Perhaps her father was the evil witch in the story. After all, he was the one who insisted she remain trapped inside the palace. Her mother was only following his ruling that she and her sisters be kept hidden from the world, never to ride in a golden carriage, never to climb a tree in the forest and never to call to a Prince from her window and have him climb her hair. How many other fourteen-year-olds had never set foot outside their home? It was just as well her home was so large and filled with so many people, even if the walls were made from stone.

Her stomach growled, despite the early hour. Soon the Whisperer would be here with her breakfast.

She missed being able to wander down to the kitchen and sit on one of the benches and talk to the cook while she made her breakfast. Nobody even told her where the cook had gone. Where anybody who worked in the palace had gone. Most of them had simply vanished one night, while these strange Whisperers moved in and took their place.

And now she had to wait for her breakfast to be delivered to her on a tray. It didn't seem enough lately for her to be kept hidden in the palace. More and more often now, she was being confined to her bedchamber. And although her room was large, there was not a lot for her to do in there, except look out the window and dream of the day her mother would tell her to run. She was painfully lonely.

The Whisperers were her father's idea, although she'd noticed that all his good ideas came from someone other than himself. Usually her mother. It would be wrong to call him stupid, as that wasn't true. He was intelligent enough to recognize a good idea when he saw one, just not quite capable of having too many of them himself.

She startled as someone opened her door. Slowly. Silently. Her father's Whisperers weren't allowed to make a single sound, which meant they were unable to knock. Their sounds were to be saved and harnessed to increase their power when they were unleashed on her father's wishes.

Her heart rate increased as she leaped from her bed, relishing the idea of a visitor, no matter who it was. She'd spent an hour the day before, talking to a butterfly that'd flown through her window, that's how desperate she was for a friend.

She knew immediately this was a new Whisperer, despite not being able to see his face. It was the shape of him that was new. The last one to bring her breakfast had been short and stocky. This one was tall. His hood was pulled low and his eyes cast down, fixed to the breakfast tray he carried.

There'd be no point asking her mother what happened to the last Whisperer. She'd only get the same sad look in return, and she hated to see her mother's eyes fill with tears.

This new Whisperer's hands were shaking ever so slightly, the only sign that he was afraid. The other Whisperer had been like that too. She didn't want them to be afraid. Surely this man couldn't be afraid of her? If they slipped up and made a sound or even spoke to her, she wouldn't tell anyone. Although they didn't know that, she supposed. She might be an innocent girl, but in their eyes, they must only see her as the King's daughter.

She went to the door and closed it behind her visitor, curious to look at a new face, undisturbed.

"Hello, Whisperer," she said, keeping her voice low so that nobody outside her bedchamber could hear.

His eyes flicked up to meet hers for only the briefest of moments before he remembered himself and looked away.

It was a moment enough. She felt everything change in just that one flash of time. Her mother had once described eyes as the window to the soul. She'd never understood that before now. But when he'd glanced at her, with those eyes that were the bluest eyes she'd ever come across, she hadn't seen a Whisperer. She'd seen *him*. A boy, not too many years older than her. Sixteen perhaps?

This shocked her. She'd never thought of the Whisperers as actual people. They were so alien in their robes, with their shaved heads and silent voices. It'd never occurred to her that they were individuals, with their own personalities. Except she'd never seen a Whisperer like this one.

Maybe he was her Prince who'd come to take her away? And he'd come for her from outside the palace, just like the Prince in the story. Only he wasn't blind, he was mute. Would her tears one day restore his voice, just like the girl in the tower had restored her true love's sight?

She scolded herself for being so dramatic. She didn't know one single thing about this Whisperer. Her fascination was due to her loneliness. This was the only other teenager she'd seen for months now. Possibly years. Of course she was making up stories inside her head about him. He was no more her Prince than her mother was a witch.

"What's your name?" she asked, desperate to know more about him, even though she knew he couldn't answer her.

He set her tray down on her table and stepped aside, looking out the window while he waited for her to take her plate.

She had no interest in her breakfast today. Sausages, eggs, and tomato couldn't compete with a new face, especially one as appealing as this. Her eyes trailed across the square line of the Whisperer's jaw, then up the smooth skin of his face, to settle on his eyes. Those blue, blue eyes that refused to look at her.

"Is it Harry?" she asked, studying him for a reaction.

He didn't flinch. Surely, he'd have flinched if she got it right.

"Harry?" she tried again.

He remained still, his eyes fixed to the window, still waiting for her to take her breakfast from the tray.

What made a person want to become a Whisperer? Who would choose this strange life for themselves? She understood that even less than she understood why they needed them. The servants who'd worked in the palace before them had done a perfectly good job. An even better job perhaps. As had her father's army. She'd felt much safer when she could see soldiers patrolling the grounds with their swords, ready to protect her at all costs.

Her father insisted they weren't needed anymore. The Whisperers were protecting them. This made no sense to Rose, although her mother said it was true. Nobody could hurt them now. She could see no reason for her mother to make this up.

She took her plate from the tray, although her hunger had vanished, as if it'd been somehow replaced by her fascination with this Whisperer.

"Thank you for my breakfast," she said.

The Whisperer almost nodded. It was a movement so slight, it was invisible to anybody who wasn't searching for it. More like a leftover reaction that he wasn't able to suppress than a deliberate movement.

"Please look at me," she said, desperate to see the real him again. That one glimpse she'd had earlier wasn't enough. There was so much more to this boy than the statue who stood before her.

He shifted his gaze and she held her breath, preparing to look into his eyes once more.

Instead, he looked toward her table and seeing that she'd removed her plate, he picked up the empty tray and stole silently toward the door.

"Harry!" she cried.

His silent steps shuffled faster and she noticed the tray shaking in his hands. He was afraid someone would hear her.

"I'm sorry." She let her voice fall to a hush, not wanting him to be punished for her crime of speech.

He left the room, closing the door behind him, the breath of air it displaced the only sound he gifted her.

She made a wish. The first wish she could ever remember making. Normally, it was her father making the wishes.

Let this boy be her Prince.

Let him rescue her from the palace. When the day came and her mother told her to run, let him be by her side.

She felt something wet on her cheeks and realized she was crying.

Life wasn't like that. It didn't deliver you something, just because you wished for it. She didn't care what her father had to say on that matter.

This strange Whisperer wasn't her Prince. He was her father's solider. His name wasn't Harry. She didn't even know what it was.

And she never would.

ROSE

THE AFTER

*R*ose's eyes snapped open at the first sign of daylight. Her sleep had been dreamless, and she was glad of it.

Her Prince would be here soon with her breakfast. She knew it was wrong to call him that, but what else was she supposed to call him? He wasn't Harry, like she'd guessed the first day she met him all those years ago. Nor was he James or Robert or Carl. He definitely wasn't Bruce or William or Marcus. And she was sure he couldn't be Peter or Simon or Frank. She'd tried every name she could think of. Only yesterday she'd also ruled out Thomas. She'd been certain that must be it, wondering why she hadn't tried it earlier. It was so obvious! Only that hadn't seemed to be it either.

Her Prince had been bringing her breakfast for five years now and she'd tried a new name each day. That was nearly two thousand names and none of them had sparked even the smallest reaction.

So, she'd taken to calling him her Prince inside her head. It was easier that way. She could hardly think of him as *Breakfast Bringer*.

Although soon there'd be a real Prince inside the palace. Her mother was pregnant and certain that this time it was a boy, just like her father had always wanted. There'd been a Whispering about it, which meant her mother was right. A Prince would soon be born and she'd have a brother to sit beside her three sisters. Not that they sat beside each other very often. It was a bit hard when they were all locked inside their rooms. The only contact they were allowed was at dinner, when they gathered around a huge table with her father at one end and her mother at the other.

Whisperers stood next to the table, waiting for them to drop something or attend to their glass if it needed refilling. Her Prince was never there though. His only job seemed to be to bring her breakfast each morning. He brought her sisters their breakfast too. And her mother. She wondered if any of them had tried to talk to him and if he'd replied, but she'd never dared to ask. It would make it too obvious that this was what she'd been doing and it would only put him in danger.

She hoped they hadn't tried to get him to talk. He was *her* Prince. She didn't like the idea of him talking to one of her sisters or her mother, and not to her.

In the five years she'd known him, she'd never heard him say a single word. And never again had she managed to catch his eye like she had that first time she'd met him. Of course, this only made her try harder. Sometimes she'd jump on her bed and pretend to fall or spill her orange juice on the floor to see what he'd do. Not once did he break and fix his gaze on her. If only she knew what her father had threatened him with if he did. She could make a good guess, only it wasn't a nice one.

Every day when he walked into her bedchamber holding that tray, she breathed a sigh to see that he was still alive. The faces of the Whisperers changed often in the palace. Her Prince was one of the only Whisperers left from the early days. When they'd first started appearing in the palace, she'd only been young and had naively thought they were there by their own choice. She no longer believed that. Nobody would become a Whisperer by choice, she didn't care how much her father insisted on it. They were as good as slaves. Who would choose that life for themselves?

When she was Queen one day, she'd set the whole lot of them free.

If not *when* she reminded herself. *If.* Becoming the Queen was another thing she wasn't sure she believed in anymore. Even though she was next in line to the throne, she couldn't help thinking that her father had other plans about this. When her brother was born, he'd find a way to change the rules to push her aside. It was no secret that he believed men to be far superior to women.

Ironic really, given that all the best decisions he'd ever made had come from ideas given to him by his wife.

The door to Rose's room opened, slowly, silently. She held her breath, waiting to see him, hoping nothing had happened in the twenty-four hours since she'd last laid eyes on him.

It was her Prince. He was still here. Still alive. Only he was different somehow. Unhappy in a deep way his normal misery had never seemed to reach.

She got up from her bed and closed the door.

"What's wrong?" she asked. "Something's happened, hasn't it?"

He placed the tray on her table and looked out the window, waiting for her to take her food.

She wasn't interested in her food. She was going to make him talk. Today. Right now. No more waiting.

"I'm not going to guess your name today," she said. "You're going to tell it to me. And after that, you're going to tell me what's wrong."

He blinked slowly, his gaze still focused on the window and not on her. There were dark circles under his eyes, like she got when she let herself cry. The whites of his eyes were pink, ringing his blue irises like a soft flame of misery. Her poor Prince. Something *had* happened. She was certain of it. She'd seen him every day for five years, and she'd never seen him like this.

"I can't help you if I don't know what's wrong." She stood between him and the window, interrupting his line of sight.

He looked to the floor.

She reached out her hands and placed one on each of his shoulders. He was taller than her, although not by much. She felt him flinch at her touch. Never before had she touched him like this. She wondered how long it'd been since anyone had laid their hands on him. He must've had a mother once.

"Tell me your name," she said, tilting her face to try to catch his eye.

He looked away.

"I want to help you," she pleaded.

Slowly, as if time had fallen asleep for a moment, he lifted his gaze.

"Let me help you," she said.

Then his eyes were locked with hers. Not a glance like the first time they'd met, this time it was a stare. She had his eyes, his focus, his soul laid bare.

Her hands dropped from his shoulders and ran down his arms to his hands. She held them. His skin was warm and soft. She squeezed gently, still keeping his gaze. He squeezed her hands in return, his gaze still locked with hers.

"Talk to me," she said. "Please."

He swallowed. Hesitated. Gathered his strength.

"Please," she whispered. He was so close to speaking. She could feel it. The words were in his chest, waiting to spill out.

"Tell me your name," she said, trying to coax them out.

He blinked, squeezing her hands gently once more. His lips parted.

She held her breath, not wanting to spoil the moment.

"Jeremiah," he said, his voice so soft, she had to strain to hear it.

But hear it, she did. The air rushed from her lungs and she broke his gaze to tilt forward and rest her forehead on his chest, for fear she was about to collapse. The moment she'd dreamed about for five years was here at last. Her Prince had spoken to her. More than that. Her Prince finally had a name.

"Jeremiah," she said, feeling the sound of his name on her lips. "Jeremiah."

Worried he'd retreat back into himself and be lost to her forever, she lifted her face and looked into his eyes once more.

"I knew you had a name," she said. "You've never been a Whisperer to me. I've seen *you* every time I've looked at you. And now I know your name. Jeremiah. Such a beautiful name."

"My sister's here." His voice was croaky, like opening a rusty gate that hadn't been used for an age.

His sister? It was strange to think he had a sibling. Was she younger than him? Taller than him? Did she have the same pale irises that drew you in and made you feel like you'd seen an angel?

"Please," he said. "You must help me get her out."

"Oh, Jeremiah. I don't even know how to get myself out. Don't you see I'm as much a prisoner as you are?"

He shook his head and his brows knitted together. He'd risked everything by talking to her. She knew she owed him more than the response she'd just given him.

"I'll think of something," she said. "We'll think of something together. We'll get your sister out. We'll get you out."

Tears welled in his eyes, spilling out and pouring down his cheeks. She lifted her hand and wiped them away with her fingertips, hoping she could find a way to fulfill this impossible promise.

"There's just one condition," she said.

He raised his eyebrows. "Anything, Princess."

"When we get you and your sister out ... I come with you."

She wasn't going to wait for her mother to tell her to run. The time to run was now. There was a whole world out there calling to her. She wanted to go to it. Feel fresh air in her hair, dirt under her feet and hope in her heart. And she wanted to do all of this with her Prince—with Jeremiah—by her side.

Let her brother be the King. Let her father have his army of Whisperers. Let her mother tell her sisters stories and whisper in their ears to run.

"Jeremiah," she said, wrapping her arms around his waist.

He flinched, stiffened, then melted.

"Yes, Princess?" he asked.

"My name is Rose. Please call me Rose."

"I know," he said.

She broke away and looked at him to see he was smiling. It was a smile that changed his whole face, like his soul was suddenly on the outside of his body, not hidden deep within.

And it was the most beautiful thing she'd seen in all her life.

She just hoped she could find a way to make sure she'd see that smile again. Because he'd smiled at her for promising to do something she shouldn't have. She had no idea how to escape the nightmare they were both trapped in.

She reminded herself that the girl in the tower had found a way to do the impossible. She'd escaped and run deep into the forest with her Prince.

Rose and Jeremiah could do that too.

KING VIRTUS

THE BEFORE

King Virtus woke to the sound of his army marching in the grounds below. He liked hearing their heavy boots connect with the earth, as if stamping their authority. *His* authority. Forte Cadence was his kingdom as it had belonged to his father and his father's father before him, going back for over twenty generations of men. All named Virtus.

He was the first King not to produce a son as his heir. Well, the first not to do away with his daughters to ensure the heir was a son. He was too kind-hearted to take his daughters' lives as babies. Best to let them live until he needed them to step aside. He had no brothers, so if he had no surviving children, the throne would pass to his twin sister. And that would be an even greater tragedy than the female fruit of his own loins taking over. His daughters could live for now.

His Queen had told him Forte Cadence needed a merciful king, so this decision seemed to make her happy. The Queen told him a lot of things, which was irritating, as of course, he'd already thought of them all first. Women didn't have original ideas. They weren't leaders. Men had always had far superior thought processes. It was the way their brains were wired. That was why it took a man to rule a King-dom. If he let his daughter take over from him, Forte Cadence would be invaded in no time, and all that work over the generations to build what he had before him would be ruined.

He reached under the covers and scratched an itch in the coarse hair below the generous girth of his stomach, aware of his manhood standing to attention, ready to serve him if required, much like his army below. That was what was needed to get respect. How could his daughter possibly rule a kingdom? What would drive her to attack, to protect, to succeed? Nothing. This wasn't a job for a woman.

"Queen!" he bellowed, waiting for her to appear by his side, as he was certain she would. She knew better than to keep him waiting. He had an itch he needed scratched and it was her job to do it. There were plenty of other women who'd gladly take her place if he grew tired of her. And with her pregnant belly and sagging tits, he was already starting to think that way. Perhaps it was time for a new Queen?

Where the hell was she? He needed her now.

"Queen!"

The door to his bedchamber opened and in stepped his Queen, still wearing her nightgown. She'd been so beautiful when he'd first met her. It was such a shame he couldn't have frozen her looks in that exact moment of time. Still, putting up with her aging was probably easier than training a new woman to satisfy his needs.

"My Lord," she said, stepping into the light. Her face was pale, in a way he was familiar with. She'd had one of her *visions*, which clearly were his departed ancestors talking to him, choosing to use her as a vessel, so as not to exhaust him in the way it seemed to exhaust her.

This was another reason he kept the Queen around. Without her, how would his ancestors talk to him?

He sat up in bed, forgetting his primal urges of only moments before. If his ancestors needed to talk to him, then he needed to listen. He was no fool.

She lay down on his bed next to him, her long blonde hair haloing her face, contrasting against his dark bed linen. She always looked younger after a vision. Like a tired, pathetic little girl.

"Speak!" he said, wishing she'd hurry up. "We must hear the message now."

"Give me just a moment, please, My Lord." She closed her eyes and drew in a breath. Hopeless woman. He'd never once seen a man behave like this. Such theatrics!

He clutched her nightdress at the neckline, drawing the fabric together.

She gasped at the tightness around her throat. Good. Let her feel some anguish too. It wasn't fair for her to make him suffer like this. She knew he didn't like to be kept waiting.

"We cannot wait all day," he hissed, loosening the fabric to allow her some air that might bring with it some words.

"It was a big vision this time," she said, gasping for air between words. He noticed the lack of oxygen had brought some color to her face. It'd done her some good. It was just as well he knew what she needed.

"It was an important vision," she said. "The most important I've ever had."

"Speak to the point! We can't understand such nonsense." Why couldn't women say what they meant? Why so many words to say so little?

"There's a way for you to rule all the kingdoms." Her eyes glazed over, as if his ancestors were speaking to her still.

"All of them?" This was impossible. Nobody could rule all the kingdoms. No King had ever come close. Forte Cadence was already the largest of the five kingdoms. If he could take over just one more, he'd be the most powerful ruler of all time.

The itch in his groin returned and he reached down to adjust his manhood.

"There's a power greater than swords," his Queen said. "Greater than combat with the most skilled set of hands. No King has discovered it. You can be the first. And with it, you can be untouchable. The greatest King the world has ever seen."

"Speak! What power is this? We must know. Tell us immediately."
He grabbed at her throat again, trying to force the words from her
mouth, wishing his ancestors had taken a more direct route this time
than to use this stupid woman as a conduit.

"Words," she said, grabbing at his hands, trying to draw them away
from her neck. "Please, my Lord, let me speak."

"Then speak!" He spat at her as he released her throat, watching his
saliva land on her forehead and run down her nose. It was an excellent shot. "What power is it that we must get our hands on?"

"Words are the power. Words. Spoken words. They hold all kinds
of magic." Her eyes were wide open, only she seemed to be looking
straight through him. She often looked at him in this way and he
didn't like it. She should be honored to look directly in the face of her
King. It was a privilege not extended to many.

He leaped from the bed and paced the room, wondering how he'd
been so foolish to make such an idiot woman his Queen. Words!
Ridiculous. What use were words in a battle?

"You put the words out in the air and leave them there for the
universe to hear," she said, daring to wipe the saliva from her face
with the hem of her nightdress. This annoyed him further. He liked
seeing the stain of spit on her forehead, as a reminder of who had
control over this situation.

He picked up the sword he kept next to his bed and waved it in the
air, pretending to battle an imaginary solider. "So, we ask the other
army nicely to pretty please put down their swords?"

The Queen stared at him, knowing better than to interrupt when
he was enjoying himself with her like this.

"Please sir," he mimicked in a high-pitched voice, not unlike the
Queen's annoying tone. "Would you mind please putting down your
sword, so we can kill you and take over your kingdom? Why, thank
you. Much obliged."

"That's not what I mean." Her voice was quiet, like the small child's
intellect she possessed.

He swung his sword to point at her chest, directly over her heart.
"Then what exactly do you mean, Queen?"

"If you say something out loud, the universe hears." She grasped the blade of his sword and tried to shift it from her chest. He held it firm, her pathetic hands no match for his brute male strength. *He would be the one to decide when the sword moved.* A bright red drop of blood dripped from her hand to her nightdress, landing on the white fabric and expanding to a large blotch over her pregnant belly. The belly that held what he hoped would be a son this time. A son that was keeping his mother alive just as much right now as she was giving him life.

"Keep talking," he said. "Use these words you speak of to tell us what you mean."

"When we speak, the universe hears. If we speak of something as if it's already happened, then we can fool the gods, and it will become reality." Another drop of blood landed on her nightgown and he removed the sword, not wanting her mess on his bedsheets.

"This sounds like nonsense." He was disgusted by this woman before him. Perhaps he should make a big mess of her and be done with it. After his son was born, of course.

"The more people who say it, the more likely it will come true." She wrapped her hand in the fabric of her nightdress, her blood mingling with his spit.

"Give an example of how this might make King Virtus the ruler of all the kingdoms in the world." He really was a merciful King, hearing her out like this. The fact that every single one of her previous visions had proven to be correct was what was weighing on his mind. Why would all of them be true and this be utter nonsense?

"Instead of training fighters to protect our land, you train an army to say, *"Our Kingdom is free from invasion,"* over and over and over. The universe hears this and makes it true. We will be free from invasion for the rest of our days."

He rubbed at his chin, wondering if it could be as simple as this. "And how does this stretch the borders of Forte Cadence?"

"You have your army say *'The kingdom of Wintergreen belongs to King Virtus.'* And so it will come to be." She smiled as if this would make him believe.

He considered what she was saying, liking the idea of it. And how could it hurt to have his soldiers wish as they marched?

"We will speak to the Commander," he said, taking steps toward the door. "He can instruct the army on what they must say."

"My Lord," the Queen said. "Not yet. You need a new army. A special sort. The most powerful army the world has ever seen."

"Our army is the most powerful."

"No, my Lord. Our army isn't the most powerful." She shook her head, her blonde hair shimmering over her shoulders, reminding him why he'd called her in here in the first place. Except this didn't excuse what she'd just said.

"It's not *our* army, you idiot woman!" he said, leaning in closer so she understood. "I said *our* army to mean *my* army. It's not yours or your stupid daughters' army. It's mine. Do you understand?"

She nodded, pulling away from him ever so slightly, as if he wouldn't notice. "Sorry, my Lord. However, there's a special type of soldier needed for this. Soldiers who have a gift even they don't know they possess. Your army won't be useful for this. But I know how to find your new soldiers."

"Then they must be found. King Virtus must be the most powerful King the world has ever seen."

"Yes, my Lord. You must." She bowed her head and he went to her and tore her blood-stained nightgown from her hand and lifted it over her head. She may be fat with his child, but she belonged to him. It was his right to take her.

He was the King. The ruler of Forte Cadence and soon to be the ruler of the world. The world had never seen anyone like him. As he positioned himself above the Queen, he imagined himself through her eyes.

Strong. Powerful. Merciful. Masculine. It was no wonder she was so keen to bear his children. A woman's purpose was to find herself a man who could spill the highest quality seed inside her. And his Queen had done better than any woman who'd ever drawn breath. He had to give her credit for that. She'd fulfilled her quest as a female to perfection.

Clever whore.

KING VIRTUS

THE AFTER

"*The Whisperers are whispering. The Whisperers are whispering.*"

King Virtus stood on the balcony of the arena and clasped his hands. Whisperings never failed to send shivers down his spine.

From where he stood, the Whisperers looked like an army of beetles with their hoods pulled over their heads. He loved it. A thousand filthy insects ready to whisper for whatever his heart desired.

When his grandfather had this arena built, it was for fighting with swords instead of words. As a small child, he'd loved watching the soldiers train, knowing they were learning skills to protect him. He'd thought there was nothing more magnificent he could ever see. Except he'd been wrong. Because this sight was far, far more magnificent.

He'd done well to immediately recognize the truth in the message from his ancestors about the power of speech. His stupid Queen had had no idea of the importance of the message she was passing on. But he'd known as soon as he'd heard it. Perhaps he should whisper for his ancestors to go directly to him the next time they had something important like that to say. It was odd that they trusted a woman with something like that. Especially one as stupid as his wife.

He'd never admit to anyone that he'd tried to bring on the visions himself, lying in his bed and staring into the darkness, waiting for something to appear. Much to his frustration, nothing had ever happened. Clearly, his ancestors were protecting him. The visions would be too draining. He needed his strength to rule the kingdom. There was no other explanation.

At least he'd been clever enough to select a wife who could do this for him. Not that he'd known it at the time. He'd married her because the first time he'd seen her beauty, he'd been unable to stop imagining the handsome son she could produce for him. And after the son, perhaps a few pretty daughters to show off at parties. He hadn't realized it would happen the other way around, with the daughters coming before the son.

He watched the Conductor lift his sword above his head, scanning the room for any disobedient beetles. They all seemed to be in line. Pity. It was always such good sport to see one of them lose their head.

As the Conductor's eyes continued to scan the room, King Virtus cursed his great-great-great-great-grandfather who'd changed the law, so the first-born child would be the heir, no matter their gender. Apparently, that particular King Virtus had a daughter, who was both his first-born and his favorite child. He claimed she was the most intelligent of all his children, which seemed impossible given he also had several sons. So, he had the law changed. Then the daughter had died in her sleep one night and her younger brother had ended up as heir, making the change completely unnecessary and extremely bothersome for the generations to follow. His great-great-great-great-grandfather had been so distraught at his daughter's death that he'd thrown himself out the window and killed himself. The only silver lining in this whole sorry tale was the hopeful thought that maybe the daughter had been poisoned by her brother, which would prove that he'd been smarter than her after all. Young girls didn't usually die in their sleep without at least a little help.

The King cleared this throat, impatient for the Conductor to finish checking his beetles. They all seemed to be doing what they were supposed to do at this stage of the ceremony, which was precisely nothing.

That ridiculous new law designed to protect the King's precious daughter had really only served to do the opposite, not just to her, but to all his first-born granddaughters of the future. This included the girl the Queen had given birth to, not long after she'd told him of her vision of the Whisperers. His fourth daughter. His fourth disappointment. And now the Queen was pregnant again, this time with his son and finally his plan was back on track. Soon a Prince would be born and he'd make certain he became the next King. It was a little bit of a shame, though. His daughters were pleasant distractions. His eldest daughter, Rose, was brighter than most girls her age (not that that made her especially bright, of course). She'd seemed particularly happy when he'd seen her earlier in the day, humming to herself. Perhaps her mother had bought her a new dress or tried a new style in her hair. He had no idea how a teenage girl's mind worked. Seeing her happy like that had convinced him that he'd done the right thing. Nineteen years of life was far better than no life at all. He was a good man.

At last, the Conductor brought down the sword and lifted his face to lock eyes with the King, waiting for his signal to start.

As keen as he was to get started, King Virtus decided to wait a few moments, just to prove who was really in charge here.

If only he could change the law back. It wasn't that simple or he'd already have done it. Nobody alive today had been around in his great-great-great-great-grandfather's days and his people had been led to believe that the laws of Forte Cadence were firmly set and not up for negotiation.

If he changed one law, it wouldn't be long before they demanded other changes. He knew the laws around property ownership were particularly contentious, especially for families without a son. They'd insist on handing down their properties to their daughters and this was as ludicrous an idea as a woman ruling a kingdom.

The Conductor held his gaze as he waited, with no sign of any impatience.

He really was a good Conductor. The best one he'd had. The two who'd come before him had been useless. Soft. Treating the Whisperers like humans instead of the nameless insects that they were. One Conductor had been a woman. No surprise she'd lasted the shortest time of all. He'd been saying it his whole life... women were for breeding, not for leading. He'd had both those Conductors killed. But not this one. He'd been conducting for five years now and had a skill for it. He didn't just do the job—he enjoyed the job. The first Conductor to realize he had the best job in the world. After the King himself, of course.

King Virtus continued to take his time. So many bodies frozen, waiting for his command.

He'd given the Conductor his Whisper earlier in the day. The Queen was getting very close now to giving birth. Soon, his greatest wish would come true. He needed to make sure nothing went wrong.

He stood up straight, smoothing his robe over his flat stomach, glad he'd had the Whisperers sort out his physique early in their service. With his full head of hair and muscular build, the Queen couldn't get enough of him when he called her to his bed. He'd never looked so good. Neither had she since he'd whispered for her looks to be restored. It was incredible to have such a young-looking woman convulse with pleasure underneath him again.

Taking in a deep breath, he nodded. Only a slight movement, yet enough for the Conductor to see.

"The Prince is a healthy and strong baby," the Conductor whispered.

The first row of beetles lifted their heads and slipped off their hoods, looking up at their leader.

"The Prince is a healthy and strong baby," the Conductor whispered again.

The first row stood, so silently that it felt for a moment as if the King had lost his hearing.

"*The Prince is a healthy and strong baby,*" they whispered.

At the command of their Conductor, each row stood to join the chorus of whispers, until finally, one thousand beetles were sending the King's wish rising into the air, swirling above the golden roof of the arena and flying out for the universe to hear.

He was going to have a healthy and strong son. He was going to be a father! Well, a father to a boy for the first time and it was the greatest feeling he'd ever known. How proud his own father would be if he were here to see this.

The Whisperers chanted his wish, over and over and over, until each of them had spoken it one thousand times. The King always stayed until the very end, reveling in the sound of his heart's desire echoing off the walls. It was just as well it was the Conductor's job to keep count, as he'd get lost in a fantasy, visualizing his wish coming true.

Today he was seeing his son standing by his side. He pictured him with dark hair that fell in waves around his face, as his own hair had done when he was a child. There was no sign of the Queen in the boy's face in this fantasy. He was a replica of himself at around ten years of age, still young enough to be a boy, yet old enough to understand the responsibilities that lay ahead of him. He was sensible, wise, fair, handsome. So much like himself that the King just knew people were going to stop and stare when they saw him with his son.

The Conductor tapped his sword on the floor in front of him and the front row fell into silence, pulling their hoods back over their hideously bald heads and kneeling.

The second row finished at the end of the next Whisper and did the same. Row by row, the beetles ceased their Whispering and returned to their mats, until the arena was silent once more.

Their deed had been done in just the way his ancestors had instructed. Well, not exactly. His ancestors hadn't instructed him on the finer details of how his army needed to be housed and treated. He'd improvised that part himself and was proud of what he'd come up with. The rules he'd put in place made sense. It was important that these beetles know their place in the palace and in life. And there was no doubt that it was working. Every single one of his wishes had come true. It seemed his ancestors didn't know everything. Fortunately, he did.

And any day now, his son would be born, healthy and strong, just as he'd wished for. The future ruler of his Kingdom. A child with enough intellect and courage to be exactly the kind of leader needed for a role this important. A child just like himself. His long-awaited son.

AURELIA

THE BEFORE

*T*he Queen never thought of herself as the Queen. She was Aurelia. A woman. A person with blood in her veins who felt all the same emotions as anyone else. Only she wasn't allowed to be Aurelia anymore. She was *the Queen.* Except to her husband, who called her any name he liked. And to her beautiful daughters, who called her Mother. And there was nothing or no-one she loved more than her daughters. Rose, Eliza, and sweet little Tash. Three perfect human beings, who were kind, clever and ... well, scared.

She could see the fear in their faces whenever their father was near. They sensed how disappointed he was in them, not for anything they'd done, but simply for who they were. Girls.

She was pregnant with her fourth child, already knowing it would be another girl. She could feel her new daughter's spirit bonding with her own as she nurtured her inside her womb. Another girl to love and protect. Another girl who she'd need to prepare to run when the time came, as she knew it would.

As soon as she gave her husband the boy he wanted, her daughters' lives would be in danger. This was why she'd begged the universe for girls, over and over, hoping that by the time a boy arrived, Rose would be old enough to take her sisters to safety. And so far, the universe had been good to her.

The universe worked in such mysterious ways. Sometimes it was easy to trust in, and other times it took all the strength in each and every cell of her body to let it sweep her along its path.

She had an angel, who talked to her and led her in whatever direction she needed to go—sometimes for her own good and sometimes for the greater good.

When she was a young girl, her angel told her she'd marry a Prince, who'd one day become the King. She'd been elated. Despite being from one of the wealthiest families in Forte Cadence, what little girl didn't dream of marrying a Prince?

If only she'd known back then what she knew now. Although, thank goodness she hadn't. It would've given her nightmares and no child deserved that. Yet did she deserve the life she'd been given? Married to an evil man who let his people starve and plotted to murder his own daughters. A man who beat her, raped her and called her a whore. He was detestable. Thankfully, he was also stupid.

She lied to him. Often. More often than she told him the truth. He thought he knew her, but he didn't know the first thing about who she was. For a start, he believed she saw visions. And he did exactly what the visions told him to do. Which meant that really, he wasn't the King and ruler of the Kingdom like he believed he was.

She was. And she was playing the long game.

Aurelia made her way down the dark stone staircase, holding a lantern in front of her, stepping carefully so she didn't slip.

She shivered. The dungeons always made her feel like this. She'd hate to be trapped down here, like so many innocent people were.

One day, she'd see them all go free. But for now, they must suffer, as she was herself. When she unlocked their cells, as she hoped she would, she herself would also be free. The day was drawing closer.

She got to the bottom of the stairs and turned left, reaching into the large satchel slung over her shoulder. As she passed each cell, she flicked her wrist, sending a peach flying into the waiting hands of the prisoner. She did this every week and they came to expect her. Never did she look at them, never did she stop and speak. If she saw their suffering directly with her eyes, her soul would break along with her heart. These people didn't deserve this. It was an even worse life than that lived by the Whisperers.

If the guards had ever noticed what she was doing, they didn't say anything. Not to her and not to the King. Perhaps, unlike her husband, they had an ounce of compassion left to hold onto.

She reached the end of the corridor and turned right, approaching a guard at a station.

He nodded and she slipped a gold coin into his hand. His treat needed to be made with precious metal instead of fruit.

The guard led her to the cell at the very end of the next corridor. The cell she'd come here to visit. This one didn't have bars. It was a stone box with a wooden door and not even a window to let in some air.

He unlocked the door and swung it open, stepping back to let her pass.

She slipped inside and he locked the door behind her.

Holding her lantern out in front of her, she swept her eyes across the cell until they landed on the angel sitting in the corner on a worn mattress next to a bucket of her own filth.

"Hello, Gabrielle," Aurelia said, crouching down to sit beside the old woman.

She reached into her bag and handed the woman a flask filled with orange juice. The woman pressed it to her lips and drank with long gulps until the liquid was drained.

"Let me comb your hair," said Aurelia, handing her a peach, then reaching back into her bag for a comb.

"Thank you, child," Gabrielle said, cradling the peach as if it were a precious gem.

"I'm no longer a child," Aurelia said, smiling.

"You were the last time my eyes saw you." Gabrielle turned her cloudy eyes toward her. "And a beautiful child you were."

Aurelia blinked back tears, remembering the day she'd come

across Gabrielle at the markets, reading fortunes from a tent. Not being able to resist the temptation, Aurelia had slipped away from her older sister, Lily, and into her tent.

Gabrielle had laughed to see such a small girl in front of her, until she'd produced a silver coin and laid it on the table and Gabrielle had agreed to see what future lay ahead for her.

The old woman, who'd not been quite so old back then, had opened her eyes wide and gasped when she realized who sat before her. The future Queen of Forte Cadence.

Aurelia knew that her father moved in important circles and had hopes for Lily to marry the Prince, although this was the first time she'd been told that it wouldn't be her sister who'd steal the Prince's heart, but rather, Aurelia herself.

She knew now, of course, that it wasn't her husband's heart she'd stolen. That man was incapable of love, except if it was for himself or his imagined son. It was another body part of his altogether that'd won her his affections when he first saw her. A body part that she'd grown to despise almost as much as the man himself.

Gabrielle sucked on the skin of the peach, softening it with her toothless gums.

"I'm sorry," Aurelia said, just as she said every week. She'd never get over the fact that she'd been the one who'd put Gabrielle in here.

After meeting her at the markets, Aurelia had returned to her often, seeking advice and guidance, quickly becoming dependent on her wisdom and vision. It was in this way that she began to think of her as her own personal angel.

As she'd grown older, Gabrielle had gently told her that her life with the future King wouldn't be the happy one of her dreams. Aurelia had wanted to run and hide, but Gabrielle had encouraged her to stick to her path because it was an important one. She needed to go through the bad to get to the good. Because when she got to the good, it would make the bad so much better for everyone in Forte Cadence. Everyone, except the King.

When the years passed and her future transpired exactly as Gabrielle had told her it would, Aurelia had stopped visiting her.

What was the point in knowing the future if it turned out to be filled with misery? Ignorance was better than fear.

The first time her husband beat her, breaking three ribs and turning both her eyes black, she sent for Gabrielle, wanting to hear that her bad was soon to turn to good. She couldn't bear to suffer like this much longer and needed to know it was coming to an end.

Gabrielle had held her hand and wept by her bedside. Aurelia had thought she was weeping for her, but when the guards burst in and dragged Gabrielle to the dungeons, accusing her of being a witch, Aurelia had realized she'd been weeping not just for her. Her tears had also been for herself. Gabrielle had known what her own future held, and as wise and mystical and brave as she was, she too was still a human, and knowing you were about to be confined to life in a dungeon must certainly be a frightening thought.

Gabrielle hadn't run from her future. She'd walked toward it. And so must Aurelia. If they were going to turn bad to good, she must keep stepping forward.

"Did you tell him?" Gabrielle asked, wiping peach juice from her lips and leaving a streak of dirt across her cheek. "About the Whisperers."

Aurelia nodded, as she reached out to comb the old woman's hair. "I told him."

"And did he believe you?"

"Not at first, but yes, he did. He'll start recruiting his new army immediately."

Gabrielle smiled. "It's happening. It's really happening."

Aurelia hoped so, for many lives depended on it. Hers. Gabrielle's. The other prisoners. The Whisperers. Her beloved daughters. And this child who kicked her from the inside, letting her know that soon everything would be all right.

"And did you tell him how it needs to be done?" Gabrielle was watching her carefully.

"I did. One thousand Whisperers in rows of ten. All with the gift, whispering for whatever the King desires."

Gabrielle nodded.

"Are you sure, Gabrielle?" Aurelia asked. "Are you sure this is what will turn the bad to good?"

"It will." Gabrielle grabbed her hand and held it. "We must be patient. It's all part of the plan. Change won't come quickly. It'll still be years, not days or months. But it will happen. We must trust in the Angels."

Aurelia tried not to let her disappointment show. Years! How could she survive years married to that monster? Surely, he'd kill her long before then with one of his beatings. When Gabrielle had first told her what she must do, she'd thought change was on its way a lot sooner than that.

Gabrielle coughed and vomited into the bucket beside her. This often happened. Her stomach wasn't used to food and didn't know what to do with it anymore. Yet it never stopped Gabrielle from eating what she brought her.

Aurelia reached out and stroked her friend's back.

Of course, she could survive years. She had no choice. How could she complain when Gabrielle was prepared to do her part, locked away down here, suffering far worse than she ever had?

At least, as the Queen, she had a soft bed, clean clothes, as much food as she desired and a warm bath to soak in. And she had her daughters. Down here, Gabrielle had nothing.

If Gabrielle could do it, then she had no excuse. She could put up with her husband for a little longer. Or a lot longer. She could.

Couldn't she?

AURELIA

THE AFTER

Five years could feel like a blink. It could also feel like an eternity. Sometimes it could feel like both.

Aurelia wasn't sure if she wanted time to pass quickly or for it to stretch out. When the bad turned to good, as Gabrielle said it would, her life as she knew it would be over. She'd be safe from her husband, however, her daughters would no longer be by her side. And for this reason, she wasn't sure if she wanted to hold on tightly to the days she had left or watch them slip through her fingertips.

Her son should've been born many days ago now, but her belly was still full with him, her skin stretched so thin now that spidery red lines had made a map across her middle. Her husband had been sure to tell her how ugly this was. She didn't care. She liked being ugly to him. Not that it was enough to keep him from her bed.

It'd been a difficult pregnancy. Not physically—that'd been the same normal discomfort as her other pregnancies—but emotionally. Much like she couldn't work out how to feel about the passing of time, she couldn't decide how to feel about this child she nurtured in her womb.

Ever since Rose's birth, she'd dreaded the arrival of her son. Rose had shown her the true meaning of love. Before her, Aurelia hadn't had a clue what it felt like for someone to fill all the spaces of her heart. She'd been so alone in the palace, surrounded by servants who treated her with fear and a husband who she herself feared.

The King didn't like her family visiting and after what he did to Gabrielle when she'd brought her into the palace, she dared not let them come near her, for fear they'd be sent to the dungeon too. She missed her sister, Lily, most of all.

She'd felt so alone before Rose. Then came Eliza and Tash and her heart expanded to make room for them too, proving that love isn't finite. There's always room for more. After the Whisperings started, she'd had one more daughter, Cara, who she'd been pregnant with when she'd told the King about Gabrielle's vision for a new army, passing it off as her own.

He wanted his first Whisper to be for a son, but she'd lied to him, convincing him that her visions had been clear about this. He'd have a son, although for him to be wise and strong, he'd need to come about naturally. Being the fool her husband was, he'd believed her.

The truth was, she'd needed more time. Rose was now at an age she'd be able to take her sisters and run before their father did the unthinkable. She wanted to run with them. Maybe she would. Except she also wanted to stay to make sure her son would grow to be kind and merciful. If she left him with his father to be raised, there was no hope for him, which meant there was no hope for Forte Cadence and all the people who lived in it. Her people. She had a responsibility to them. She was their only hope.

As much as it shamed her, she'd thought about killing her husband. It would be so easy. But Gabrielle had warned her against this. It wasn't written in the plan. And to deviate from the plan would mean bad would never turn to good. She had to hold steady.

Since Cara's birth, she'd been pregnant once more, only her body hadn't been strong enough to hold onto this child. So, the King had Whispered for her health to be restored. And her beauty. She looked and felt like she had twenty years ago and it upset her. She didn't want to be beautiful for him. She wanted the privilege of growing old and he'd taken that from her, just as he was preparing to take her daughters.

She leaned back on her pillow and rubbed her hand across her stomach, her son kicking her in response. She wished he'd never be born. She loved him, of course, but his arrival would herald the departure of her daughters. So, there was resentment wrapped up with her love and it felt cruel to resent a child.

Her stomach cramped and she drew in a deep breath, recognizing the feeling. Her son would be born today. She looked out her window at the rising sun. Before it set once more, life would be different. Today was the day when everything would change.

Tears sprouted from her eyes and ran down her face, dripping to her chest. Time hadn't stood still for her. Change was upon her.

Swinging her legs out of the bed, she stood and clutched at her belly. *Rose.* She needed to go to Rose. It was time for her girls to run.

Aurelia placed one hand on her back and the other on her stomach and slowly made her way to Rose's room, opening the door quietly.

Rose was lying on her bed, staring at the ceiling. She was smiling in a special kind of way that only certain people smile. The realization hit Aurelia at the same time as the next cramp that swept through her middle. Her daughter was in love.

"Mother." Rose sat up, the smile falling from her face. "What is it?"

"Who?" Aurelia sat beside her on the bed, leaning back and groaning at the growing pressure on her pelvis. "Who is he?"

"What are you talking about? Are you okay? Is the baby coming?" Rose reached out and touched her belly.

"Who put that smile on your face, my sweet daughter?" She put her hand on Rose's and they looked at each other. Rose seemed to be deciding if she could trust her. Surely, she knew she could tell her anything!

Rose shook her head. "Nobody."

"Do you remember the story I told you of the girl in the tower?" Aurelia asked, squeezing Rose's hand.

Rose nodded. "Of course."

"It's time for you to cut off your hair and run far from here. Do you understand me? Your father will be so distracted by the birth of his son, he won't notice immediately. It's the perfect time."

Rose shook her head. "I can't."

"You can. I need you to take your sisters and find your Aunt Lily in Aria Flats. She'll know what to do. She'll help you. I know she will. You can't stay here." She tried to sit up and more cramps washed over her. Soon the cramps would become contractions, then contractions would become a baby. Time was running out.

"I can't go yet. I made a promise to someone." A faraway look washed over Rose's eyes once more. Aurelia didn't know how it was possible, but someone had stolen her beautiful daughter's heart. If the Prince in the story could find a girl in a tower in the middle of the forest, it made sense that someone could find her daughter here.

"Who is he, Rose? You can trust me. Who? Maybe he can help you get out? There's safety in numbers."

Rose shook her head. "He can't."

"Why, Rose? Why can't he?" Who could her daughter possibly have met, locked in her room? Not one of the guards, she hoped.

They both turned their heads as the door pushed open again. It was the Whisperer who brought them breakfast each morning. The one with the kind face.

He startled when he noticed her there and looked to the floor, seeming unsure if he should continue on in or leave.

"You can come in," said Aurelia. Rose was going to need her breakfast today.

He approached and set the tray down silently on the table.

"Thank you," said Aurelia. Even though she knew he wasn't allowed to reply it hadn't stopped her from thanking him each day.

She looked across at her daughter, wondering if Rose ever thanked him for his trouble.

Rose was looking out the window. Her cheeks were flushed and her breath coming in shallow gasps.

"Are you all right, Rose?" she asked, touching her on the arm.

Rose nodded, glancing at her briefly, then back out the window. "I'm fine thanks, Mother."

Aurelia looked back at the Whisperer and noticed his hands were shaking. And his legs. He finished with the tray and left as quietly as he'd arrived.

"Oh, Rose." She reached for her daughter again, forcing her to look at her. "Oh, Rose. It's him, isn't it? That's who you've made your promise to."

Rose shook her head, quickly and firmly. "No, it's not him."

Words may hold power in the arena, but right here, right now, they were useless. For Rose's face spoke far louder than her words were able.

"I won't tell anybody," Aurelia said, ignoring the growing pains in her middle. "It's okay. I'll look after him when you're gone. I'll find a way to get him out. I promise. But first, you must leave. And take your sisters with you."

"I can't. I can't leave without him." Her daughter crumbled, putting her head in her hands and letting sobs wrack her slender frame.

How could she deny her daughter this love? A love she'd always wanted for herself and never experienced. Except it was hard to be in love when you were dead. And that was most certainly what the King had planned for her.

"Let's go to your sisters," she said. "We must ready you for your journey. I've organized for your safe travel to Aunt Lily's. Everything's going to be okay."

She stood and pain washed over her, sending her back to the bed, groaning. Her other babies hadn't come this quickly. She hadn't counted on this.

"Rose," she said, clasping her daughter's hand. "Listen to me. Go to your sisters. Take them to the dungeon and find the guard named Tyron. He's waiting to take you to Aria Flats. Your Aunty Lily will take care of you."

Rose shook her head. Stubborn! Just like her father. This was no time for stubbornness.

"Your father is going to kill you," she choked out, wincing as a strong contraction gripped her.

Rose reeled back, unable to speak as she processed what she'd just been told.

It broke Aurelia's heart to have to be the one to spell it out to her like this. "He will. He insists his son will be King. You must leave."

"I'm his daughter," said Rose, biting her lip.

"Listen to me. He's going to kill you. And your sisters. You must run."

"I'm calling for the doctor." Rose slipped out of bed and left the room.

Aurelia screamed, not from the pain in her belly, but from the pain in her heart. Her son was coming into this world to breathe air that her daughters would be denied. She clenched every muscle in her body trying to hold the baby in. He couldn't come out. It wasn't supposed to happen like this. Gabrielle had promised her that her daughters would be safe.

"Rose!"

Her daughter didn't answer her call and instead, she was joined by a doctor who told her to push and wiped the sweat from her brow.

The labor was short and intense and as her son slipped from her body, she felt herself go numb, the pain in her heart outweighing the pain she felt anywhere else.

The doctor placed her son in her arms and she looked down at his face, not wanting to love him, yet unable to deny that she did. As much as her daughters were her children, so was this small pink boy.

He let out a cry and she held him immediately to her breast. He wasn't just precious to the father who was yet to meet him, he was precious to her.

The King burst into the room, just as her son attempted to suckle. He was a hungry baby, almost as if he knew he was going to need sustenance for the life that lay ahead.

"Where is he?" the King asked, rushing to the bed and tearing her son from her arms. His tiny lungs screamed in protest.

The King held him roughly, with no idea how to correctly cradle a newborn, having never held one before.

"Careful!" Aurelia cried without thinking, her concern for her son outweighing her concern for herself. "You must support his head."

The King looked at her, his eyes flashing with fury, and she flinched. He didn't like to be told what to do. Please let him show her mercy now. The doctor hadn't even finished attending to her yet.

But instead of hitting her, as she'd feared he would, he handed the baby back to her. It seemed he cared more for the welfare of his son than he did about his ego right now. She didn't think she'd ever seen him put anyone else's needs before his own.

She smiled as she pressed the baby's tiny lips to her breast once more. Her husband might think he needed this son, but right now their son needed only her.

"I love you, baby," she whispered, not wanting to use the name she dreaded having to give him. He may be forced to carry his father's name, but he'd never carry the coldness of his heart. She'd raise him better than that.

She touched his cheek with the tips of her fingers. He was so soft and innocent. That was what she loved most about babies. They were all born without sin. Even her husband had been born this way, as hard as that was to imagine. Had his mother loved him with the same force she loved this small child? She never met his mother. She'd died not long after giving birth to her twins, leaving them to be raised by their father. Aurelia had always wondered if the timing of her death was a coincidence. She hoped so, or her own future didn't look particularly bright.

"He looks like his father," the King said, leaning over her, and pushing her hand aside so he could get a better look.

"He does," she lied, seeing no resemblance whatsoever. He looked exactly like his sisters had at their birth.

Please let Rose be taking her girls to safety. Her heart couldn't bear to lose them when she'd only just found another piece of it that she hadn't even known was missing.

Whether or not her son ever ended up being King, he'd already changed the world for everyone in Forte Cadence.

Now it was time to find out exactly how. Whether she wanted to or not.

JEREMIAH

TEN

*H*e spoke to her.
        Was he crazy?

No, not crazy. He'd had no choice. He'd had to speak to her. Who else could he talk to, if it wasn't Rose? Not the Conductor, that was for sure. And none of the other Whisperers would help him save Micah. They wouldn't know how, even if they wanted to.

When Jeremiah arrived back in the arena, he noticed his mat had been moved to the front row, making him the tenth longest serving Whisperer in the palace. That was how they were ordered for the Whisperings. Rows of ten, with the most experienced at the front and the newer Whisperers at the rear. As one would leave, the ones who came after them would move up a place. On the rare occasion, when a Whisperer was returned from the dungeon, they'd have to take their place at the back of the room as if they'd only just arrived.

He lay down on his mat, feeling strange in this new position in the arena. It was hard to tell how the other Whisperers felt about moving up a place, but Jeremiah hated it. The worst times were like today when the new place also moved him up to a new row. Each time that happened, he'd carry the weight of ten departed Whisperers on his back like a sack of stones.

When the first Whisperers were brought to the palace, they'd been arranged in order of age, which placed Jeremiah in the last position in the very back row. So, it was with great dread that Jeremiah took his new place in the front row, knowing that nine hundred and ninety of his peers had fallen before him. He knew he was supposed to be honored to make it there, despite not being allowed to show it. When it was time for the Conductor to step down from his role, whoever was in the first position would take his place. Jeremiah knew that could never be him. He'd sacrifice himself before he ever became the Conductor, hopefully being sent to the dungeon rather than losing his head. It was one thing to do the King's bidding by whispering his wishes, it was another altogether to punish innocent people, stripping out their insides and leaving empty, obedient shells in their place, much like the walnut he used to wear around his neck. No, he could never be the Conductor.

His time was running out. He was now ten places away from having to act. For five years, he'd passively accepted the rules and kept himself out of trouble. But in ten places ... all that must change.

And although the Whisperers in front of him were the hardiest of all and Jeremiah should feel safe for years to come, it weighed heavily on his mind. His time in the palace had taught him that Whisperers could fall faster than expected. He certainly hadn't thought he'd move from the last row of the arena to the front this quickly.

He closed his eyes, pretending for a moment that he was back in the rear of the arena where he could hide. He felt so exposed in the front row with nobody to stand between him and the Conductor.

Although, now that Micah had appeared, the time for change wasn't in ten places. It wasn't even in three. He could no longer wait quietly for change to come to him. He had to go and get it himself. And talking to Rose had seemed his safest choice. Nobody had treated him like she had since he'd arrived here. Her sisters were frightened of him, hiding under their blankets when he set down their breakfast trays each morning. Her mother had the same kindness in her eyes as

Rose, and would thank him for his trouble, except never had she asked him a question or tried to get him to speak. Perhaps she understood the consequences better than her eldest daughter.

This was just one of the reasons Jeremiah had fallen in love with Rose. She was so pure of heart that she couldn't possibly believe he'd be killed for speaking to her. She was reckless too and as much as that had put him in danger, he liked it. She was the only person he'd seen in the palace brave enough to defy her father's rules. She was also the only person who'd treated him like a human. Without the few minutes he spent with her each day, he wondered if he'd have lost sense of who he was. Those few minutes were what had helped him keep hold of himself. And as much as he hadn't wanted Rose to guess his name, as she'd tried out each new guess he'd been screaming silently at her, telling her who he was, which of course had reminded himself that he was Jeremiah.

Was that what'd happened to the other Whisperers? Without someone to remind them of who they were, they'd somehow let go of themselves and accepted their lives?

He longed to know what was going on inside their heads. But not one of them—not one!—had ever tried to talk to him. Then again, nor had he tried to speak to them.

He owed Rose his life and for that reason, he'd decided to put it in her hands. If she betrayed him, he was dead. Although wasn't he as good as dead anyway?

He'd seen the uncertainty in her eyes as she'd promised to help him and that was okay. Because her uncertainty was still far more likely to help him than his certainty that he was unable to help himself.

He pulled his woolen blanket up to his shoulders, nestling down so his face was obscured. Closing his eyes wasn't enough to block his reality out. When he'd first arrived, he'd thought this blanket was harsh and scratchy. Not now. He loved his blanket and the small amount of privacy it gave him in the monotony of his life.

His days in the palace passed like clockwork, each one the same as the one before and certain to be the same as the one that followed.

He'd wake at sunrise and head to the bathroom with the other male Whisperers for hygiene time. At all other times, the Whisperers were treated like name-less, gender-less, everything-less servants, but at hygiene time a distinction was made. Perhaps if they were to see the opposite sex without their robes, they'd be reminded of the differences that existed between them.

They'd shuffle naked in single file through a long passageway, with freezing water pouring over them to wash the stink and disease from their bodies. Palace groomers awaited them at the end to inspect for any illness, sprouting hair or injury, like they were some kind of farm animals, which perhaps they were.

After hygiene time, they set out to do their morning chores. Delivering the royal breakfast trays had to be one of the easiest assignments in the palace, once Jeremiah got used to carrying the trays with a steady enough hand that he wouldn't make a single noise. Each step was fraught with danger and his stomach would groan at the delicious smells. He'd never get used to that.

After his deliveries, he'd go to the dining hall for his own breakfast, then back to the arena for rest time, as was happening now.

He shifted on his mat, peeking out from his blanket to look at the glass window at the very top of the arena's domed roof, waiting for the sun to hit the high point in the sky. This would tell them it was time for the female Whisperers to have their hygiene time and for the afternoon chores to begin.

Jeremiah worked in the laundry, which was tiring and lonely and he'd have to drag himself to the dining hall afterward for his watery soup, before collapsing in the arena for his night's sleep.

At sunrise, the clock would re-set and an identical day would begin. Only today the clock had been broken. By him. He'd broken it and ground the pieces beneath his foot by speaking to Rose. No day was ever going to be the same again.

He tried to stretch out on his mat as much as possible while remaining within its confines. His mat was the one place in the world that was his. A rectangle, five feet by three feet. That was all he had. His one little space on this enormous planet. He envied some of the smaller Whisperers who could stretch out their legs while they slept. That was one bonus of being in the front row at least. If his foot came off his mat at night, it was less likely to poke another Whisperer in the ribs.

The arena was also the one place where there was noise made by Whisperers. Snoring wasn't technically allowed, of course, however there was little the Conductor could do about it. At first, he'd dragged the offending Whisperer from their mat and beaten them. Or worse. But the Conductor soon realized that although there was a steady supply of replacements as needed, if they were to replace each one who snored, they'd never be able to keep up. So, only the heaviest snorers were punished now. And the sleep talkers, of course. Jeremiah had no idea if he was one of those who quietly snored. He doubted it, certain that he slept in silence. It wasn't like he could ask *Worried One* who'd slept beside him for over three years now. So perhaps he'd never know.

Snoring had quickly become Jeremiah's favorite noise and he'd lie awake at night, wondering what dreams were attached to these slumberous sounds. Did these Whisperers speak in their dreams like he did? Did they visit their families, have long hair and wear clothes without hoods made from fabric that was any other color but gray? He hoped so.

Or did they dream of taking the Conductor's sword and killing him with one stroke? Because more than once this had been the subject of Jeremiah's dreams and he'd woken in a sweat, disappointed to realize it was only a dream. He tried to feel bad about this. The Conductor was just as much a prisoner as they were. If he failed to do his job, the King would have him killed. There were a thousand Whisperers lined up to take his place. But he just couldn't feel bad for him. The Conductor was evil, taking pleasure in the punishments he dished out. Jeremiah could never do that. He'd rather die.

Ten places from certain death. That's all he was.

He'd been right to talk to Rose.

He froze in his thoughts, as he felt a Whisperer walk past his mat. With the absence of the sound of footsteps, as bare feet padded silently through the palace, he'd gotten used to sensing people were near, rather than hearing them.

He was certain it was Micah, yet he didn't look up. That would only endanger both her and him. He could never risk her safety. Which meant that now he was unable to take risks himself—for her survival depended on him. He must get her out of here.

It was crazy that she was in here anyway. He'd told her about the test, even though he wasn't meant to. She should've known how to answer the questions to keep herself safe.

Feeling certain that Micah had passed by, he peeked out from under his blanket. Almost all the Whisperers had finished their morning chores and were back on their mats by now. From the corner of his eye, he could see Micah making her way to the back of the arena, to the very last row, the one furthest away from him.

He startled to see something white on the edge of his mat. A folded piece of paper. A note from Micah? He hoped not. That would be far too risky. If the Conductor found a note being passed between Whisperers they'd both be killed.

Careful not to react too quickly, he reached out and picked up the paper, taking it under his blanket and clutching it in his palm. If the crinkling of the paper hadn't been heard, then surely the sound of his heart hammering was echoing around the arena? It sounded like a hundred drums beating in his ears. If the guards suspected something was wrong, he was done for.

Taking his time, in case his behavior had been noticed, he stared at the ceiling with a bored expression and counted to one thousand.

He loosened his hold on the note, frightened that the sweat from his palms would obscure the message. If indeed that's what it was. It could be anything really. Actually, no, it couldn't.

Whisperers weren't allowed access to paper. Or pens. Or the fancy feathers the palace workers used. Or anything they might use to communicate with each other. There was no way this note falling on his mat was an accident. It was meant for him. He hoped none of the other Whisperers in the room had seen Micah dropping it, although he doubted they'd squeal on him. It was hard to squeal when you had no voice.

He unfolded the note under his blanket as slowly as he could, keeping his eyes on the ceiling. It was a high ceiling with timber rafters that crossed at strange angles beneath the golden dome of the oval shaped roof. He knew these angles better than the lines on his hand, he'd spent so much time staring up at them. The arena was long and relatively narrow, and as he'd moved his mat up a row, he'd stare at a new set of rafters. He was certain he could sketch them perfectly if required.

When he was sure he hadn't aroused any suspicions, he took a deep breath, preparing to position himself in such a way that he could read the note. Would he even remember how to read? It had been such a very long time.

He turned to his side, slowly, carefully, as if he were going to sleep, and lifted the blanket slightly to let in a small amount of light.

He *was* holding a note. A small piece of paper that looked like it'd been torn from a larger piece.

The first thing he saw was a letter on the bottom of the paper, drawn in a large childish hand.

It was the letter M.

Micah. Thank goodness she hadn't been foolish enough to sign it with her name. Although, he would've preferred it if she hadn't signed it at all. He'd already known who it was from.

She'd risked everything to deliver this note to him. Both her life and his. It was the most selfless and selfish gift he'd ever received. And as much as he wished she hadn't done it, he was so glad she had. Because right now, as frightened as he was, he felt more alive than he had in the five years since he'd come to the palace. More alive even than when he'd talked to Rose.

Micah was his family. She represented everything about his life before he came here. Rose might claim to have always seen him as a person, not a Whisperer, but it was Micah who knew him as the person he was. Rose would never get the chance to do that. Unless somehow if he did manage to escape, he could take her with him as she'd asked.

He relaxed his face, closing his eyes almost all the way, to look like he was sleeping and fixed his eyes on the paper. There was only one word on it and it was smudged, as if written in a hurry. Still, he could make out what it said.

Surprise! M

He shook his head and suppressed a laugh. She'd risked her life— and his— to say that. Although if he thought about it, the note said a whole lot more than one word. It said that Micah was still… Micah. Still his little sister, ready to jump out from behind a corner and announce "Surprise!" He was certain she was telling him not to cry over her like he had in the dining hall.

Micah had been here two days. Two days! And already she was far braver than he'd been in five years. He'd always loved her fighting spirit, but now he was in complete awe of it. She could—and would— do anything she wanted to.

He held in a gasp as a wave of truth washed over him.

Micah was in here on purpose. She'd wanted to find him and had passed the Whisperers' test intentionally. She'd known exactly how to answer the test questions. And she'd chosen to answer them in such a way as to put her here.

What did that mean? Was she trying to save him? Or had things gotten so bad outside the palace that she was trying to save herself? How could she leave Ma, Da and the baby like that? Dread punched him in the gut. Maybe there was no Ma, Da or baby for her to leave. Why else would she be here?

No, he shouldn't be so negative. His parents were fine.

Whatever Micah's reasons, she was serious about what she was doing and clearly, she wasn't going to waste any time doing it.

Soon he would find out. Either that, or soon he'd be dead.

MICAH

NINE

*M*icah settled down on her mat at the back of the arena and carefully arranged the blanket over herself. She hated this blanket. It was itchy and she longed to be back home in the days when her parents were alive and she had a soft quilt on her bed.

Hopefully, Jeremiah had found her note by now. If not... she shuddered. As long as he found it before a guard did. Surely, he would. She was certain he'd been aware of her walking past his mat. He'd frozen, as if holding his breath, until she'd passed.

Her beautiful, brave brother. It'd taken all her strength not to fall to the floor, throw her arms around him and whisper *surprise* directly in his ear. For as different as he looked on the outside, she could tell he was still the same person. The King may own his body, but he didn't own his soul.

She smelled like last night's soup, which wouldn't be so bad if it were the kind of soup her mother used to make, not the revolting slop she'd been assigned to dish into bowls as each Whisperer approached for their second and final meal of the day. It was a horrible job, although not as bad as her morning chore of chopping up the ingredients that would be used to make it. Cutting a carrot without making a sound was impossible. Thankfully she hadn't seen the Conductor in the kitchen yet. Potatoes were quieter, and onions quieter still, even if they made her cry. Not that there were many ingredients to cut up, given the amount of people they had to feed. The soup was mainly water with a few herbs she'd seen the cook stir in and the small pile of vegetables she prepared. To think she and Tallis had imagined Jeremiah in the palace eating a roast chicken!

She wasn't allowed to eat any soup herself, until the last bowl had been served. And as much as she detested the foul liquid, her stomach disagreed and growled at the smell of it, not fussy about what it was she put in it, just as long as she filled it with something.

A growling stomach was a dangerous thing for a Whisperer. Thankfully the sound must have been muffled under her heavy robe. Any louder and she'd really be in trouble. The Conductor had made that very clear in her training. No noise was acceptable, bodily functions included. An attack of the hiccups could be deadly, as could their twice-daily toilet breaks, which needed to be kept as quiet as humanly possible. A true Whisperer needed to be in control of their minds, their bodies and their voices. No exceptions. Ever. Although she noticed that snoring seemed to be conveniently ignored.

There'd been four of them in her training group. Only three had made it through with their heads attached to their necks. The unfortunate fourth one had been used as an example very early on when she'd asked the Conductor for some water. She was a woman who'd had long dark hair before they'd been lined up and shorn bald, leaving scalps as smooth as the oranges that'd lured them there. The woman's mouth had dropped open after her head had fallen to the floor, as if still seeking the water she'd asked for. Micah hoped that wherever her soul traveled after this life, it was to a place filled with water and she could swim and drink and live a life that'd been robbed of her too soon.

The Conductor had smiled at them after the deed was done and asked if they understood the consequences of not following the rules.

It was the first time he'd smiled and Micah had been horrified to see his yellow teeth clicking. She wondered if he did that in every training group, as a way to ensure full compliance. Because it was extremely effective. Before the beheading, they'd been reluctantly complying. And after... Well, after, things were different. They'd actively complied—watching their every movement, every sound, every reaction. The risks were too high.

She'd seen fear in the faces of her two remaining companions and wondered what they saw when they dared to look at her. They may mistake it as fear, but it wasn't. It was anger. How dare they trick her brother and take him from his family like that! How dare the King treat people as pawns in his sick game. She didn't care what he had to wish for. No wish could be so important it was worth taking the lives of so many innocent people.

And as much as fear may drive compliance, anger drives rebellion. And she intended to waste no time.

As she'd dished up Jeremiah's bowl of soup, he'd looked directly into her face and they'd asked each other a thousand questions without saying a word. She wanted to let him know it was still her and that she was all right. He looked so heartbroken. How could she convey that in a few seconds of silence as she handed him a bowl? She couldn't.

So, as soon as the cook's back was turned, she'd torn the corner of a page from the large leather-bound book he used to keep track of supplies. The cook was the only Whisperer Micah had seen with access to such a thing as pen and paper. Assigning Micah to work in the kitchen was the universe practically begging her to make the most of it.

She'd taken the pen, dipped it in ink and scribbled her note as fast as she could, not daring to take the time to write more than the one word needed to let Jeremiah know that it was still his sister inside this Whisperer's robe.

Barely allowing the ink enough time to dry, she'd folded the note and tucked it into her armpit. With no belts or pockets on her robe, her choices were limited. This morning's rest time was the first opportunity she'd had to pass on the note. Breakfast had seemed too risky.

In a perfect world, she'd have written Jeremiah a note detailing her plan of escape. But the escape plans she'd had before coming into the palace, seemed foolish now. Knocking out guards and stealing their keys so they could run into the darkness of the night was just a fantasy. It wasn't possible. Nor was setting fire to the palace and escaping during the chaos. Everything was too tightly locked down. There were too many eyes watching and too much silence to make any sudden moves. She needed a new plan. Jeremiah had been here for years now. He must have some idea of what they could do. Or at least tell her what he thought of the new idea she'd been busy forming in her mind. An idea that would save more than just her and Jeremiah. An idea that could save them all. The more she thought about it, the more she thought it had potential.

Micah lay as still as she was able, waiting for the sun to hit its highest point in the sky, which would announce the female Whisperers' hygiene time. Not that being squirted with cold water and having a razor scraped all over your body seemed like great hygiene, although she had to admit she was cleaner here than she'd been when sleeping under bridges. Or even cleaner than she'd been in the Before, when Jeremiah would tell her that the dirt was making her freckles join up. She smiled at this memory.

Sunshine burst through the apex of the arena's dome, announcing the midpoint of the day and Whisperers began to rise from their mats. Slowly. Quietly. Micah stretched and got up, her body moving at the opposite speed to her brain, as she psyched herself up for what she was prepared to do. It was time to give Jeremiah another surprise. A proper one this time. The sort that made him jump.

She made her way up the side of the arena, glancing as quickly as she dared at Jeremiah's mat. He was still lying with his head tucked inside his blanket. The note was gone. She hadn't heard the guards making a fuss, so he must have found it.

She left the arena and padded down the hallway, following the trail of female Whisperers, keeping her eyes cast down. A palace worker stood at the bathroom door, with a whistle around her neck, ready to alert the Conductor should any Whisperer step out of line.

There were no mirrors in this bathroom, for that would mean appearance was important. The lack of mirrors would work in Micah's favor today, to help her pull off her surprise.

Micah took off her robe, slipping something out of the hood as she did so. The magic tricks she'd performed at the market had served her well. Her sleight of hand so precise that she could take the belt from someone's waist without them noticing. She placed her robe in the washing crate, careful to conceal the hidden object she kept in her hand. Her nakedness was of no concern to her. She'd already become used to seeing the other females naked, just as she'd become used to them seeing her. Their skinny bodies all looked much the same without curves and bumps to define them. There wasn't much to look at apart from their varying heights and the shapes of their breasts.

As Micah approached the shower tunnel, which was more like a torture chamber than anything resembling a shower, her wrist flicked so quickly that only the most trained set of eyes would ever notice.

She hesitated, slowing her pace, waiting for the worker to see what Micah hoped she would think was a pool of blood seeping from the shower tunnel, but was in fact concentrated raspberry juice she'd pilfered from the kitchen and carried with her in a small jar, releasing the contents to create the distraction she needed.

The workers would never be able to figure out what that mess was and how it got there, even once they realized it wasn't blood. The women had no injuries and there was far too much of it to be explained away by a woman's cycle, if the bitter-tasting shot of liquid they were forced to swallow each week had failed to prevent it. It was just the sort of confusion she needed.

At the exact moment the worker blew her whistle, Micah dove into the crate of discarded robes and buried herself. She was so fast, she doubted any of the other Whisperers saw her, let alone the worker. She carefully wriggled herself into a robe, made sure she was covered and created a small pocket of air, listening to the commotion in the bathroom as the guards ran in. It was hard to make out each spoken word, just enough to glean that her plan seemed to have worked. The voices were nowhere near the crate, which meant that nobody had seen her climb inside.

She waited. Minutes felt like hours as the commotion in the bathroom settled. Then she felt herself moving as the crate was wheeled from the bathroom. She'd seen Jeremiah collecting the full crates the day before and had immediately decided this would be the best way to speak to him. Perhaps the only way.

The movement paused, then took off again. She was certain she must be in Jeremiah's hands by now, as she rolled silently along the passageways. Very slowly, she moved the robes out of her way, so she could get a glimpse of who was pushing the crate. She had to be sure it was him.

Light broke through the small space, as she shifted a piece of fabric and brought her face closer to the top of the crate.

She peered out and there he was. Her beloved brother, pushing the crate. He looked less sad and more frustrated since the last time she'd seen him. This was a blow. Surely her note should have reassured him that she was okay. He should be smiling to himself.

She watched him and waited, needing to be sure they were alone before she let him know he had some extra cargo today.

He turned a corner and parked the crate. She peeked out a little more and saw him opening a door. He returned to the back of the crate and pushed it through. The room they were in was warm and smelled damp. It must be a laundry. She only hoped he worked alone.

He closed the door behind him and wheeled the crate over to a row of large vats, stopping the crate in front of one of them.

Throwing aside the robes that were still covering her, she leaped to her feet and waved her hands over her head.

"Surprise!" she called, as loudly as she dared.

Jeremiah jumped in just the way she'd hoped. But as he spun around and looked at her, the expression on his face the opposite of what she'd hoped for. It was the face of anger. He didn't find this as funny as she'd hoped he would.

"Micah! Get down before someone sees you." His voice was not so much a whisper, it was more of a hiss.

"I had to see you," she said, crouching down. "I didn't mean to make you mad."

"You could get us both killed." His face softened just a fraction. He was clearly finding it hard to stay angry with her.

"Aren't we dead in here already?" she asked.

He went to answer her and stopped himself. Perhaps he knew she was right.

"Please give me a hug," she said, climbing out of the crate. She needed to feel her brother's love. She'd waited so long and been through so much to get to this moment.

Jeremiah's eyes pricked with tears and he reached out for her, wrapping his arms around her and pulling her close. It felt strange. The last time she'd hugged him, he'd been so much taller than her. Now her forehead rested on his shoulder.

"You're crazy," he said.

"I'm crazy about surprises." She giggled. It felt so good to laugh again. She couldn't remember the last time she'd laughed about anything. Perhaps not since she'd last seen Tallis.

Jeremiah pulled away, so he could look at her. "You came to the palace on purpose, didn't you?"

He'd figured it out. She knew he would and didn't want him to feel bad for having told her exactly how to pass the test.

She nodded. "I came here to get you out."

"Don't you think I would have gone already, if that were possible?" He kept his hands on her shoulders. She was glad. It steadied her. The relief of having him back by her side was making her feel faint.

"I have a plan," she said, aware that they were running out of time before their absence was missed. She needed to get to the point. "It came to me this morning and the more I think about it, the more it makes sense."

She felt him sigh, rather than heard it.

"You need to become the Conductor," she blurted out.

"No!" His hands dropped from her shoulders and he stepped away.

She flinched at the certainty in his response.

"Think about it," she said. "It makes sense. It's the only way we can take control. You're so close to the front."

"There are ten people in front of me, including the Conductor himself," he said, crossing his arms. "It could take years. And the last thing in the world I want to be is the Conductor. It's a position of pure evil."

"I know that." She reached out a hand and touched his cheek. "You don't have an evil bone in your body. That's why it has to be you."

"The King would have me killed. What good would I be to you then?" He took her hand from his cheek and held it.

"Think about it," she said again. "Together, we can figure this out."

"I'm already figuring it out." He squeezed her hand. "There's someone here we can trust. She'll help us."

"Who?" Micah tried not to feel put out. She wanted to be the one to help Jeremiah.

He hesitated. Surely, he knew he could trust her!

"Who?" she asked again. "One of the Whisperers?"

He shook his head. "The Princess. Rose. She's... my friend."

"Whoa!" Micah was genuinely lost for words. Jeremiah knew the Princess?

"Surprise!" Jeremiah smirked.

"I think you've topped all my surprises put together." She shook her head, trying to take all this in. "You sure she's good? You trust her with your life?"

"I trust her with both our lives."

There was a look in his eyes she hadn't seen before. Was Jeremiah in love with the Princess? This was another thing she'd joked about with Tallis. Surely it couldn't have come true. Princesses didn't fall in love with Whisperers.

Jeremiah smiled at her, and she knew what he was saying was more than possible. All the girls in the valley had been in love with her brother. The Princess may be a princess, but she was also a girl. Why should she be any different?

"Tell her about my idea," said Micah. "She'll agree with me. I'm certain of it."

"I need to get you back to the bathroom," he said, not seeming to want to discuss her idea any further. "You've taken a big enough risk already. Please don't do this again."

"I can't promise you that." She grinned, not wanting to lie to him.

"First, quickly, tell me how Ma and Da are. Was the baby a boy or a girl?" His face lit up in a way that broke her heart. What words could she use to tell him that awful truth?

She shook her head, quickly, looking to the floor, not wanting to see his face as she gave him this news. "It's just us now. Da didn't last long. Ma joined him shortly after, before the baby had a chance to be born."

Jeremiah stood very still, clearly needing a few moments to compose himself after hearing this news.

"No," he said, tears spilling from his eyes. "No, it can't be true. What about the food and medicine the King promised?"

She shook her head again, not needing words to let him know the King's promise was a lie.

"And our house?"

She shook her head once more, wishing she had some better news for him.

"So, I came here for… nothing? I knew I shouldn't have trusted the King." He stepped away from her and paced the room. It was a lot for him to take in. But she'd had to tell him the truth. Lies were for the King. She was better than him. They all were.

"I've been on my own this whole time," she said, going to him and putting her hand on his arm. "Now do you understand why I came for you? You're all I've got."

He nodded, wiping his tears with the back of his hand and pulling himself together. She knew he'd grieve properly later when he had a moment to let his thoughts settle. "I'm not happy you came… I wish you didn't… although…"

"You're happy to see me?" she prompted.

He nodded and drew her into an embrace again. "I didn't think I'd ever see you again."

"You might not, if I don't get back to the bathroom."

"How were you planning on that?" A frown crossed his face.

"I didn't really think that far ahead," she admitted.

He rolled his eyes. "Help me get these robes into the water and fill the crate with yesterday's dry towels. You'll have to hide in it again when I take it back to swap with today's wet towels. If you climb out at the bathroom wearing a towel you should be able to join the others."

"Looks like I'll be staying dirty for another day," she said, helping him remove the robes from the crate and dropping them into the vat of water as he added some powder from a bucket. "No shower for me."

"Since when did that bother you?"

"Hey!" She breathed a sigh, glad to see him joking with her again. The news she'd just given him had been a massive blow. He was going to need time to process it all.

"Have you seen Tallis?" he asked, as they worked.

She nodded. "Yes."

"Did he take care of you? Because if he didn't, then—"

"No! Jeremiah. He did. He was wonderful. I shouldn't have said that you're all I've got, because honestly, he was so good to me. I lived with his family for a while, but I was a burden to them and I ran away. He came to find me. He's been a good friend to me."

He really had. The best kind of friend. He was the only thing she missed outside the palace. Her dragon, who'd carried her on his back when she was a child, then did his best to look out for her when times got even tougher than before. The only reason he hadn't done more for her was because she hadn't let him.

Jeremiah was looking at her with a strange expression.

"What?" she said.

"Nothing. I'm just glad he took care of you when I couldn't."

She nodded and added another robe to the vat of water.

"I meant it when I said not to do this again," he said, reaching the bottom of the crate. "Emergencies only."

He was right. Being caught would be disastrous. Her plan depended on Jeremiah becoming the Conductor. If he was sent to the dungeon and placed in the back row again, they were doomed. He was so close. Tenth in line to the top job.

"Look away for a moment," she said, reaching for a towel and adding her own robe to the vat. She wrapped herself in the towel and climbed back into the empty crate.

"Pass the bucket of soap powder," she said, reaching out her hand.

"You're still bossy," he said, bringing her the powder. "Why do you need this?"

"Might come in handy." She took a large handful and held it tightly in her palm as she climbed into the crate and positioned herself in a corner. Jeremiah filled it with dry towels, which had been neatly folded, presumably by another Whisperer during their morning chores.

"I missed you," she said, as Jeremiah was about to place the final towel on top of her head.

"I missed you, too." He winked as he covered her over and pushed her from the room.

It'd been a risk, but one that was worth taking. If the Conductor killed her now, she couldn't say she'd die happy, however, at least she'd die with a little closure. It'd been so good to be back by her brother's side once more.

Jeremiah wheeled the crate through the palace and Micah closed her eyes and enjoyed the feeling of being safe, despite that not being the case at all. But for the moment, she was buried among clean towels being wheeled through a palace by her brother. Her brother who was in love with the Princess! It was going to take her a long time to come to terms with that as an idea. There was no doubt that the Princess would be a very powerful ally. If she agreed with Micah's plan, then there'd be no stopping them.

The crate came to a stop and Micah's eyes sprung open. Jeremiah tapped the towel on top of her head to indicate he was leaving her, and she waited for the palace worker to wheel the crate back into the bathroom.

Once back inside, she peered out from beneath the towels, waiting for an opportunity to escape.

The last of the women were emerging from the shower hall and heading toward their hygiene inspection with their towels wrapped around them. This was Micah's best chance.

The moment the palace worker turned her back, Micah jumped up and threw the washing powder across the room. It landed on the opposite wall and exploded like a water bomb completely covering the Whisperer at the front of the queue, waiting for her hygiene check.

The worker blew her whistle and Micah slid from the crate and joined the back of the queue. The Whisperer in front of her shifted her head slightly, making Micah wonder if she'd noticed, but she remained calm. It wasn't worth the risk for this Whisperer to draw any attention to herself. There was enough happening in the bathroom already.

Two guards came running at the sound of the whistle, their attention focused on the Whisperer with powder stuck to her damp skin.

"Again?" said one of the guards, taking her roughly by the arm. "What is it with you Whisperers today?"

"Congratulations," said the second guard, grabbing her other arm. "You're off on a little holiday."

Guilt wrapped its way around Micah's middle. This was her fault. She'd caused this. The fear on the woman's face, not understanding what had just happened to her, was an image Micah was going to need to learn to deal with. Because something told her that it was an image she was never going to be able to get out of her mind. Her need to talk to her brother had cost that poor woman a trip to the dungeon. It had perhaps cost her even more than that.

As she caught a glimpse of the woman's frightened face when she was dragged away, a memory turned over in the back of Micah's mind. She knew that woman. She'd seen her sleeping by Jeremiah's left side in the arena. That meant she was the ninth Whisperer. With her in the dungeon, Jeremiah was no longer tenth in line. He was ninth.

A small smile wrapped its way across Micah's face and she suppressed it, forcing her guilt to the surface once more to remove it completely from her face.

Without even meaning to, she'd gotten Jeremiah one step closer to taking on the most powerful position in the palace.

One down. Nine to go.

But how?

ROSE

EIGHT

*R*ose hid from her mother in Eliza's room. Not that it was particularly hard to hide from a woman who'd just given birth. Her mother couldn't exactly go looking for her. Although, it was a bit of a shame that the actual birthing bit happened in her bedchamber. Or perhaps *ironic* was a better word than *shame*. Ironic that her father's chosen heir was born in the bed of the true heir.

That was if what her mother had told her was true of course. Was her father really planning to kill her and her sisters?

She wrapped her arm around her younger sister's waist and drew in the smell of her freshly washed hair. Eliza liked to sleep late, not necessarily because she was tired, but because there was nothing else for her to do. Rose and her sisters hadn't been outside the palace since their birth. Not even to walk in the palace grounds.

She'd never understood why, although the reason was becoming clearer by the moment. Their father hadn't wanted anyone to see them. Perhaps if the people didn't see them, they'd forget they existed. They would certainly mourn them less if something *unexpected* were to happen to them.

She wondered why he hadn't just had them killed at birth? Although that reason was becoming clearer too. Until her father had a son, there was a chance he'd need his daughters to prevent his much-detested twin sister getting anywhere near his precious throne. Rose may be blind to some of the inner workings of the palace, but to this, her eyes were wide open. There was nothing her father hated more in this world than his sister.

Rose had met her Aunt Georgia a few times and couldn't understand what the problem was. She was everything her twin brother was not. Kind. Warm. Intelligent. If only she'd pushed ahead of him on their race to exit their mother's womb. Aunt Georgia would make a far better ruler than her father. Perhaps that in itself was what his problem was with her? He was threatened.

As much as Rose had hated hearing her mother tell her the truth about her father, she knew she was right. Her father wanted her dead. The only reason she was still alive was because her father had needed her in case something happened to him before his son was born. She was his insurance. An insurance that was no longer needed.

She'd heard her brother squawk through the walls of the palace a few hours before sunrise. Her innocent brother whose birth would cause her death. Prince Virtus. It wasn't his fault, although she was going to have to try hard not to resent him. If her father got his way, she wouldn't be resenting him for long. It was hard to resent someone when you were dead.

Maybe she should have taken her sisters and run? Maybe she still should? But how could she leave without Jeremiah after she'd promised him she'd get him and his sister out?

She let out a slow breath as she realized she couldn't get anyone out of the palace if her father succeeded in killing her.

There was only one possible solution to this. She needed to kill her father before he had the chance to kill her. It was time for the prey to be the predator. She was smarter than him, of that she was sure.

Eliza groaned in her sleep at the exact moment Rose remembered that killing her father was impossible. One of his first Whispers had been for his safety. He was untouchable. There was no point in even trying. She had to be even smarter than smart to figure this out.

What she needed was to put out a Whisper of her own. One more powerful than her father's Whispers. But how? The Conductor worked for her father alone. And he didn't seem to be the sort of man who could be corrupted or bribed. Perhaps she needed to kill him first.

At the thought of all this killing, she looked down at her hands, turning them to study her palms. Were these the hands of a killer? Was she capable of doing such a thing, even to someone as evil as the Conductor?

The door to Eliza's bedchamber opened, slowly. She looked across to see Jeremiah standing there holding her breakfast tray.

His eyes widened at the sight of her, then he broke into a grin.

"I was worried about you," he said quietly, glancing at Eliza to be sure she was asleep. "Your bedchamber was empty."

Rose crawled out of bed, careful not to wake her sister.

Jeremiah set the tray down on the table and she smiled to notice he'd done it silently, despite there being no need.

"I thought my mother was in my bedchamber," she said, taking him by the hand, so grateful that he'd spoken to her again. She was afraid he'd have thought about it and regretted his decision and would fall silent again. "She had the baby in there, so I stayed with Eliza last night."

"The Queen's been moved back to her own room." He ran his thumb across the back of her hand, sending warm waves down her spine. Was this what it felt like to be in love? Had her mother ever felt like this about her father? She doubted it. Perhaps her father had once felt like this for her mother, if his heart was indeed capable of feeling things like love.

"How's your sister?" she asked, keeping her voice low.

"I saw her," he said. "We spoke."

"How did you manage that?" Rose could hardly believe it.

"Doesn't matter." He shook his head. "She has a crazy plan. She wanted me to tell you about it."

"You told her about me?"

"Just a little. You can trust Micah." Rose wondered what he'd said to her. Had he talked about his feelings, or just stuck to the facts? Did he even have any feelings for her or was she just a way for him to get himself out of here? No, she could see the way he felt in his eyes. He loved her. She was certain of it.

"What's her plan?" Rose asked. "Maybe it's not so crazy."

The truth was that Rose didn't have any kind of plan. Perhaps Jeremiah's sister's idea would give them a place to start.

Jeremiah lifted his free hand to brush some hair away from Rose's face, a gesture only her mother had used with her before. She caught his hand and lightly kissed his fingertips.

He drew in a breath and held it, his eyes never leaving her own.

"She thinks I need to be the Conductor," he said.

At these words, Rose dropped his hand and stepped back, needing some air to think. She'd only just been thinking about killing the Conductor. Was this a sign that she was supposed to do exactly that? Still, she didn't think she had it in her.

"Don't tell me you think it's a good idea too?" He ran his hand over his shaved head and Rose wondered what his hair had looked like before it was taken from him. Hopefully one day she'd get to find out.

"What position are you in the arena?" she asked. "It has to be close to the front. You've been here for so long."

"I was tenth until last night, when I moved up a place. I'm ninth now. See, it's impossible. It'll take ages for me to move up any more places."

"If we can somehow get those who are in front of you sent to the dungeon and gather the courage to kill, or at least injure the Conductor, then maybe—"

"Rose!" He shook his head. "You're sounding like Micah now. She said you'd like her plan. I can't believe she was right."

"Maybe she's right about everything. Maybe this is the only way we can turn the tables on my father. Surely that has to be better than running and hiding, hoping that things get better when they're only going to get worse with my father on the throne. This evil has to end sometime." She had to find a way to make him understand.

"How does me being Conductor turn any tables?"

She took a step closer to him again. "Because if you're Conductor, you can change the Whisper. Think about it."

"Between you and Micah, I already have too much to think about."

"I like Micah." Rose grinned.

"She'd like you too." He quickly took Eliza's breakfast items from the tray and set them on the table.

Rose glanced at her sleeping sister. She'd wake soon. It was surprising she hadn't woken already with all the excited talk around her.

"I'd better go," Jeremiah said. "I'll return with your breakfast, although your sister will probably be awake by then."

Rose nodded. "Just one more thing then…" She stood on the tips of her toes and quickly kissed his cheek.

He flushed at the contact, went to say something and lost his words.

"Go," said Rose. "And think about it. Please."

He left and she climbed carefully back into bed.

It was time for her father's reign to end. And she was going to be the one to do it. Not alone, for that was the way her father had chosen to rule his kingdom—alone—she was going to do it with help. If everyone joined together to work against her father, surely even the most powerful Whispers in the world wouldn't be enough to protect him? She had Jeremiah. And his sister. And she had her mother and sisters. They could do this. This plan could work.

"He's cute," said Eliza, her eyes springing open.

"You were awake?" Rose swatted her playfully across the top of her head.

"Of course I was. You were just too love drunk to notice."

"You can't tell anyone about this," said Rose, gripped by sudden concern. "Not even Mother."

"I won't," said Eliza. "Promise."

"Thank you. It's very important. Not anything you heard or even that you heard Jeremiah speak. He could be killed for it. Do you understand?"

"I'm not stupid," she said, sitting up and crossing her arms. "Tell me, are you really going to kill the Conductor?"

"I don't know." This was the most honest answer she could give her. She hoped she'd have the courage to do it, but she couldn't be sure. "We have to do something, Eliza. There's more going on here than you understand. Please trust me. I'll always look after you."

Eliza nodded. "I do trust you."

"Thank you. I'm counting on you to keep quiet." Rose looked toward the door thinking she heard Jeremiah returning, but it was too soon for that. Perhaps she imagined it.

"Just one more thing then," said Eliza, leaning across to give Rose a peck on the cheek.

"You're teasing me!" said Rose, laughing.

"Not really. I'm happy for you. I've always liked that Whisperer, although I usually hide from him. He was a lot less scary when he was talking to you just now. Like a real…"

"I know. Like a real person," Rose finished. Her nose crinkled at the smell of something she couldn't place at first. She sat upright when she realized what it was.

"Eliza! Do you smell that?"

Eliza sniffed deeply. "It's smoke."

She was hoping she'd imagined it. This couldn't be good.

"There's a fire. Quickly now." She took her sister's hand and dragged her from the bed. "We need to leave."

Was her father wasting no time in dispensing of her?

Eliza started to cry, seeming so much younger than she had only moments before. "I'm scared. I don't like fires."

"I know. Me neither," she soothed. "It's okay. We'll stick together."

She went to the door and turned the handle, only to find it was locked. That must have been the sound she'd heard at the door. She didn't even know their doors locked. How was this possible? She tried again. No, it was definitely locked.

The smoke was creeping under the door now and billowing into the room. Eliza coughed. Her lungs had never been strong. Being kept indoors her whole life, instead of being allowed to run and play, hadn't helped her.

Rose dashed to the window, threw open the shutters and looked to the ground below. They were too high up to jump. Three men could stand on each other's heads and still they wouldn't reach their window from the ground.

"We can't jump," shrieked Eliza.

"No, we can't." Rose looked around the room for ideas. If only the girl in the tower was here to let down her long hair.

With a sudden idea, she reached for Eliza's bedsheets and stripped the bed. She tied one end to the bedpost and joined the sheets together, dangling them out the window, dismayed to see they didn't even reach halfway to the ground below. She pulled her makeshift ladder back up, looking around the room for anything else she could use.

"Take off your nightgown," she said, already unbuttoning her own. "Quickly."

Eliza was coughing now, blinking her eyes and not moving.

"Quickly! Eliza!"

She tied the sleeve of her gown to the sheet and removed Eliza's to add to the end. Dangling it out the window once more, she saw she was close. Perhaps they'd only break their legs if they fell now, instead of their necks.

"You go first," she said, pushing Eliza toward the window. "You need to climb down."

Eliza shook her head. "I can't."

"You can. And you will."

"I'm in my unders!"

"Nobody cares about your unders! When we get to the bottom, we'll put our gowns back on. You trust me, remember? You need to trust me now."

Eliza nodded, clutching at her body, like she had a secret to hide.

Her poor sister. If she didn't move quickly now, her little body would never grow old enough to develop any curves worthy of hiding. And anyway, their unders—as her sister liked to call them—covered everything that needed to be covered, reaching from their elbows to their knees.

"Eliza. I'm not leaving without you. If you don't climb down, then we both die. We're not dying today. Do you hear me, Eliza? Climb down!"

She was shouting now. It wouldn't be long before the flames broke down the door and once that happened they had no hope. If the sheets caught alight, then there was no way they were ever getting out of here alive. Her father would win. And she couldn't have him win. She'd already decided that she was going to win this game.

The door cracked and flames licked their way at the edges.

"Go! Now! Please! Just hold the sheets and slide your way down. You can do this. I'll be right behind you."

Eliza blinked once. Twice. Three times. Her body still, her mind undoubtedly racing. Then she moved.

She swung her little body out of the window, clinging to the sheet and sliding down fast. Too fast perhaps. Or maybe it wasn't fast enough. They only had seconds now.

Rose was right behind her. Gripping. Sliding. Screaming. Raging! How dare her father do this to them!

The fabric slipped from her hands and she fell the last few feet, landing partly on the ground and partly on top of Eliza.

"Are you okay?" she asked her sister, reaching for her and cuddling her close.

"No." Eliza sniffed, burying her head in Rose's chest. "My foot hurts."

"You're okay," said Rose. "We're both okay. We got out of there."

"What about Tash and Cara?" Eliza asked.

Rose jumped up, ashamed for forgetting about her younger two sisters for a moment. She looked up at the palace, directing her gaze to the window to the right of the one they'd just climbed out of.

There, looking out at her, were two little faces. Two frightened little faces.

"Tash! Cara!" she called, stretching out her arms. "Jump to me! Jump!"

She wasn't certain she could catch them, but jumping had to be a better chance than letting the flames eat them alive.

The noise of the fire was roaring now, drowning out any hope of her words reaching her sisters' ears.

Then a face appeared behind her sisters. A man in a robe. A Whisperer. What was he doing there? She peered harder to see if it was Jeremiah, but it wasn't. This was a face she knew though. It was the Whisperer who worked in the garden. She'd seen him outside her window. He'd been at the palace for years. Only now his face looked different. Like there was a man inside the robe, instead of an empty soul.

"Save them!" she called, even though she knew he wouldn't hear. "Save them!"

He reached for the girls, cradling them in his arms and sat on the window ledge. The girls were screaming, clutching onto him.

"Throw them to me!" Rose called, waving her arms now. Soon it would be too late. "Eliza, help! We need to catch the girls."

Eliza limped to her side.

The Whisperer pushed himself off the edge, holding the girls tightly. The next few moments in time seemed to pass in slow motion. He fell, turning himself in the air with the screaming girls holding the front of his robe. When his back hit the ground, it was chaos. Bodies scattered and separated. There was screaming. So much screaming.

Then Rose realized the screaming was coming from her own lungs. She reached Cara first and scooped her into her arms. She was alive. Her arm and possibly a leg were bent at strange angles and most certainly broken, but she was alive.

"I have Tash!" Eliza called.

Rose turned her head to see Eliza cradling their sister in her arms, in much the same way she'd held Eliza only moments before.

They were injured. Only time would tell just how injured. However, they were alive. All of them. Her father had failed.

She crawled to the Whisperer to see how he'd fared, still clutching Cara in her arms.

He was lying on his back, his breathing shallow. Death hadn't claimed him, but it was certain to. He was in terrible shape with blood pouring from a wound on his head.

"Thank you," Rose said, taking his hand. "You saved my sisters. Thank you."

He shook his head, the movement slight as he groaned from the effort.

"I didn't." His words were hard to make out, so she came closer, her face only inches from his.

"You did save them. I saw you."

"No." His breathing was raspy now, with blood bubbling in his lungs. "I tried to kill them."

"No! I saw you. The way you jumped. You protected them with your fall."

"I lit the fire. King's orders." His head fell to the side. "I'm … sorry."

"No, Whisperer!" Rose said again, placing a hand on his cheek. She'd seen him try to save her sisters. Seen the pain on his face. Except there'd been something else in that pained expression. There'd also been guilt. Clearly, he'd been forced to light this fire.

"What's your name?" she asked him, wanting him to leave this earth as a man, not a nameless servant.

"Jack," he choked out, before closing his eyes.

"Thank you, Jack. You saved my sisters' lives. You're a hero."

His chest fell still and she was unsure if he'd heard her words before he'd gone.

Why hadn't she listened to her mother and run when she'd had the chance? If one of her sisters had died today, it would've been all her fault. She may as well have lit the fire herself.

Instead, a determination lit inside her. Her father may have avoided war with the other kingdoms since he'd had his Whisperers in the palace, but right now, he had a war raging inside his kingdom. A war with his own daughter.

She knew right then that she had the strength to kill the Conductor. She'd kill ten conductors if she had to.

Evil wouldn't win this war.

She would.

JEREMIAH

SEVEN

*J*eremiah could smell smoke. Lots of it. It unsettled him, even more than Micah had with her crazy plan for him to become the Conductor. More than Rose seeming to agree with it.

He'd gone to the kitchen to collect Rose's breakfast tray, only to find it gone, which meant he was no longer required to deliver it. So, he'd gone to the dining hall to queue for his own breakfast with a heavy heart. He'd been looking forward to seeing Rose for a second time that day, even if her sister would have been awake by then. He hoped Rose knew how lucky she was to have a sister to sleep safely by her side.

When his own sister had jumped out of the crate and called *"Surprise!"* he'd had a thousand thoughts race through his mind. None of them good. And none of them were about her asking him to become the Conductor. That'd been the greatest surprise she'd ever given him. And ironically, it'd been the one time she hadn't prefaced it with the word surprise. She didn't seem to understand what it would take for him to make it to the top of the chain of Whisperers.

But Rose did. She'd made that clear in their rushed conversation just now, with her idea to have the Whisperers before him sent to the dungeon. Was that really the only way? He was desperate to come up with a better idea, only so far hadn't thought of anything. He needed to keep thinking. And fast. Because somehow, he was already one step closer to becoming the Conductor. *Worried One*, who'd slept beside him for five years now, had gone. Her mat had been taken from the arena and he'd had to move up one place. He wondered what could have happened to her and if Micah had somehow had a hand in it? For he was now one place closer to the position she and Rose seemed to want him to take. In his mind, this was only one place closer to death.

It'd felt odd last night without *Worried One* there, a woman who he never once said a single word to but had known her all the same. The thought of what might have happened to her sent pain shooting to his heart, to sit beside all the other information Micah had given in that brief time they'd spent in the laundry.

His parents were dead. And the baby had never lived to draw breath. And he and Micah were just as good as dead living here in the palace. His whole family wiped out by King Virtus and his lies. At least Tallis was still alive. The only one of them left in the Valley of the Blessed. The name of his former home had never felt more ironic.

It was strange to see Micah again. It was her, but not her. He wondered if she felt the same about him. So much about her had changed, yet so much remained the same.

His nose twitched as the smoke smell got stronger. This wasn't just a small fire. Something had gone horribly wrong. The palace was on fire!

The Conductor had been very clear in their training about what to do in an emergency.

Nothing.

He was to do nothing. If the flames reached him, he was to let them lap at his sides and eat him alive. He doubted if he would even be allowed to scream. Not that the Conductor would be able to do much about it if he did.

How could he do nothing when he was certain that the flames had something to do with Rose?

He touched his cheek where she'd kissed him and tried to hide a flush from creeping up his face. The feelings he had for her seemed to be mutual. Feelings that stretched beyond friendship or admiration into the realm of… love? Was that what this was? He definitely loved Rose and couldn't deny it was a very different kind of love than what he felt for Micah. Was this the feeling he'd been waiting for when the girls in the valley had paid him so much attention? He now knew that the reason he hadn't pursued any of them wasn't because he hadn't wanted a family of his own. It was because none of them had been Rose.

Which was why not being able to run to her side to save her was so hard. The Prince had been born. Rose had told him so, and he'd heard a baby crying when he'd passed the Queen's bedchamber on his way back to the kitchen. That small set of lungs howling had nearly made him howl himself. For surely, now that he'd been born, Rose and her sisters were in danger. This fire could be no coincidence.

He heard the familiar tapping of the Conductor's sword as he paced the dining hall, reminding them of their punishment if any of them dared to react to what they must all be able to smell by now.

Jeremiah's heart was beating fast now. He had to get to Rose. How could he stand here and do nothing? Although, he didn't suppose he could save her if he was already dead or locked in the dungeon. He had no choice except to stay here for now. Besides, if anyone could save themselves, it was Rose. She was strong, feisty and brave. If there was a way to get herself to safety, she'd do it.

He collected his breakfast and ate it even more slowly than usual, his appetite having vanished as his concern increased. However, not to eat would only draw attention to himself. He could see Micah at a nearby table, so at least he knew she was safe.

On his way back to the arena, he tried to figure out which direction the smoke was coming from. The smell of it was so strong, it was impossible to tell. Please let Rose be safe!

He reluctantly took his place on his mat and lay down, begging the universe to let Rose be okay. She didn't deserve her father's hatred like this. She was a good person. Too good to have such a malicious father.

From the corner of his eye, he saw the Conductor approach the first row of mats. He swooped down and picked up the mat in the second position and tucked it under his arm, tapping his sword three times on the floor as he waited for the Whisperers to silently assume new positions.

The slow and careful shuffle began. What had happened to *Blue Eyes*? It wasn't normal for two front-row Whisperers to leave in such quick succession. Had Micah had a hand in his departure, just as he suspected she'd had something to do with *Worried One*'s absence? Except *Blue Eyes* worked in the garden. Micah couldn't have gotten anywhere near him. Was this just a coincidence? He needed to find a way to talk to Micah again. A safer way than last time. She'd taken far too many risks that time. Her plan wasn't a good one. She didn't know the palace like he did. He couldn't possibly be the Conductor. He didn't have it in him. The King would have him killed in no time. There wouldn't be time for him to change the Whisper like Rose had suggested.

Unless...

He could find a way to kill the King before he killed him. The Conductor carried an awfully sharp sword around. If somehow, he could use that sword to take off the King's head, then perhaps Micah and Rose would be safe. He would certainly be put to death himself, but he was as good as dead anyway. Why not use his life to save others? If Rose were to become Queen, maybe he could even escape death. It was hard to imagine her having him killed.

He turned this idea over in his head, savoring it in the same way he'd seen Micah do with the orange on that fateful day. He was going to kill the King. It was time to see if the sword was mightier than words.

He pulled his face under his blanket to hide his smile.

But his smile was wiped off his face by the sound of sobbing. Large sobs that quickly became uncontrollable howls.

His spine turned to ice. This wasn't allowed. Someone was going to die today. The Conductor would never stand for this.

As subtly as he could, he lifted his face from his blanket and turned his head toward the noise. It was close. A woman. Definitely the sound of a woman.

"Jack!" she gasped. "What did you do to Jack?"

Oh, no. It was *Fair Face*, the Whisperer who'd been made to take *Blue Eyes'* place. Only five mats down from his own.

"Jack!" she sobbed again, clearly unable to control herself, as she reached out her hand to her right, in the place *Blue Eyes* had once slept.

Jeremiah looked away as the Conductor hurried toward *Fair Face*. She'd broken too many rules to be taken to the dungeon. She'd spoken. She'd shown emotion. She'd made a noise. And worse than any of those crimes, she'd known *Blue Eyes'* real name.

Jeremiah wondered how *Fair Face* and *Blue Eyes* had managed this. They must've spoken. Perhaps done more than speak. How? Where? Micah had found a way to talk to him, he supposed. There must be other ways he hadn't thought of.

He'd spent the past five years with these two Whisperers and never once noticed anything unusual between them. Or perhaps *special* was a better word than *unusual*. Because what they must've had was something he'd never seen in this palace before. Love. Although, he was sure the other Whisperers would be just as surprised if they knew what had transpired recently between him and Rose. Perhaps even more so. Love could exist in the darkest places. This, right here, was proof of that.

He turned his face back under the blanket and put his fingers in his ears. He liked *Fair Face*. He didn't want to hear her final moments.

However, fingers in his ears or not, he thought the whole kingdom would've heard her final moments.

"I hate you!" she screamed. "I hate all of you, lying here, accepting this. I don't accept it. I don't accept any of it. It's too late for me, but it's not too late for you. Band together and fi—"

An almighty crack echoed around the arena, followed by a thud.

Then silence. The kind that brought new meaning to the term *deathly silence.*

Jeremiah had no doubt *Fair Face* was gone. She hadn't wanted to live without *Blu*—Jack. That had been his name. Jack. A man, not a Whisperer. A man who *Fair Face* had loved more than her own life.

He heard the shuffling of what no doubt were guards. Whisperers would never make that much noise as they walked.

The smell of smoke was worse now and Jeremiah wondered if that was because the fire was still raging or if it was because it'd been put out.

As he shuffled one place closer to the Conductor's side, his determination of earlier built.

Fair Face was right. It wasn't too late. He didn't accept what was happening to him. He never had. And if he felt like that—as *Fair Face* had—and clearly, Jack had too, then how many more of them were there? And how did he find out who they were without following down the same path as *Fair Face?* Because as brave as she'd been, she hadn't been wise enough to bide her time to do more damage before she was killed.

Or perhaps her words had done damage enough? Surely his mind wasn't the only one buzzing here.

And who knew how he'd react if someone he loved was killed. If Micah's mat was taken away without a word, would he be able to lie there in silence or would he erupt as *Fair Face* had done?

He hoped he never had to find out.

Please universe, let Rose be okay.

MICAH

SIX

*I*t was happening. Faster than Micah ever expected. Three Whisperers in three days. Had Jeremiah had something to do with the second one? The Whisperer that woman had called Jack. She doubted it. Jeremiah hadn't seemed keen on the idea of becoming the Conductor at all. The thought of it had horrified him.

She could understand why. It wasn't a job she wanted—for herself or for Jeremiah. But there was no other choice. It was the only way they'd ever be able to make the change that was needed in this hell-hole of a palace. They needed to be in a position of power and trust. Unless the Princess could help them out, although it didn't seem like she had a position of either power or trust. Micah wasn't even sure she was still alive after that fire. Jeremiah must be going out of his mind with worry.

She made her way down the passageway, heading from the bath-room to the kitchen where she had a tedious couple of hours ahead, dishing up soup. She was alone, which was a nice change, and getting the hang of walking quietly. This wasn't something that came easily to her. Her parents used to say they could hear her coming a mile away. But her years of busking in the market, performing tricks, had been good training for learning to control her body. If only she'd known at the time what misery it was she was training for.

She'd been so naive when she first entered the palace with her useless plans to find Jeremiah and run away together the first chance they got. Then she'd seen the Conductor remove that poor woman's head in training and she'd known she had to save more than just Jeremiah and herself.

This feeling had only grown when her training finished and she was added to the back of the arena as the newest Whisperer. The first time the Whisperers had removed their hoods and stood to grant the King his wish, she'd had to hide a gasp as the image of the back of all those bald heads branded itself into her memory. She couldn't possibly run away, saving herself and her brother and leave all these people here to suffer. It wasn't right. None of this was. Who knew what lives they'd had outside the palace. Some were surely mothers or fathers, but certainly, all of them were all somebody's child (at least once, if not still) let alone sisters, lovers, friends, and cousins. They had beds that lay empty and people who were missing them. It just wasn't right for them to be kept prisoner here.

Long gone were the days of the palace promising food and medicine in exchange for a Whisperer's service. The King had given up on that after the first wave of Whisperers were recruited. Now they were lured by an orange, then taken by force. Instead of promising to keep their families alive, they were promised their deaths if they didn't comply. This really didn't bother Micah. At least it was honest. The way Jeremiah had been fooled only seemed to make what had happened to him even worse.

Micah's foot caught on the bottom of her robe and she stumbled, catching herself just in time and taking a deep breath to still her racing heart. She needed to be more careful. Smoothing down her robe, she slowed her pace as she rounded another corner, almost at the kitchen now.

She could still smell the charred ashes from the fire, reminding her that her plan was more urgent than ever. The fire had been put out eventually, but not before destroying several rooms and taking the life of the Whisperer called Jack. That scene in the arena, when Jack's true love had sacrificed herself, had been difficult to witness. Not that she'd looked directly at it. Although she'd witnessed it with her ears and that'd been more than enough. The sound of that poor woman in so much pain at the loss of her beloved. And then the silence, which was even worse than her screams.

The fire definitely wasn't a good sign. Could it really be a coincidence that the Princesses' rooms were the ones affected, so soon after the birth of the Prince? The King may think his people were too stupid to link these events, but it seemed obvious to her.

Although, whatever he'd been planning had backfired. She had proof of that approaching her in the opposite direction in the passageway. The four princesses were walking toward her, the youngest two being carried by their elder sisters. Micah had never seen them before and her eyes were glued to Rose.

Micah could see immediately why Rose had won her brother's heart. She was pure, raw beauty. Even more beautiful than her mother, the Queen—something Micah hadn't thought was possible. She had long, blonde hair, the palest blue eyes and skin the color of milk. Micah felt hideous in comparison, with her bald head and ugly, shapeless robe. It was the first time since entering the palace that she'd given her appearance any thought. She scolded herself. How she looked had never been important to her. Why should she start caring now?

She tried to drag her gaze away as she passed, but Rose caught her staring and locked her eyes on her.

"Are you Jeremiah's sister?" she said, keeping her voice low.

Her sisters widened their eyes at the sound of Rose speaking to a Whisperer.

"Hush," she said to them.

"How did you know?" Micah asked the question before she could stop herself. Speaking to the Princess was a crime punishable by death. Although, Jeremiah had said she could trust her. And it seemed rude not to answer.

"It was the way you looked at me. And you have the same eyes," said the Princess. "You're lovely."

Micah liked that. Not the lovely bit, as that was clearly a lie, but the bit about having Jeremiah's eyes.

"You're safe?" Micah asked the question Jeremiah was unable. Maybe she'd get an opportunity to pass on a message later.

Rose shook her head. "Not safe, although we survived." It was obvious she knew exactly what had happened. This princess was no fool. Micah felt sorry for her, before reminding herself how lucky this girl was. Even if her father was trying to kill her, her life was still better than her own. After all, in many ways, the King had already succeeded in killing Micah. She certainly felt like she was dead.

Micah stepped away. She'd risked talking for long enough.

"Wait," said the Princess, tugging on her robe. "I like your idea. Jeremiah told me. Just before the fire."

Micah's eyes lit up and she dared a smile. Perhaps she wasn't quite dead just yet. "But there are still seven places to go."

"We'll work it out," said the Princess, her voice a hush. "If all of us try, we can surely get him to move up that line faster. However, we all must do our bit. Nobody can achieve that alone. I'll help. I promise. But you must help too."

Micah nodded. So, the Princess was brave as well as beautiful. She was pleased it wasn't just her looks that'd drawn Jeremiah in. There was a lot more to this Princess than met the eye.

A Whisperer entered the passageway and the conversation was dropped. The Princesses continued on their way, as did Micah. It was as if nothing had ever happened.

Only it had. The Princess had made Micah more determined than ever to succeed in her plan. She wanted nothing more than to bring this palace down.

Micah went to the kitchen and saw that the Cook had placed the pot of soup on the servery, ready for her to dish up.

Micah collected the wooden bowls and set them beside the pot. Soon the dining hall would fill with hungry Whisperers, who would leave almost as hungry as they arrived.

Her conversation with the Princess had gotten her fired up. She had to figure out how to remove another Whisperer from their position in the arena. The Princess had said it herself. They all needed to do their bit. And they had no time to waste.

But how to get another Whisperer sent to the dungeon, to join that poor woman whose fate Micah was already responsible for? She refused to believe that the Whisperer in the bathroom had been killed. The guilt of that would be too much to bear. It was easier to imagine her in the dungeon, as awful as that thought was. She really hadn't meant to get anyone in trouble. However, if they could succeed in getting Jeremiah to be the Conductor, hopefully, they could also succeed in getting the prisoners in the dungeon released. These Whisperers wouldn't suffer for too long.

When the cook's back was turned, Micah acted swiftly. It was a plan she came up with as fast as the movement of her hand. She picked up the tin of rat poison and sprinkled a dose into the palm of her hand, tipping it into one of the soup bowls. The poison was back on the shelf in a matter of seconds. She'd taken so little of it that the cook would never realize, not even the next time he went to deal with an unfortunate rodent. The dose in her hand wasn't enough to kill a person, yet enough to make someone sick so that they'd surely cry out in pain and be sent to the dungeon for their noise. This was her plan and she felt awful about it. It wasn't the right thing to do at all. But she was going to do it. She was desperate. They must all do their part. When the Princess heard about this, it might spark her into action to remove one of the Whisperers on her own.

Micah's heart pounded underneath her robe, reminding her that she was still very much alive, even if she was about to do something she'd never have contemplated in the Before.

The line of Whisperers came creeping into the dining hall and she carefully began dishing each of them a bowl of muddy soup water. She'd memorized the faces of the seven Whisperers who were ahead of Jeremiah and decided to hand over the poisoned bowl to whoever came to her first, simply because she needed to get this over with before she lost her nerve. Sending someone to the dungeon was a horrible thing to do. But what choice did she have? And the sooner she could get Jeremiah to hold that sword, the sooner they'd be able to have the prisoners released. Well, she sincerely hoped so. It was all still a long shot.

Her stomach tightened when she saw her target join the line. An older man with a large bump in his nose that made her certain it was him, no matter how alike these Whisperers looked. She'd noticed that the longer she was in the palace, the more unique each Whisperer looked. And this one was unmistakable.

When he reached the front of the line, she reached for the bowl, trying to hide the shaking of her hands. It wasn't too late to back out.

Yet no matter how much her mind screamed at her to abort her plans, she couldn't. She had to go through with it. This Whisperer needed to make way for Jeremiah.

She poured the soup into the bowl and watched the rat poison dissolve. Her movements were slow, careful, noiseless.

Just as she'd been trained, she held out the bowl, keeping her face down, not making eye contact with this poor man. She was grateful for that. How could you look someone in the eye as you sent them to live in a dungeon?

He took his bowl and moved away.

Micah drew in a deep breath, willing her hands to be still. She'd done it! She'd actually done it. She was fighting back the only way she knew how.

She lifted the next bowl from the pile and continued to serve, all the time waiting for the inevitable sound she knew would erupt from the poor Whisperer's mouth.

It happened faster than she expected. She'd seen a rat eat the poison before and it'd taken ages to die.

The noise was terrible. Awful. The worst noise she'd heard in her life. Worse than the Whisperer dying in the arena while calling for her love. Worse than the silence that followed it. Because this noise had been caused by her.

It was like a howl or a groan or a screech. It wasn't the sound of a man being poisoned. It was the sound of a man dying.

Micah froze, with her ladle hovering over the next bowl. Something had gone horribly wrong. Had she put in too much? This man was a hundred times larger than a rat and she'd only given him a few pellets. The cook put out far more than this for the rats. The difference must be that the rats only ate one pellet, not the whole pile. She'd obviously gone too far.

The Whisperer standing before her, waiting for her bowl, had dared to glance up at her. To catch her eye in a way that was strictly forbidden.

Micah locked eyes with her and silent words passed between them. Words that Micah didn't deserve. This Whisperer was looking at her with sympathy, as if telling her that it wasn't her fault the soup had made him sick. How little she knew.

The Whisperer nodded at Micah, urging her to continue with her task before the Conductor felt the need to discipline more than one Whisperer today. This silent communication was new to Micah. In the short time she'd been at the palace, this was the closest she'd come to having a conversation with anyone, apart from Jeremiah. Had the dying words of the woman in the arena had some kind of effect? Were people starting to rebel, just like the woman had begged them to?

The awful noise continued. The man was standing now, clutching at his middle and vomiting up a horrible red liquid. Blood. It had to be blood.

Micah blinked back tears as she poured soup into the bowl.

The man was going to die. Nobody vomited up blood like that and lived. She thought of her mother and the way she'd died, lying in a pool of her own blood.

It was too much.

She handed the soup to the Whisperer, who mouthed the words *"It's okay,"* at her. But it wasn't okay. She'd just killed a man. It didn't matter that she hadn't meant to. It was what she'd done. He'd taken a bowl of soup from her and eaten it, trusting that it would strengthen his body, not rob it of life.

The Conductor went to the dying Whisperer and smiled, standing over him as he fell to the floor. He didn't take his sword to him, as he didn't need to. This Whisperer was being punished already and no doubt his punishment would soon be over.

The screaming turned to silence, just as it had in the arena. And as Micah continued to serve the soup, she dreaded Jeremiah joining the line. He'd know she'd had something to do with what just happened. And there was no way he'd be happy about it. He'd be so disappointed in her. No doubt she'd have lost all respect in his eyes. It was too much to bear.

She saw him join the line and with each step he took closer to the front, she felt her legs weaken.

When he got to her, he looked her straight in the eye, confident the Conductor was otherwise occupied with removing that poor man's body.

"Did you do it?" he whispered, his voice little more than a breath.

A tear escaped down her cheek as she answered. "I didn't mean to."

But instead of the hatred she expected to see in his eyes, she saw some kind of understanding.

He nodded, and as he took his bowl from her, he let his fingers brush against her own. It seemed the only way he could let her know he still loved her. How could he possibly love a murderer? For that's what she was, wasn't she?

It wasn't until Jeremiah walked away that she realized she forgot to tell him that the Princess was alive.

How could she be expected to remember anything ever again? She'd just killed a man. It didn't matter that it was an accident. He was dead! She'd made a huge mistake and it'd cost that man his life.

She couldn't take it back. The only thing she could do to honor his accidental sacrifice was to move forward. If Jeremiah didn't become the Conductor now, then this man's life had been taken in vain. She couldn't let that happen. If she could set the Whisperers free, then it made this man a hero. She'd honor his memory for the rest of her life, however long that was.

I'm sorry! she called inside her head as his body was carried from the dining hall.

As she served the next bowl of soup, she pushed more words from her mind. *Four down. Six to go.*

ROSE

FIVE

*R*ose couldn't sleep, but that wasn't unusual. She felt like she hadn't slept in days, not since the fire, only that couldn't be right. She must've dropped off for at least a few seconds at some point.

It didn't help that her bedchamber had burnt down and she was bunked in with her three sisters in the servants quarters. They were taking up a room once occupied by palace workers before the arrival of the Whisperers, who'd put nearly all of them out of a job. The workers who remained were paid from the royal purse and lived in rooms just like this one.

There were four tiny beds in the room the princesses now occupied, lined up neatly with barely an arm's length between them. She didn't mind though. She liked being close to her sisters to make sure nobody was trying to murder them in their sleep. She was certain that if so many people hadn't seen them since the fire, her father would have had them killed already and pretended they perished in the flames.

The sisters ate all their meals in the royal dining room now, including breakfast. It was nice to be able to eat in company, but she missed Jeremiah desperately. She hadn't realized how much her happiness depended on seeing him each morning.

She was even angrier now than she'd been during the fire. So angry that the idea of leaving had become impossible. Her father couldn't be allowed to get away with this. Whether he was King or not, he was still a man and men shouldn't try to kill their innocent daughters. Running away from this wouldn't solve anything for anyone.

First thing in the morning, she planned to take her sisters to the dungeon to find the guard called Tyron and send them away to Aunt Lily. She knew her mother wanted her to go with them, except that was impossible. If she went, then nothing in the palace would ever change. There were many thousands of people counting on her, even if they didn't know it right now. Although one person knew it. Jeremiah. Actually, no, there were two. Micah knew it too. And there was no way she could let either of them down, especially after what she'd said to Micah when she'd met her in the passageway. They all had to do their bit. She couldn't run away now.

It'd been strange to meet Jeremiah's sister. She'd known immediately it was her, not just from her eyes, which were so much like her brother's, but because of the way she'd looked at Rose. No other Whisperer would dare to meet her eye like that. She was a pretty girl, and no doubt with ordinary clothes and her hair allowed to grow, she'd be even prettier. This hadn't been a surprise. A man as handsome as Jeremiah was unlikely to have an ugly sister.

Her own sisters were pretty too, but in a different way. They had a delicate and fragile beauty, quite different to Micah's. Although, they were still young. They had time to grow courage and strength to give them the sort of powerful beauty Micah possessed.

Eliza was twelve now. Old enough to care for her sisters on their journey to Aunty Lily's house in Aria Flats. All they had to do was sit inside a carriage. Eliza had shown just how capable she was during the fire. She could do it. There was no other choice. Rose would've sent them away sooner, however, Cara's injuries from the fall were too severe and she'd needed time to regain some of her strength. She was far from better now, yet well enough to survive the journey. And that's exactly what this was about. Survival.

If only she could speak to her mother about everything. She still hadn't been allowed anywhere near her since the baby had been born. She hadn't even seen this mysterious brother of hers yet.

She turned over in bed, wondering if sleep would come if she were to lie on her back.

The shadows were darker in here. Back in her bedchamber, she could leave her shutters open and let the stars light a path across the darkness. But in here, the windows were small and let in nothing except the night.

Tash whimpered and Rose reached out for her, unsure if her nightmares were the sort you had while you were awake or asleep. Lately, it was hard to tell the difference. Her sister quietened, so Rose tucked her arm back under the blanket and tried once more to sleep.

"Rose?" Eliza said. "I heard something."

"Hush now," said Rose. "Go back to sleep. It was only Tash."

She could hear Eliza fiddling with her lantern.

"I said it's okay." Rose sat up. "There's no need for the light. You'll wake your sisters."

As soon as the words were out of her mouth, the room filled with light and Rose looked across to see Eliza sitting up in her bed with her lantern held out before her, blinking rapidly as her eyes adjusted.

"I told you not to." Rose rolled her eyes.

"Look." Eliza was pointing.

Rose glanced around the room, only she didn't see anything. "Nobody's here. Turn it off now."

"Where's Tash?" asked Eliza, pointing to the empty bed beside Rose.

Rose's hands raced to the sheets of the bed she'd heard her sister sleeping in only moments before.

The bed was warm, but Tash was definitely not in it.

"We must find her," said Rose, reaching for the dagger she'd stashed under her pillow and looking underneath the beds. Her heart was beating so fast, she had to stop to take a breath.

"Tash!" Eliza called.

"Look after Cara," Rose said over her shoulder, leaving the room just in time to see a robe disappear around the corner of the passageway.

She raced after the shadow. How could she have let Tash be stolen from right under her nose? They'd had the door locked too!

As her feet pounded forward, she knew she shouldn't be surprised she hadn't heard anything. The Whisperers knew better than anyone how to be quiet. They were experts at it. And by the look of the robe she was chasing, that was exactly who'd snatched Tash from her bed.

She got to the corner and saw the figure disappear around another bend. A figure that was holding the unmistakable form of her sister, who was wriggling against his grip.

She resisted the urge to call out to Tash, not wanting the Whisperer to know he was being followed.

This part of the palace was labyrinthine, but she'd grown up here, allowed to play in these hallways when she was young. She knew every twist and turn. And she was betting that she knew them better than this Whisperer.

Quietening her footsteps, she continued forward, knowing she had the advantage. Not only did she know where she was, she wasn't carrying a struggling child. If she played this right, she'd catch up to them before it was too late.

I'm coming, Tash. She grabbed her dagger more tightly.

A few more corners and she was now as close as she dared without revealing her position. Hopefully, the Whisperer thought she'd lost him and had slowed his pace.

She pressed herself against the wall as she saw him turn to look behind him. Poor Tash was still struggling, pummeling his chest with her little fists. She must be so frightened! She should've sent her sisters away earlier, despite Cara's injuries. Traveling injured was better than not having the chance to travel at all.

The Whisperer reached a door at the end of the passageway and

Rose drew in a breath. It was the Conductor's private chambers. Clearly, her father had failed at his attempt to burn his daughters alive, so had demanded the Conductor finish the job himself. And it looked like he'd decided to do it one Princess at a time.

The Whisperer opened the door and as the light caught his face, she recognized him as the Whisperer who served her family in the dining room each evening. She'd never paid him too much attention before now.

He stepped inside, leaving the door ajar.

Rose quickly followed, getting as close to the door as possible without being seen.

She had to choose her moment carefully. The Conductor was a trained fighter and she was a mere girl, who'd never even been able to so much as twist the neck of a rat found in her bedchamber, instead, letting it out her window to return at a later time.

Except the Conductor wasn't a rat. That likeness was far too kind for him. He was a monster. She didn't care if he was only acting on her father's orders. You had to have a large share of evil in your soul to carry out the deeds he was instructed to. Rose didn't believe there was anything in the world that could make her slice off the head of an innocent Whisperer, no matter what personal threat was made against her. She'd have lasted five minutes in her father's army. How had Jeremiah possibly managed to survive five years?

"Excellent," she heard the Conductor say to his silent soldier.

"Let me go!" Tash yelled. Her words made their way straight out the door and into the center of Rose's heart. This could *not* go on.

"Do it quickly before somebody hears her," said the Conductor.

Rose knew she could wait no more and burst into the room with the dagger held in front of her.

"Oh, how wonderful," said the Conductor, leaning on a large desk, with his arms crossed and a smirk wrapped across his awful face. "Two for the price of one!"

The Whisperer was crouching, his strong hands pinning Tash to the floor.

"Help me, Rose," said Tash, struggling to push out her words. "He's squeezing…my neck."

"Get your hands off her!" said Rose, her shaking hand waving the dagger at the Whisperer. "She's only a little girl."

"He's not going to listen to you," laughed the Conductor. "He's going to kill her, then he's going to kill you."

The Whisperer looked up at Rose. Sweat was dripping from his brow and his mouth was a grimace. But there was something else hidden in his eyes. Just a flash of it, yet it was enough to tell Rose that he didn't want to do this.

"Do you have a sister?" Rose asked, deciding her words would be a more effective weapon than a dagger she had no idea how to use. "Or a daughter?"

There was that flash again, and she knew she'd struck a chord.

"You have a daughter, don't you? She's no different to my sister here. My sister's name is Tash. She's five years old, her favorite color is yellow and she loves to draw and sing and would like to learn how to dance. She's not a pawn in my father's sick game. She's a little girl and you can't kill her. You can't!"

The Whisperer's expression didn't change, but Rose saw his grip on Tash loosen ever so slightly.

"Do it now!" bellowed the Conductor, holding up his hand to silence Rose's words. She'd needed to humanize Tash to wake this Whisperer up to what he was about to do. It seemed it was working.

"You're better than this," said Rose. "I know you are. You aren't this person he's trying to make you be. You wouldn't kill a little girl before you came here. Don't do it now. Please don't kill my little sister. She's an innocent child. How would you feel if someone did that to your daughter?"

With these words, the Whisperer let go of Tash. She wriggled free and raced to Rose, burying her face in the skirt of her nightdress.

Rose put her free hand on Tash's back, still holding out the dagger with her other hand.

The Conductor reached for his sword, which was lying across the desk, turning his face for only the briefest of moments.

The Whisperer chose this moment to leap to his feet and wrap his hands around the Conductor's neck, choking him in the way he'd been instructed to do to little Tash.

Rose covered Tash's eyes with her hand. She'd been traumatized enough tonight. She didn't need to see this. But Rose did. She couldn't turn away now. She needed to know the deed was done.

The Conductor, who hadn't had time to grasp his sword, was struggling now, however the Whisperer had him firmly in his grasp, choking harder.

"I nearly killed her," said the Whisperer as he squeezed his hands tighter, turning the Conductor's face a deeper shade of purple. "I nearly killed a little girl."

It was strange to hear a Whisperer talk. For five years Rose hadn't heard any of them utter a word. And then there was Jeremiah, then Jack, then Micah and now this man. Change was in the air.

The Conductor let out a gurgling noise, his fingers clawing at the Whisperer's hands now.

Rose winced. As much as she hated the Conductor and wanted to see him dead, it was hard to watch. Somehow, as the life was draining from this evil man's body, his humanity was rising to the surface. Once this man had been an innocent child, but clearly, something had happened along the way to strip him of that innocence. Life was trying to restore it to him in his death.

She just hoped the Whisperer wasn't seeing what she was seeing. Because she didn't want him to let go. If the Conductor survived, then she and Tash were as good as dead.

The Conductor's body fell slack in the Whisperer's hands and he slumped to the floor. Rose let out a breath, clutching Tash closer to her side.

"I-I-I killed him," said the Whisperer, looking at Rose, wiping his hands on his robe as if he could wipe away the act of what he'd just done.

"You did," said Rose, leaving Tash to go to him and take his hands in hers. "And I thank you. Killing him saved my sister's life. And mine.

And I promise you that I'm going to save yours in return. I'll get you back to your daughter."

The Whisperer's eyes filled with tears and he nodded. "I have two daughters and a son."

"Who knows you're here?" asked Rose.

The Whisperer pointed a shaking finger at the Conductor's body.

"Well, he's not going to tell anyone and neither am I."

He nodded again, clearly not in the habit of using words.

"Go back to the arena. Freedom is coming. Prepare for it. Tell the others if you get the opportunity. Everyone must be ready."

This time his eyes filled with an emotion she'd never seen on a Whisperer's face before. Hope.

"Prepare for freedom," she said.

"Prepare for freedom," he repeated, leaving the room, pausing only to glance at Tash who shrank away from him, still not prepared to offer him her trust.

"Let's go," Rose said to her sister, tucking the dagger into her undergarments and scooping her sister into her arms.

"Where are we going?" asked Tash, nuzzling her face into Rose's neck.

"We're going to get Eliza and Cara, then you're going on a little trip." She had to get them to safety. Not soon, but now. Because once the Conductor's body was found, who knew what was going to happen. Change certainly was coming, and not like a gentle breeze, it was charging at them like a cyclone.

Her sister's arms tightened around her shoulders. "Not going anywhere without you."

"It's just for a little while."

"No little while."

"I'll explain when we get back to our room." Rose feathered kisses on Tash's cheek as she carried her down the hallway and back to where their sisters waited.

Please just let them still be there. She needed to get them to safety as soon as she possibly could.

JEREMIAH

FOUR

*J*eremiah still had no idea if Rose and her sisters had survived the fire. He was no longer required to bring the princesses their breakfast, which wasn't a good sign, yet he refused to believe they were dead. They were probably just eating somewhere else now that their bedchambers had burnt down.

Besides, he couldn't think like that. Rose was his last hope. If she was dead, they were all doomed. Until he knew one way or another, he wasn't going to let himself get too worked up about it. His sanity depended on that.

He noticed the Whispering flags as soon as he entered the dining hall. They were at half mast, which meant that when the sun was at its highest point in the sky, there would be a Whispering, pushing the rest of the daily routine back by a few hours.

For once he was glad there'd be a Whisper, because with any luck, it would give him a clue as to what was going on with Rose. Unless the King whispered for fuller hair or a trimmer waistline again...Jeremiah thought he might choke on his words if he had to whisper for that again. Although it was better than some of the alternatives, he supposed. Superficial and selfish, but not evil.

Breakfast dragged as he knew the coming hours would too. The Conductor wasn't in the dining hall this morning, which was unusual. The King must be providing him with the words of his Whisper.

There was something else unusual that Jeremiah couldn't put his finger on. As he silently scooped his porridge into his mouth, he carefully looked around the room. Everyone looked the same, so that wasn't it. It was an energy in the room. He'd been noticing it building ever since *Fair Face* died. It was nothing that anybody could be punished for, but it was definitely there. Perhaps he'd underestimated his fellow Whisperers, because there was definitely the smell of change in the air.

It wasn't until he was taking his bowl to the cleaning area that he realized just how much change was in the air. As he carefully placed his empty bowl on the table, the Whisperer next to him spoke to him. It was *Freckle Nose,* one of the last Whisperers he'd expect to break the rules like this. She'd never even looked at him before.

"Prepare for freedom," she said, softly. Jeremiah strained his ears to catch any further words. "Pass the word."

Not daring to reply, Jeremiah nodded, as much as he was able without seeming to be moving his head.

He wondered how *Freckle Nose* of all people knew what was happening. Or if the freedom she spoke of was even the same one he was working toward with Rose and Micah.

He walked quietly to the arena, noticing that his blanket had been removed for the Whispering, leaving one thousand mats lined up neatly in rows. Some Whisperers were there already, preparing to wait the hours it would take for the sun to reach its highest point in the sky. Other Whisperers were still in the dining hall, taking their time finishing breakfast. Yet more would still be finishing their morning chores— tasks that would take half the time if not needed to be done in silence.

The Conductor wasn't here either, which again was unusual. Normally he was pacing the arena before a Whispering as if psyching himself up for a performance. Well, that's what it really was, Jeremiah supposed. A pretty powerful performance though. One that could change the world in unexplained ways.

Jeremiah took his time going to his mat, missing the days when he could walk all the way to the back of the arena. His position was so close to the front doors now.

A male Whisperer was walking behind him. Without turning his head, he thought it might be *Round Face*.

"Prepare for freedom," was hissed in Jeremiah's ear. He stiffened, hoping the guards hadn't heard this not-so-quiet whisper. "Pass the word."

Jeremiah knelt on his mat, keeping his eyes focused on the floor, holding his breath as he waited for any repercussions. None came. What was going on here? No Whisperer had spoken to him for five years and today two had spoken the same words aloud to him. Freedom was coming, if only everyone remained calm. If a group of Whisperers had another plan, it could jeopardize his own.

The minutes ticked by, stretching out into an hour or more. It was hard to tell sometimes. Time had a new meaning in the palace than it'd had back home in the valley.

Eventually, he heard the familiar tapping of the Conductor's sword on the floor as he walked. Jeremiah kept his gaze down, not wanting to attract any attention, particularly on a day when so much danger was present.

The tapping of the sword was also unusual today. It wasn't the Conductor's usual rhythm. And it was getting closer to him. Soon he wouldn't be able to ignore it.

Tap. Tap. Tap. Each tap louder than the one before it. Then a series of taps in front of Jeremiah's mat to attract his attention.

Jeremiah raised his face, sweeping his eyes up the Conductor's robe, being careful not to reach his eyes.

Or not his eyes. *Her* eyes.

Jeremiah stifled a gasp and concentrated on drawing in a deep breath to still his shock.

It was *Mean Mouth* standing before him. Whisperer number one.

Why did she have the Conductor's sword? Was this the change he was sensing rippling through the palace this morning?

As he drew in a second breath, he cursed himself for his stupidity. *Mean Mouth* didn't have the Conductor's sword. She *was* the Conductor. Something must've happened to the former one. It was the only explanation, even though this hadn't occurred in all the time he'd been here.

What did she want with him? Had she heard *Round Face* talking earlier and thought it'd been him to speak? How was he going to explain? It was an impossible task when you weren't allowed to use words.

She tapped her sword in front of him again and pointed to the position to his left. There was no mat there. He hadn't noticed everyone moving up a place.

Relief slid down Jeremiah's spine. Of course. If she'd moved into the Conductor's role, then her place was vacant. It was time to move up again, to fifth position.

When Micah had told him her plan and he'd imagined ways they might be able to get those ahead of him sent to the dungeon, he'd never thought about the possibility of the Conductor himself being taken away. Or killed? He was unlikely to ever find out what really happened to him.

He quickly picked up his mat and assumed his new position. *Mean Mouth*—the Conductor—walked on, no doubt to make sure everyone else followed suit.

As he knelt back down, he wished he'd paid more attention to *Mean Mouth* over the years. Despite living in such close quarters to her since his arrival at the palace, he'd never really thought about her too much. Perhaps because she was one of the Whisperers he'd never warmed to, hence the unflattering name he'd pinned on her. It wasn't just that her mouth was pulled into a permanent scowl, it was her... aura? Was that the right word? It was the energy she put out around her, just like the energy he'd picked up on in the dining hall this morning, only it held a negative charge instead of a positive one.

As much as he couldn't help but be glad that the Conductor had gone, he doubted this new Conductor was going to be any better. She might even be worse. Which meant of course that the King was going to love her. She'd do his bidding without an ounce of remorse.

The sun was getting higher now and soon all positions in the arena were filled.

The heavy doors at the back of the arena opened with a loud clunk, as they always did. There was only one person in the palace who dared to make such a noise. The King, who was no doubt making his way to the balcony for his observation.

The Conductor returned to the front of the arena and tapped her sword seven times, waiting two seconds between each tap.

"*The Whisperers are whispering. The Whisperers are whispering,*" the chant began.

Jeremiah noticed his voice warming with each word he spoke. His vocal chords felt like a bird being let out of a cage. Free to stretch and fly.

The Conductor swept her sword across the arena with a little difficulty. She was far shorter than the previous Conductor and she made the sword look heavy. It had seemed to have been made from feathers, the way the previous Conductor had held it.

Jeremiah dropped to his knees, alongside the other Whisperers in the first row. He waited for the rows behind him to follow, wondering if the new Conductor had the capacity to discipline them, mentally as well as physically. Taking someone's head from their shoulders was something he felt firmly he'd never be able to do.

The Conductor raised the sword above her head. Jeremiah braved a glance up at her and saw her eyes darting across the arena, looking for anyone out of place. Her mouth was pulled into an even tighter grimace than usual.

It seemed she was satisfied with what she saw. No matter how much the Whisperers were holding onto the hope of freedom, none of them were willing to step too far out of line just yet. Or perhaps they felt as confused and sorry for this new Conductor as Jeremiah. No matter how mean she looked, she wasn't in a position he envied. Despite his realization that the only way for change to properly occur was for him to be Conductor, he dreaded that day rather than relished the idea of it.

The Conductor brought her sword down and from Jeremiah's position in the middle of the front row, he could see her shaking hands.

Jeremiah waited for her to receive her signal from the King and begin the Whisper. He realized he'd never heard *Mean Mouth's* voice before and hoped it didn't match the shape of her mouth.

"The Conductor is resting in peace," she whispered. Her voice had a higher pitch than the previous Conductor, yet still quite deep for a female.

Jeremiah lifted his head, along with the rest of the first row, and removed his hood. What a strange whisper. Just to add to the list of unusual things for the day, it was rare for the King to wish for something that didn't directly involve himself or his needs. To offer up a wish that was completely for the benefit of someone else—even if it was just for their soul—was surprising. At least Jeremiah now knew what'd happened to the Conductor. He was dead. Oh, how he'd love to know how he died. They may be about to wish for his eternal peace, but Jeremiah hoped that his death had been the opposite. He didn't deserve to have left this earth in peace after the suffering and pain he'd caused so many innocent people.

"The Conductor is resting in peace," came the whisper once more.

Jeremiah got to his feet, his movement in perfect synchronicity with the rest of his row.

"The Conductor is resting in peace," they chanted.

Row after row joined in the chant, each voice whispering for peace for a man none of them had ever cared for, knowing that the universe would grant this Whisper, whether they wanted it to or not. The Conductor would soon be resting in peace.

They chanted over and over, their fragile voices cracking under the strain of delivering a thousand whispers. Yet as always, they did it, with each row falling silent one by one under the Conductor's command as they pulled their hoods back over their heads.

Now that the Whispering was done, they were allowed to rest. Most Whisperers chose to lie on their mats and stare at the ceiling.

Jeremiah glanced at the balcony and noticed the King was still standing there, observing. Was there no end to unusual occurrences today! Perhaps he was just checking on his new Conductor to assess her level of control. Although, he had a smirk on his face. An awful smirk. Something wasn't right.

A noise caught Jeremiah's attention and he carefully redirected his gaze to scan the room. Would this be the Conductor's first test? How would she handle the discipline of the first Whisperer to make noise in her presence?

But it wasn't a Whisperer. It was the Conductor herself. She'd collapsed on the floor and was lying completely still.

Jeremiah had seen enough death in the past five years to know it when he saw it. She wasn't unconscious. She was most definitely dead.

Two guards rushed over and lifted her from the floor, carrying her from the room. When they passed Jeremiah, he had a clear view of her face. And he noticed the strangest thing.

Mean Mouth's face was so relaxed that somehow her mouth had lost its grimace. She looked… beautiful. How strange that Jeremiah had never noticed that before. Her face was the perfect picture of happiness. She was just so peaceful.

It was this thought that made Jeremiah's heart skip a beat. She was just so *peaceful*. The Conductor was indeed resting in peace.

He looked up at the balcony and saw that the King's smirk was now a smile, so bright that Jeremiah could practically count his teeth.

He'd wanted this to happen! His Whisper had gone exactly as he'd intended! They'd thought they were whispering for peace for the former Conductor's soul, when indeed he'd tricked them into whispering for a murder.

The strange thing was that *Mean Mouth* would most likely have made an excellent Conductor if he'd given her the chance.

Jeremiah wondered what exactly it was about her that the King hadn't liked? Whatever it was, he hoped that he didn't possess the same quality. As when he got to the job, he needed to keep it for at least a little while. Long enough to raise his sword and use it against the King.

Because freedom was coming, just like *Freckle Nose* and *Round Face* had both said. And with *Mean Mouth*'s death, they were all one step closer.

MICAH

THREE

*M*icah wasn't quite sure what to make of what just happened at the Whispering. She was just glad to be tucked away in the back row and not to have witnessed it at such close proximity as poor Jeremiah had. Although, the way the Whisperers were moving up lately, soon she'd be in the second last row. The palace was churning through Whisperers, having to bring some back from the dungeon to make up the one thousand they needed.

She could tell the Whisperers were from the dungeon and not fresh recruits. There was a big difference in the expressions old Whisperers wore compared to the new. They had a hardened look about them, with all the hope having been wiped from their eyes.

Except there'd been something different in the air today. The Whisperers had started whispering to each other, speaking of freedom and spreading the word. It seemed that Whispering ceremonies weren't the only way for words to own their power. She wasn't sure how or when this had all started, but it was good. When Jeremiah became the Conductor, they were going to need the Whisperers on their side, ready to act.

She'd already learned that overthrowing the King and gaining freedom for the Whisperers wasn't a job that could be done alone. They needed to band together, just like that poor Whisperer had told them to before she'd died. All of them. It was the only way.

Micah stretched out on her mat, glad she wasn't tall. She had no idea how Jeremiah got comfortable on these things.

As much as she thought what the King had done to the new Conductor in the Whispering was a cruel trick, she couldn't help but be a little glad. That new Conductor had had a mean face. Micah hadn't trusted her. She was likely to be even worse than the previous Conductor. Plus, her removal meant that the next Whisperer in line would take her place, which moved Jeremiah into fourth position now. It was happening faster than she expected.

She still felt sick about what she'd done to that poor man with the rat poison. It was hard to believe she'd actually killed a man, whether it had been accidentally or on purpose. And that poor woman in the bathroom, who was hopefully still alive in the dungeon. Once Micah escaped this hell, if there was another hell in the afterlife, then she was certainly destined to go there.

She knew exactly who the next Conductor was going to be, having studied the faces of the four people she needed to remove to get Jeremiah where they needed him.

The next in line was a man. He appeared to Micah to be too weak for the position, yet despite this, she suspected the King would like this one better. She couldn't help thinking the problem he'd had with the last one was her gender. Because that was the only obvious difference between her and the last Conductor. They both had the same vicious streak in them. And the way the King was so desperate to have a son and do away with his daughters told Micah that he valued males over females.

She heard the familiar tapping of the sword on the floor as the new Conductor entered the room. She rolled over and chanced a glance. Two seconds of observation told her that she was right. He was most definitely too weak for this position.

The way he was walking and tapping his sword wasn't the way a leader should do it. It lacked authority and power. He tapped his sword like he was petrified of using it, not waiting for the first opportunity, like the past two Conductors.

A ripple spread over the sleeping Whisperers. None of whom were actually sleeping of course, yet all doing a fine job of pretending they were.

"Freedom is coming!" called a Whisperer from the opposite side of the arena to the new Conductor.

The Conductor snapped his head in their direction and marched forward, looking for the source of the outburst. It seemed Micah hadn't been the only one to sense this new Conductor's weakness.

Micah's heart beat so hard it felt like it was going to burst from the strain of the blood flowing through it. She lifted her head slightly to see the Conductor studying the Whisperers on their mats, but all were feigning sleep and she was too far away to see their faces to work out for herself who had dared to speak.

Before she knew what she was doing, Micah rested her head on her mat, cleared her throat and called out as loudly as she could, "Freedom is coming!"

She stilled herself, trying to steady her breathing, closing her eyes to add to the innocent facade. What had she done? She was losing her mind! But at least her actions had saved the Whisperer who'd spoken first. Maybe that would help to make up for the life of the Whisperer she'd taken away.

The sound of the Conductor's sword tapping on the floor came closer as he altered the direction of his search.

Yet he never reached her mat, for across the other side of the arena came another voice. "Freedom is coming!"

The Conductor marched away and yet another voice called out, each time on the opposite side of the arena to where the Conductor stood.

Then more Whisperers gathered their courage and instead of one voice calling at a time, there were many.

Micah called out a few more times and soon the whole arena was shouting, no matter whether they were near the Conductor or not.

They rose to stand and their voices grew louder, shouting in unison in the way that their Whisperings had trained them to do.

"Freedom is coming! Freedom is coming!" Micah wondered if this would be as powerful as a Whispering. Their voices were certainly louder, so surely the universe had to hear their pleas.

The Conductor's face had turned red now. "Stop this!" he shouted, his voice lost over the din of the Whisperers' chant. "Stop this!"

But nobody stopped anything. They just got louder. There was safety in numbers. The Conductor was hardly going to kill the whole army. Micah doubted he had it in him to kill one of them, let alone a thousand.

"Freedom is coming! Freedom is coming!" the shouting continued.

Micah stood on the tips of her toes, tempted to do a cartwheel. Her body ached to move in the way it was accustomed. The energy in the room was incredible. It wasn't just Micah who wanted this madness to end. Or Jeremiah. It was everyone. This cruelty had to stop. She felt happier right now at this moment than she thought she'd ever been in her life.

A hush rippled across the room as Whisperers sunk back to their mats. From the back of the arena, Micah couldn't see what was happening. However, as more Whisperers pressed their bodies to the floor, it became clear.

The King was here. And he looked the complete opposite to how he'd looked standing on the balcony at yesterday's Whispering. There was no smile on his face now.

He went directly to the Conductor and took the sword from his hands, without speaking a word.

The Conductor knelt at the King's feet and clasped his hands in front of him.

"I'm sorry, my Lord," he said. "Please show mercy."

Even from the back of the arena, Micah could see the tears pouring down the man's face.

Any of the happiness that'd filled Micah's soul only moments before, evaporated in an instant, the space it left being flooded with guilt. The King was going to kill the Conductor. There was no doubt.

He was begging for mercy that the King didn't possess. This man was going to be murdered in front of them all for the crime of weakness. Or kindness perhaps. He was going to be killed, because he himself had refused to kill. This wasn't right. And every one of them who'd called out for freedom, was responsible for his death.

No, that wasn't right. It wasn't! They weren't responsible for his death. They weren't responsible for any of this. The King was the only one with blood on his hands here.

The former courage of the Whisperers had vanished, alongside their happiness. Nobody dared to defy the King himself. Micah considered speaking up, but what if nobody followed? Then her death would follow this Conductor's. And she had no doubt Jeremiah would follow suit after that. She couldn't risk it. She had to keep him safe, so they could put a stop to this.

"Please, my Lord!" the Conductor said, as the King raised his sword high above his head.

Seeing he had no chance of survival, the Conductor turned his eyes to the Whisperers.

"Freedom is coming!" he called out, letting them know he was still one of them.

Micah looked away as the sword swung down. She didn't need to see this. She'd already seen far too many things that she was unable to erase from her memory. She didn't need to add to her collection.

As the guards came closer to clean up the mess, Micah curled herself into a small ball, ashamed of how her actions had contributed to this man's death.

The silence that'd fallen over the arena was haunting. She wasn't sure if the King had even left yet. Until she heard his voice.

"This must never happen again, you ungrateful beetles," he said, the high pitch to his voice revealing his anger. "We clothe you, we feed you, we give you somewhere to sleep and a place to wash and *this* is how you repay us?"

Micah wondered if the King was speaking of the palace or himself. It was so hard to tell coming from a man who spoke about himself in the third person.

"It wasn't our fault that we had to remove the Conductor's head."

Himself. He was talking about himself.

"It was your fault. And you'll be punished for it. If you don't live by the rules, then you won't be provided for with the kindness currently bestowed upon you. Do you understand?" His voice rose to an impossibly higher pitch as he waved the sword in the air, blood dripping from it, droplets flying across the arena.

"Do you understand?" he said again. Did he actually expect them to reply?

They responded by their actions, keeping their heads down and their voices quiet.

"Excellent," he said. "We are pleased. Go and do your chores now, and don't bother going to the dining hall tonight. You must think on this with empty stomachs."

Then he pointed his sword at the first Whisperer in the first row.

"Come with us now," he said.

The Whisperer got to his feet. Another man. This one had a determined look plastered to his face. Micah wondered how long that expression would last and what it would mean for them.

Jeremiah would move up yet another place.

Seven down. Three to go.

ROSE

TWO

*A*fter leaving the Conductor's lifeless body on the floor of his study, Rose had taken Tash back to find Eliza and Cara, who were huddled together under one of the beds. Clever thinking on Eliza's behalf. At first Rose hadn't thought they were there and her heart had skipped a beat, until her sisters had shuffled out of their hiding place and wrapped their arms around her.

She'd tried to take them immediately to the dungeon to get them on their way to safety, but Tash had started shaking violently, clearly traumatized by what'd just happened to her. Every time Rose tried to put her down, she'd strengthen the grip she had around her neck. She just didn't have the heart to send her away, deciding she was going to have to somehow just keep them alive for another day.

They'd left the room they'd been sleeping in and gone to a cupboard under a staircase that Rose had discovered once as a child. It was empty, apart from a thick coating of dust, and the four girls had crouched in there for the night, holding each other close as Rose whispered to them, preparing them for the journey they had ahead and promising they wouldn't be apart for long.

Eventually, Tash's shaking stopped and she fell asleep in Rose's arms. Eliza was holding Cara, who despite being the youngest, seemed so much less vulnerable right now, not having suffered the same ordeal as Tash.

When Rose's sisters woke and complained of hungry tummies and needing to use the bathroom, she left them to fetch a bucket and a tray of food she found sitting on a table in one of the servant's bedchambers. She paced out the route to the dungeon, figuring the safest time to walk her sisters there would be when the Whisperers were moving about the palace, performing their afternoon chores. The more people around as witnesses, the safer they surely were.

She'd returned to the cupboard and together they waited. Rose told her sisters stories of Aunt Lily, who she'd met as a young child, telling them how she was beautiful and kind. Her own memories of Aunt Lily were vague, given she hadn't visited the palace for many years, so she made up the details she couldn't remember, reassuring the girls that she'd take great care of them.

She talked non-stop as a way to prevent herself from wondering if the Conductor's body had yet been found. Surely it had. His absence wouldn't go unnoticed for so long, especially if her father had a Whispering planned.

The day passed slowly, but instead of being resentful, she tried to be grateful of her sisters' company, hoping these weren't the last moments they'd spend together.

When Rose was certain it must be afternoon, she opened the cupboard door a crack and glued her eyes to the passageway until she saw a Whisperer walking past.

"It's time," she said to her sisters.

"Please come with us," said Tash, giving it one last try.

"Now, now," said Rose, wishing she could see her sweet little face in the dark. "You're a big girl. You proved that to me last night. Aunt Lily will love seeing what a big girl you are."

"Want Mother!" said Cara, not understanding what was happening. She was still very much a baby herself. How was she to understand that their Mother had a new baby to care for now?

They stepped out of the cupboard, just as a Whisperer turned into the hallway. Rose noticed his eyebrows shoot up, before he composed himself and kept walking with his eyes cast down, as if nothing unusual had happened.

Rose took her sisters directly to the dungeon, telling them to act as normal as they possibly could, which of course meant that they walked on exaggerated tip-toes with their index fingers across their lips. It was pretty cute and Rose didn't have the heart to tell them to stop.

When they got to the dungeon steps, her sisters' mood changed. The guard looked at them strangely but let them pass. A princess outranked a guard in the palace, even if she was a princess with a death warrant pinned to her back.

Rose had never been down these steps before and was glad of it. With each step she took, the air grew thicker with the smell of human waste and decay. The stone walls dripped with condensation and it was dark. Her sisters clutched at her skirts, clinging to her legs as they walked. She wished she had a pair of legs to cling to. She was just as scared as they were. The dungeon was no place for little girls. It was no place for anyone, really.

They reached the bottom of the stairs and approached the nearest guard, who was standing in the light of a lantern, staring at them like four ghosts had just appeared before him. In their white nightgowns, with their long blonde hair, they must've looked exactly like some kind of strange vision. They were such a contrast to anything else down here.

"Are you Tyron?" asked Rose, getting straight to the point.

He licked his lips. "I can be anyone you want me to be, baby."

She took a step closer to him and looked him square in the eye. "I am Princess Rose, heir to the throne of Forte Cadence, and I demand to be spoken to with respect."

A look of horror spread across his face and he dipped to a bow. "Forgive me, your Highness."

"Take us to Tyron, immediately." She had no time to waste, and no time for lowlifes like this guard. If ever she became Queen, he'd be the first person she'd have banished from the palace.

"This way," said the guard, taking the lantern from the wall and leading them down several corridors.

"You were scary," whispered Eliza.

Rose squeezed her sister's arm. "You'd do well to learn to be scary sometimes, too."

They passed several cells and Rose tried not to look at the people trapped behind their bars. None of them called out to her, which worried Rose even more. What poor treatment had they endured to take all the fight out of them like that?

"Wait here," the guard said, coming to a halt.

They stopped and Rose caught the eye of a prisoner, the whites of his eyes looking like the winter snow in comparison to the filth covering his skin.

The guard scurried away, hopefully to fetch Tyron.

A few minutes later, a tall, well-built guard appeared. He was squinting, with his hair sticking up in all directions. Clearly, he'd been woken. Yet his eyes opened widely when he saw Rose and her sisters standing before him. Rose was relieved to see kindness in his startled eyes.

"Princesses," he said, dipping to a bow. "At your service."

Better. Much better. Her mother had done well to place her trust in this guard.

"The Queen said you've been waiting for us." She kept her voice authoritative, not wanting a repeat of earlier.

Tyron nodded, running a hand through his hair, trying to flatten it down. "Very well. Let's be on our way. I have my instructions. The Queen was very clear."

"I won't be coming," said Rose. "You have just three passengers. Eliza will care for the younger two."

She pushed Eliza forward, only for her to take a step back toward Rose.

"We can't go without you," Eliza pleaded, grabbing for her hand.

"You must. I'll come and find you as soon as I can. I promise." She bit her tongue at these words. Why must she continue to make impossible promises?

"Very well," Tyron said, motioning for them to follow him.

"No, Rose! No!" Tash wrapped her arms around Rose's legs. "I told you no!"

She may have stopped shaking, although the poor girl was still traumatized.

"Hush, Tash." Rose kissed her sister on the top of her head, before opening her arms to draw all three of her sisters close. "Aunt Lily is waiting for you. She'll take excellent care of you until I get there."

"Want Mother," said Cara, tears streaking their way down her face.

"I told you, Aunt Lily is Mother's sister," said Rose. "And her name is a flower, just like mine so you know she's going to be nice."

Even though that made no sense whatsoever, it seemed to soothe Cara and she nodded her head bravely.

"You take good care of them, you hear me," Rose said to Tyron. "If anything happens to them…"

"They're in safe hands," said Tyron. "No harm will come to them. I'll see to their safe delivery."

Rose nodded her thanks and the three girls took a tentative step toward him.

Eliza turned back and looked at Rose. "You make things better here, okay?"

Rose nodded, relieved that Eliza understood, and blew her sisters kisses.

"Be safe," she called, begging the universe to please let her see them again one day. They disappeared down the passageway.

As Rose turned to make her way back up to the palace, she reminded herself that her mother loved them. She trusted her mother. And just like Jeremiah had put his trust in Rose, she also had to put her trust in someone. Their mother would never hurt them. No doubt she'd paid Tyron handsomely to take care of them. And Aunt Lily was their flesh and blood. She'd take care of her sisters even better than she could.

Besides, what choice did she have? At least now they had a chance. The further away they were from their father, the better.

She slowed her footsteps, realizing she'd made a wrong turn. This wasn't the way to the stairs that would take her back up to the palace. The cells here were unfamiliar, filled with the desperate faces of people she hadn't seen earlier.

"Princess!" one of them called. "Save us!"

"I'm trying," she said, pleased that at least one of them still had the courage to speak. She avoided the prisoner's eye. Her heart was already broken enough. "Freedom is coming."

She hurried on, reaching the end of the corridor, only to find it was closed off by a door. Thinking it might be another way back up to the palace, she tried the handle, jumping back in surprise when a hatch in the door opened and a face peered out at her through a set of bars.

It was an old woman, her eyes a cloudy blue, luring Rose back to her to take a closer look. So much for not directly looking at anybody. Did it count if they were unable to look back at her?

"Princess Rose," the woman said, her fingers reaching through the bars. "Is it you?"

"How do you know me?" Rose asked, standing far enough away so as not to be reached, now certain that this woman must be blind.

"I've seen you in my dreams," the woman said.

"Can you see me now?" Rose asked.

"I can see you inside my head. And you look like your mother. You're kind like her, too."

"How do you know my mother?" Rose was certain this woman hadn't been a Whisperer. She'd recognize her face from around the palace. Besides, they'd never had anybody this old whisper for her father. Her voice was croaky and hollow. Rose doubted she'd even know how to whisper.

"Your mother visits me," said the woman. "She calls me her angel. My name is Gabrielle."

Rose gasped. She'd heard her mother talk of an angel before and had always assumed it was some kind of made-up person, like a spirit.

"I knew you were coming to see me." Gabrielle took hold of the bars as she spoke and held on.

"How could you know?" asked Rose, keeping her voice low. "I didn't even know."

Gabrielle smiled, revealing her shriveled gums.

"I must tell you something," Gabrielle said, crooking her finger for Rose to come closer.

Rose stepped forward, unsure if it was a trick. Although, there was something about Gabrielle that made her trust her. Goodness seeped from her soul.

"You must find the Whisperer you met last night," said Gabrielle, quietening her voice. Rose had been wrong about her inability to whisper. "The one who saved your sister."

Rose nodded, not asking her how she knew about this. Was that why her mother visited her? Did she know things she couldn't possibly know?

"Find him and convince him to get himself sent down here. It's the only way."

"Why would he do that?" Rose glanced around, doubting that anybody was here by choice.

"Because he owes you. You stopped him from doing a horrible thing. Something he couldn't have lived with. And you gave him hope. Hope that he's spreading around the palace as we speak."

"Why should he go to the dungeon? What help is that?" Rose asked.

"Because he sits to Jeremiah's left."

Rose's hand flew to her mouth. This woman not only knew about Jeremiah, but it seemed she knew about their plan for him to move into the Conductor's position.

"He must make way. He must!" Gabrielle shook the bars, making the door rattle.

"Princess!" a guard called from behind her. "Is this prisoner bothering you?"

"No," said Rose. "I'm lost and was asking if she knew the way back to the palace."

The guard shook his head. "She doesn't know the way anywhere."

Rose looked into Gabrielle's sightless eyes one last time. How little this guard knew. It seemed that Gabrielle knew the way *everywhere*.

"Thank you, Gabrielle," she said, reaching out to touch her fingers on the bars.

"Follow me," said the guard.

She followed him back up to the palace, feeling guilty for the relief she felt to leave the dungeon. How awful it must be to be trapped down there. Poor Gabrielle. How had she come to be down there in the first place?

With her stomach growling, Rose decided to go to the royal dining room. Often her father didn't turn up for dinner. Hopefully, today would be one of those days. Although maybe if he did turn up and saw her there, he'd be less suspicious of her sisters having left the palace.

She sat at the dining table and waited to see if she'd be dining alone, wondering if maybe being in the dungeon was preferable to sharing a meal with a man who was trying to kill her.

Her father entered the room, glanced at her and took his seat at the head of the table.

"Your sisters are still taking their meals from their beds?" he asked.

Rose nodded. "They were quite badly injured in the fire. It's been very painful for them. They're suffering a lot."

She'd added that last bit to see if it caused any reaction. Any remorse or guilt? Her father didn't so much as flinch.

Two Whisperers crept into the room, each carrying a plate of food. She glanced up at the Whisperer who'd killed the Conductor, but he refused to catch her eye. Wise of him, especially in front of the King. She wondered how he was feeling? If he was still serving her food, then clearly, he hadn't been caught.

The Whisperers placed one plate in front of her father and another in front of her. Two plates piled with enough food to feed at least a dozen people. Rose's mouth flooded with moisture. She was so hungry. Hopefully, Tyron had food for her sisters for their journey. They must be hungry too.

She pushed her food around her plate, as the Whisperers left the room, wondering if it was poisoned. Surely that would be an easier way to kill her than setting the palace on fire? How could she possibly eat this meal, no matter how hungry she was?

Her father had already started tucking into his food, chewing with his mouth open as he skulled his wine and burped. The Whisperers may have been able to grant him a slimmer waistline and more hair, but they hadn't seemed to have been able to do much for his manners.

"Tell your sisters we'd like to see them tomorrow. Your mother will be well enough to join us for dinner again."

"If they're well enough, I'm sure they'd love to see their father." She wasn't sure why she was bothering to remind this brutal man of who he was to them. Or why he cared if her sisters joined them or not.

"We would like them to join us." He glared at her, before shoveling a few more mouthfuls of his meal into his mouth. "That's an order not just from your father. It's an order from your King."

Then he pushed back his chair, leaving the room without a word.

"Nice to see you, Father," she said, when the door closed behind him.

Perhaps tomorrow was the poisoning and he wanted to witness it first-hand and make sure he got all four of them at once? Why else would he insist on their presence like that? But it was going to be hard for him to poison her sisters when they'd be all the way over in Aria Flats by then.

She counted to ten to make sure her father had really gone and went to his end of the table, slid into his chair and pounced on his plate to eat his leftovers. There was no way anything on this plate would be poisoned.

The two Whisperers came into the room to clear the table. If they were surprised to find her in the King's seat eating from his plate, they didn't react. They stood to the side of the room and waited for her to finish. Thankfully her father hadn't been very hungry today. She'd seen him put away a lot more food than this before.

She wiped her mouth on a napkin and looked up at the Whisperers, wondering how to phrase what she had to say. Gabrielle had been very clear just now about her instructions for this Whisperer.

The female Whisperer, a short woman with a large birthmark on her cheek, picked up Rose's plate of untouched food, while the man went toward her plate.

"Freedom is coming," Rose said, standing.

The male Whisperer glanced toward the female, clearly wanting to speak, yet unsure if he should.

"I need your help," said Rose, deciding to be more direct.

He hesitated, then placed the plate back on the table and cleared his throat.

"What can I do, Princess?" he asked.

The female Whisperer's eyes flew wide open, clearly unable to believe she'd heard him speak.

"I need to have you sent to the dungeon." Rose winced as she waited for his reaction.

"Why?" His hands were shaking. "You said you wouldn't tell."

"I'm not going to tell," she reassured him. "For that would mean losing your head, not being locked away."

"Then what?"

"I'll tell them you spoke to me. That should do it." She nodded encouragingly.

"Why?" Sweat pooled on his brow.

"Because I need you to make way. Freedom is coming. It's coming soon. Except it will only come if we clear the path for Jeremiah to be the Conductor. I need you to step aside."

"Who's Jeremiah?" he asked.

The female Whisperer had frozen with the plate in her hand, unable to believe what she was hearing. Yet she didn't say a word. Rose doubted she would either.

"Jeremiah whispers on your right," Rose said.

"He's young," said the man.

Rose nodded. "He is. And he's going to save you. He's going to save us all. You trusted me last night and you must trust me again now. Freedom is coming soon and when it does, you'll be released from the dungeon. You have my word. I won't let you perish down there."

He looked at her, nodding slowly, seeming to understand, but not understanding at the same time. She couldn't blame him. It was confusing. Although, one thing he did understand was that really, he didn't have a choice. Rose could speak up about what had happened and he'd be put to death, or he could follow her plan and be sent away to the dungeon.

"I'm sorry," she said, placing a hand on his forearm. He flinched at the contact. "I wish there was another way, but there isn't. Please trust me."

"How will you move the two who stand before Jeremiah?" he asked.

"I haven't figured that out just yet," she said. "But I'll make sure it happens as soon as I can."

He nodded, more decisively this time. "Okay. I trust you, Princess."

"Guard!" she called, before he could change his mind. "Guard!"

Two guards burst into the room. "Yes, Princess."

"This Whisperer just spoke to me. Take him to the dungeon immediately." She tried to inject authority into her voice in the same way she had in the dungeon.

The guards took hold of the Whisperer's arms and the plate he'd been holding clattered to the floor. The guards dragged him from the room. Despite agreeing to her plan, she noticed his feet resisting where he was being led, as if they had an opinion different to the one he'd formed in his head.

Rose wished she'd asked his name while she'd had the chance.

The female Whisperer was still frozen, holding the plate. She let a knife with a wooden handle fall to the floor and quickly picked it up with shaking hands.

"It's okay," said Rose. "I don't mind noise. Please continue clearing."

The Whisperer looked at Rose, holding her gaze in a way that was forbidden.

"I have a son," she said, keeping her voice low as one hand brushed the birthmark on her face. "I must see him again."

Rose went to her and put a hand on her shoulder. "Freedom really is coming. I won't just be saving that man, I'll be saving you too. As soon as I find a way for Jeremiah to be the Conductor, you'll all be saved."

"Thank you," the Whisperer said. "Thank you."

Despite not using the word promise, Rose knew that was exactly what she'd done again.

She was promising the world. Now she needed to deliver.

JEREMIAH

ONE

*J*eremiah moved his mat up another position in the arena. There was only one Whisperer ahead of him now, a woman he called *Eye Twitch* for fairly self-explanatory reasons, although her eyes didn't seem to twitch as much these days as they had when he'd first seen her. Nevertheless, he'd stuck with the name he originally gave her.

He wondered how he might get her to abandon her position in the arena, so he could take her place. He didn't fancy killing anyone, having seen in Micah's face what that act had done to her, when she'd accidentally poisoned *Nose Bump* in the dining hall. She'd been devastated. She still seemed to be. Knowing Micah, she'd never get over that. Her heart was too kind to live easily with having done something like that.

Perhaps he could ask *Eye Twitch* to step aside? Or was he better off getting rid of the new Conductor and have her take over? The King hadn't seemed to like the last female Conductor so maybe he'd take care of things for them again. Although, he didn't like the idea of sending anyone to a certain death.

It was an interesting dilemma—do you kill one person to save the lives of one thousand? Logic said yes. His heart said no. He could never do that to an innocent person. There had to be another way.

He lay down on his mat and stared up at the ceiling, listening to *Eye Twitch* breathe. Perhaps he could ask her very quietly if she'd mind stepping down and have herself sent to the dungeon? He quickly pushed that thought from his mind. Nobody would ever agree to being sent to the dungeon. Nobody. You'd have to be insane.

The new Conductor was pacing the arena, watching the Whisperers as they rested. Nobody was prepared to act out this time. Not while *Strong Man* held the sword. Jeremiah had called him this when he'd first seen him in the shower. His chest was surprisingly rippled with muscles, despite the lack of exercise they got in the palace. He was frightening-looking and determined to prove his worth as the new Conductor. Within minutes of being handed the sword, he'd used it to pierce the heart of one of the newer Whisperers, announcing to the arena that he'd done so as punishment for the rebellion the day before. He was looking forward to punishing the next person who stepped out of line. And it appeared that the Whisperers believed him, for nobody was demonstrating the courage they'd displayed when the last Conductor had been in charge.

The Conductor reached the very rear of the arena and Jeremiah breathed a sigh, happy to have him so far away for a brief moment. It was such a long room that he could get away with almost anything at this distance if he dared. But did he?

He blinked as he heard something unusual. Footsteps. Light footsteps familiar of the Whisperers, except these footsteps were moving too quickly. Something wasn't right. He looked up to see *Birth Mark* moving toward him with purposeful steps and an expression of terror on her face. She was clutching a knife with a wooden handle.

Instinctively he put his hands in front of his face, certain she must be about to kill him.

She got closer and crouched to the floor. Jeremiah shuffled back on his mat, only to realize he wasn't her target. She was after *Eye Twitch,* who was still sleeping beside him.

Birth Mark's hand darted out and with one quick movement, she sliced open *Eye Twitch*'s throat. It was so fast that *Eye Twitch* barely had a chance to react. She just opened her eyes and her hands flew to her throat as she let out a gurgle. Panic and confusion filled her eyes before the life drained from them.

Jeremiah looked up at *Birth Mark* to see if he was next, but she'd already gone.

Realizing something was going on, the Conductor came running to the front of the arena. By this time, blood was everywhere, pouring from *Eye Twitch*'s throat.

Jeremiah remained perfectly still, realizing he'd be the prime suspect, and knowing that any movement now would only implicate him further. He had no blood on him, no weapon in his possession. Hopefully, the Conductor would realize it would be impossible for him to have killed her. Although Conductors weren't exactly known for handing out fair trials. Especially this one.

"Who did this?" bellowed the Conductor when he got close enough to see what had happened.

Jeremiah kept his eyes down, not looking up.

"Was it you?" The Conductor grabbed Jeremiah by the arm and pulled him to his feet.

Jeremiah held out his hands to show they were empty and kept his eyes on the floor.

"Search him," the Conductor said to the guards.

Jeremiah felt hands all over him, probing him, checking for anything he might have concealed, while the Conductor lifted his mat to check the floor beneath.

Nothing.

"Who did this?" he bellowed again. Nobody replied. How could they when they weren't allowed to speak or make eye contact? "When I find out who did this—and I will— there will be consequences! Severe consequences! Nobody takes a Whisperer's life, except me. Do you understand? DO YOU UNDERSTAND?"

Nobody answered. Nobody nodded. Nobody moved.

Jeremiah was thrown back to the floor and one of the guards landed a boot in his ribs.

He bit back a groan and curled himself into a ball, closing his eyes and pretending he was back in the Valley of the Blessed, his mother and father by his side and Micah playing on the floor beside him. If only he could go back to those days just one more time. If only he'd appreciated it when he'd been there. It had been his little piece of Evernow and he hadn't even realized it at the time. He could only hope there was a much bigger Evernow waiting for him when this nightmare was over.

Why had *Birth Mark* done it? Was it a coincidence that her very action had helped Jeremiah with his plan? Had she somehow known what they were planning? But how could she possibly know that? Unless Micah or Rose had told her...

There was so much he didn't understand. So much he never would.

One thing he did understand was that now he was first in line. If this Conductor was to meet an untimely end, then finally, freedom would really be coming. And coming soon.

The Conductor blew his whistle and several guards ran into the arena. They removed *Eye Twitch's* body and a palace worker mopped up the mess she'd left behind.

Jeremiah wished he'd given her a nicer name than that. She hadn't deserved what'd just happened. None of them did. It had been a brutal way to die, the only blessing that it was fast and she'd barely known what had happened to her. Did that make it better or worse? Was it better to know what it was that took your life and die with some understanding, or was it better for your life to be wiped out in an instant? This wasn't a simple question and unfortunately, there was no simple answer, except to say that neither option was better.

Better would be to live a happy life until you were old and wrinkled and died in your sleep surrounded by people who loved you. Was that too much to ask? In this palace, it appeared that it was.

He stood and picked up his mat, moving it one more position to the left. The last position in the arena. There were no further places to the left that he could move after this. After this, the only way was to move forward. Forward into the Conductor's role and forward into a new and hopefully better future.

MICAH

NONE

*M*icah wasn't sure how'd they'd managed it, but they had. Somehow. Jeremiah was the next in line. The only person standing in his way of being the Conductor, was the Conductor himself.

The events that'd just taken place in the arena were shocking. One Whisperer had killed another. Sliced her throat so quickly and quietly that nobody knew who'd done it and how.

Jeremiah must surely know. It'd happened right next to him. Had he done it himself? When the Conductor had pulled him to his feet to accuse him, Micah had felt her heart stop for a few beats. It wasn't him. She was certain of it. He wouldn't be that careless or callous. Especially when he was so close to his goal. Or was it being that close, that'd made him reckless? No, not Jeremiah.

But then the Whisperer who slept in front of her, returned to her mat and sat down with a look of horror on her face as she trailed her fingers over the birthmark on her cheek, leaving a line of blood on her face.

Micah stretched out her leg and kicked her to get her attention, miming wiping her face when she looked at her. She didn't want to see anyone else die today. And like it or not, this Whisperer had helped them out, even if what she'd done was beyond comprehension. The Whisperer nodded at Micah and used the sleeve of her robe to wipe the blood from her face, leaving the birthmark clear and clean once more.

How Micah longed to ask her why she'd done it. How had she known this was what was needed? Her act of violence surely couldn't have been random.

Micah didn't have long to think about this, for no sooner had they all recovered from the shock of what just happened as another shock was delivered.

A voice rang out across the arena. A female voice. A young voice, not unlike Micah's when she'd been allowed to use it.

"Whisperers!" the voice called.

Micah twisted her head to look up at the balcony at the rear of the arena, not far above from where she sat.

It was Princess Rose, standing on the balcony addressing them all. She looked different to the last time Micah had seen her. Less defeated, more ready to defeat.

"Whisperers!" she called out again. "Some of you know me. I am Princess Rose, the King's eldest child and heir to his throne."

Micah looked around the arena to gauge the reaction of her fellow Whisperers. Their faces were all turned upward, staring at the Princess, with their mouths open. Except for the Conductor. His eyes were darting around in a panic. Was this allowed? Was the Princess allowed to speak? This had never happened before.

"Despite being the heir," she continued, "I'll never be the ruler of this Kingdom. Because my father wants me dead, so his newborn son can be King in a long line of men who've ruled Forte Cadence."

"Your Royal Highness, forgive me, but I must ask you to be quiet," the Conductor called out, tapping his sword on the floor.

"I will *not* be quiet," said the Princess. "Whisperers, I need your help. I wish to be your Queen, so I can set you free. I'm being kept here as a prisoner, just as much as you are. But together we can make change. I can't kill my father, you know that. You yourselves have whispered for his protection. So, I have a plan and I'm asking you to trust me. Freedom is coming!"

A gasp swept through the arena at these words. The Princess was the key to the freedom they were waiting for.

"Save us, my Queen!" called out Micah, confident that the Conductor was too preoccupied to punish her right now.

"I need to see my son!" called the Whisperer with the birthmark, giving at least a small clue as to why she'd just taken a life in such a way.

Soon, more Whisperers were calling, begging the Princess to save them, calling her their Queen.

"Quiet!" bellowed the Conductor.

A hush fell across the room.

"Including you!" he said, lifting his sword and pointing it toward the balcony, his respect of earlier having vanished. "Or yours will be the next head that I take, Princess or not."

The Whisperers gasped. Could the Conductor talk to the Princess like that?

"What do you need us to do, my Queen?" Micah called to the balcony.

"Kill him!" the Princess shouted, her eyes aflame, her hands gripping the balcony's railing, turning her knuckles white. "Kill him and you'll all be saved!"

The Whisperers froze, not expecting these words. The Conductor held his ground, doing his best to look fearsome instead of fearful.

"Don't anybody move," he said.

"I don't condone violence, but it's the only way!" called the Princess. "Hurry!"

Micah saw Jeremiah rise from his mat and snatch the Conductor's sword from his hands so quickly that he didn't have time to react.

The Whisperer with the birthmark rose from her mat and began running to the front of the arena. But she didn't get far, stopped by a sea of Whisperers clambering to get to the Conductor.

Jeremiah was pushed back, not given the chance to use the sword he'd taken, as Whisperers piled on top of the Conductor.

From where she was at the back of the arena, Micah could hear screaming, shouting, cries of victory and one final howl that she assumed came from the man who'd commanded them not to move.

One by one, the Whisperers backed away, and soon Micah could see what was left of the Conductor. The Princess's wish had been granted. The Conductor was dead. There was no doubt about that.

The Whisperers returned to their mats, bowing their heads at the balcony and the girl they'd just pinned all their hopes on. Except for Jeremiah, who remained at the front of the arena, holding the Conductor's sword in his shaking hands.

The Princess had tears rolling down her cheeks.

"Thank you," she said. "I won't let you down. Now, do you see the man who holds the sword?"

She pointed at Jeremiah and a thousand heads turned in his direction. "He's your new leader and you must put your faith in him. Trust him as you just trusted me. Soon this—" she swept her hand across the arena— "will be finished. We may not be warring with other kingdoms, however, my father has begun a war within his own. It's not a war that he'll win."

The Princess drew in a breath so deep that the air in the arena seemed to move toward her in response.

"I need you to all continue to trust me. Even though you may not know me, you need to take a chance on me. You must pretend to fear Jeremiah. Do as he says. Appear to be giving him the respect the King expects of his Conductor. He may pretend he's about to hurt you, but he won't. He's your salvation. Be patient. Hold on. Freedom is coming!"

Micah felt something wet drip onto her lap and realized that she too was crying.

They'd done it.

Jeremiah was the Conductor. And now, not only would they soon be free, but all the other poor souls trapped in this arena would be free too.

The Princess raised her hand and blew kisses down to them, before turning and leaving the balcony, the hope she'd given them still present in the room.

"Freedom is coming!" cried one of the Whisperers. His chant was joined by others as the arena broke into the sounds of hope.

Then there was the sound of a sword tapping on the floor.

Silence spread across the room in a wave.

"You heard what our future Queen said." Jeremiah held the sword in the air. "Freedom is coming, but freedom is not yet here. Please let us have some order, so our plans don't fail. We are close, however, we're not there yet."

The Whisperers sat on their mats and bowed their heads, understanding.

Micah smiled. They were trusting him, just like the Princess had asked them to. She really was brave as well as beautiful. Forte Cadence would soon be in safe hands.

"There's just one thing..." said Jeremiah.

All eyes rose and were glued on him now.

"This." He pointed at the Conductor's body with his sword. "I need one of you to take responsibility for this. The King will demand an explanation."

Nobody moved.

"I'll have you taken to the dungeon. I give you my word that I won't kill you. You won't be there for long. I'll see to it that you're released as soon as possible."

Still, nobody moved.

"We can't succeed without a volunteer," said Jeremiah again, and Micah wondered if perhaps she should raise her hand. She wasn't needed anymore. She'd done all she could do to get Jeremiah where he needed to be. But would Jeremiah be able to concentrate on his task ahead, if she were locked away in a cell?

There was a movement in front of Micah and she realized there was no need for her to volunteer. Someone else had. The woman with the birthmark had risen to a stand and put her hand in the air.

"I'll do it. I deserve no better. We all killed the Conductor, but I alone, killed the woman who sat to Jeremiah's left. It must be me. However..."

Jeremiah nodded, encouraging her to continue to speak.

"However, if I don't make it out of here alive, you must promise to look for my son. He was unwell when I was taken from him and has nobody left to care for him. I'm so afraid."

Micah was still unsure how this woman had known that Jeremiah needed to be the one to stand before them, but her motives were now clear. She'd sacrificed the life of the Whisperer, believing her actions would be the only thing that would save her son. She was desperate to get back to him so she could nurse him to health. And now she was making another sacrifice. Herself.

Some time in the dungeon in the hope she'd live to see her son again.

A mother's love was a powerful force. Micah wondered if her own mother had loved her like that.

Remembering the last moments of her mother's life, she knew for certain that she had. Her mother's last words were of concern for her children, not herself. Once again, she hoped she'd heard her tell her that she loved her before it'd been too late.

Micah stepped forward on her mat and took the hand of the brave Whisperer, squeezing it tightly. This mother needed to be with her child. This child needed his mother. Micah didn't have a mother and she didn't have a child. She couldn't let this woman make the sacrifice.

"I'll do it instead," she called to Jeremiah. "Leave this woman alone."

She watched her brother's face threaten to break underneath his brave facade.

He bent and took the Conductor's whistle from around his neck, blowing it until two guards came running into the arena.

The guards looked at the body of the Conductor and then at Jeremiah holding both the sword and the whistle.

"That woman killed the Conductor," Jeremiah said, pointing in Micah's direction. "I am your Conductor now. Please, take her to the dungeon and send some workers to clean up this mess."

Micah took in a deep breath, still holding the hand of the Whisperer beside her, who was clutching her like a vice. She steeled herself for what was to come.

Jeremiah walked the guards toward Micah, but just as they were about to seize her, Jeremiah called them to a stop.

"No, that one," he said, lifting a finger to point to the woman beside her. "That one."

Micah barely had time to react, when the guards grabbed hold of the Whisperer—a mother who yearned for nothing more than her son—and took her away. She didn't scream or drag her feet. Instead, she walked to her fate with her head held high.

"My son's name is Samson," called the Whisperer, as she was taken through the door, her words echoing around the arena.

"Her son needs her," Micah said to Jeremiah, who was still standing by her side.

"And I need you," he said to Micah, keeping his voice low. "I can't do this without you."

She held back her tears as she nodded, ashamed that she was feeling relieved. That woman had shown so much courage. It was now more important than ever that they succeed. Too many of them had done things they'd never normally do. Lives had been taken that should never have been lost. Regrets had been made and innocence had been stolen.

If freedom was coming, it'd better hurry up and come fast. There was only so much more of this they could take.

ROSE

THE ONE

*R*ose was shaking so violently that the water in her bath was lapping at the edges and threatening to spill over.

She'd just killed a man. Not with her own hands, but certainly the responsibility for his death was hers alone.

Jeremiah was the Conductor now. Their plan had somehow worked.

She trailed her hands over her skin, trying to wash away her guilt. Was she a murderer?

Lying back in the bath, she closed her eyes and let herself sink under the water, feeling her hair float out in all directions, like it had taken on a life of its own.

A shadow moving across the washroom caught her eye and she sat up quickly, droplets of water pouring from her body as they struggled to meet up with the rest of their kind.

A Whisperer was standing by her bath, staring at her.

"Don't you touch me!" said Rose, crossing her arms across her chest to preserve her dignity. Was her father still sending Whisperers to try to kill her? And after what she'd just witnessed in the arena, did she still need to be afraid?

The Whisperer removed her hood, and Rose saw it was Micah. She let out a deep breath.

"It's only me." Micah held up her hands.

"Pass me my towel," said Rose, pointing.

Micah picked up the towel and held it open for Rose to step into, averting her gaze.

"I'm sorry to interrupt you in a ... private moment," Micah said. "I needed to be sure you were alone."

"Definitely alone," said Rose, wrapping the towel around herself and feeling instantly better once covered. "I'm just jumpy at the moment. Every shadow is someone trying to kill me."

"That's understandable. Looks like you're taking precautions though." Micah nodded toward the dagger she had beside the bath. The same one Rose had taken when she went to save Tash that night. She'd been carrying it with her ever since, not that she'd needed to use it so far. She'd killed the Conductor with her command—her words— which was sort of ironic given his position.

"Jeremiah's in the Conductor's study. His study. He wants to see you urgently. He sent me for you."

Rose nodded, still feeling shaken.

"Princess," Micah said, reaching to touch her on the arm. "Thank you. What you did today was ... inspired."

Rose smiled. "And here I've been thinking it was evil. I killed a man."

A sadness crossed Micah's eyes. "I did too," she whispered.

"This is a war. Lives will be lost." Rose touched Micah on the arm, not wanting her to feel sad. They'd all done things they weren't proud of. But they were all things that'd needed to be done for change to happen. Otherwise how many more lives were going to be taken in the process?

"Is Jeremiah okay?" Rose asked, wondering what she could expect when she saw him. It'd been so long since they'd last spoken. Seeing him in the arena had been both uplifting and heartbreaking. There really was nobody else like him. It was like he'd been born to this world, just for her.

"Yes and no." Micah both shook and nodded her head, then decided on a shrug. "He's dreading meeting with the King, your father. I don't think he's sure what he has to do. If you want him to kill him with his sword—"

"Not his sword!" Rose interrupted. "His words. Jeremiah is going to kill my father with the very weapon he's been using against all of us. Words. Come with me and I'll explain to you at the same time as Jeremiah."

Micah bowed her head. "I must go to the kitchen now and do my work. We can't let the King become suspicious."

"Then I'll go alone."

Micah nodded. "Thank you." She did some kind of strange curtsy and scurried from the bathroom, leaving Rose to get dressed.

Rose pulled her dress over her head and looked in the mirror briefly, trying to comb her hair with her fingers. Since her bedchamber burnt down, she'd looked a mess. It hadn't bothered her. Until now. She was embarrassed to admit it, but she wanted to look her best for Jeremiah. Which was crazy, as she was certain he wouldn't be looking at the styling of her hair (or lack of) when he saw her. He loved her for so much more than how she wore her hair. She could see it in his eyes.

Poking her tongue out at her disheveled appearance, she left the washroom and set off to find him.

With each turn of the corridor, each step she took, the knot in her stomach tightened.

Jeremiah. Ever since that day he'd told her his name, she'd turned it over on her lips, letting the sound caress her. The boy who used to bring her breakfast had become her whole reason to exist.

When she reached the Conductor's study and put her hand to the door handle, she hesitated. What if he didn't feel the same? What if his love for her was like a brother loved a sister—like he loved Micah— when her love stretched so much further than that. If she took every cell of her body and lined them up until they reached high into the sky and touched the sun, even that wouldn't describe how far her feelings stretched. He was threaded through her being like he was a part of herself.

She opened the door.

Jeremiah wasn't sitting behind the large oak desk, instead, he was pacing the room. His head snapped up and he turned to her, his eyes filling with surprise and anguish.

"Rose!" He went quickly to her side and placed one hand on either side of her face, pressing his forehead to her own.

She tilted her head and pressed her lips to his, desperately hoping for him to respond.

His hands slid behind her head and he deepened the kiss in a way that chased away her fears. With that one kiss, her feelings for him flew even higher than they had before, touching not only the sun but now reaching out into the far corners of the universe. He'd been made for her, just as she'd been made for him. When she kissed him, they were no longer two lonely souls, they were one being, united by love.

"I love you," she said, pulling back just enough so she could trail small kisses from his lips down to his jawline.

"Rose, you don't know me."

"I know you," she said, her kisses peppering his neck, until his head tilted back and he gasped.

"I know you," she said again. "And I want to know more of you."

"Rose, your father will be here soon," he said, pulling himself from her. "We must talk."

He was right. Deciding that the only way to be able to resist touching him was to put a large object physically between them, she went behind his desk and sat down.

"I have a plan," she said.

"I do too." He picked up his Conductor's sword. "I'm going to kill him."

"No, Jeremiah." She leaped from her chair. "You've never used a sword. My father is a trained fighter. The risk is too great."

"Then…" He ran his fingers across his scalp. "I don't understand."

"Then listen." Yet before she could outline her thoughts, the door handle turned once more and the door swung open.

Rose slid from the chair to the floor in one fluid movement, crouching under the desk, hoping she'd been swift enough that whoever had come to pay Jeremiah a visit hadn't seen her.

"Your Majesty," said Jeremiah, confirming Rose's worst fears.

"Conductor," her father said. "We are surprised to see you here so soon. You have moved up the ranks quickly."

"Yes, Your Majesty. I'm surprised too."

"Are you pleased with your new position?"

"Yes, Your Majesty. It's my honor to serve you."

"Excellent." Rose didn't need to be able to see her father to know he'd be rubbing his hands together right now. "We expect big things from you. We don't want to see another change in position for a long time, do you understand?"

"Yes, Your Majesty."

"You must regain control. I fear the Whisperers are getting restless. And THIS IS NOT ACCEPTABLE."

Rose flinched as her father shouted these last words, longing to reach out to Jeremiah who was no doubt petrified at this very moment.

"I'll do my best, Your Majesty." His voice was shaking, betraying his fear.

"We need better than your best. We need better than everyone's best. We're not happy with recent events. There will be a Whisper today."

"Today?" asked Jeremiah.

"Is that a problem?"

"No, of course not. I just didn't expect a Whisper so soon, Your Majesty."

"Well?" The King was tapping his foot on the floor now.

"I'm not sure I understand," said Jeremiah.

"Well, aren't you going to ask us what the Whisper is to be?"

"Of course, Your Majesty. What will we be Whispering for today?"

"Better. It's a simple one today. One we have desired for a very long time, and we fear it can wait no longer. We've tried other means and success has not been granted."

"I'm listening, Your Majesty. What is the Whisper?"

Rose heard her father clear this throat.

"The King's daughters are dead."

The knot that'd previously tied Rose's gut in knots released, then tightened. It was one thing to know your father wanted you dead. It was another altogether to hear him say it.

"Are you certain, Your Majesty?" asked Jeremiah.

Rose had to use all her control to resist jumping out from her hiding place and hitting Jeremiah over the head. The King didn't like to be questioned. And it didn't matter what he'd asked for. She had a plan.

"Because you are new," said her father in a snarl, "we are going to pretend we didn't hear that. Repeat the Whisper to me, so I know you understand."

"The King's daughters are dead," said Jeremiah, his voice level now. "I understand, Your Majesty. And I apologize."

"Impress us today," said the King. "We demand that of you."

"Yes, Your Majesty."

There were footsteps and the sound of the door closing.

"Rose," said Jeremiah.

"Wait!" she hissed, knowing her father well enough to know there was a good chance he might return.

The door opened again.

"Conductor," her father said. "Gather your Whisperers. We are keen to get on with this business."

The door closed again and her father's footsteps could be heard disappearing down the hallway. He didn't feel the same need for silence when the sound was coming from his own feet.

Rose came out from under the desk and returned to Jeremiah's side. His face was crumpled, his eyebrows knitted together and water pooling in his eyes.

"I'm sorry," he said, pulling her to him. "I should have killed him, but you said not to. What are we going to do? What's your plan?"

"It's okay. I told you it's okay." She ran her hands down the front of his robe, taking hold of it and pulling his ear to her mouth as she lowered her voice and told him exactly what she had planned.

With each word she spoke, she could feel the tension seeping from his body. It was going to be all right. He just needed to trust her.

"Will you do it?" she asked when she'd finished telling him her plan.

He nodded.

"Good. Because it's the only way."

He nodded again. "You're right."

Rose wrapped her arms around him and wondered how she was going to let him go when she felt like she'd only just found him. But afterward... that was what would happen. He'd leave her. Of course he would. He hated the palace. There was no way he'd hang around here to be with her. And she knew now that there was no way she could ever leave.

She either died here or she lived here. Or both. No matter if her plan worked or not, this was where she'd remain. Because leaving may preserve her life, however, it was certain death for everyone else. And she may have the death of one man to carry on her shoulders, but she didn't need the weight of a thousand. She'd never be able to stand up again.

Soon she'd know. It was time. Her future had arrived.

KING VIRTUS

THE NOW

King Virtus sat outside the balcony room in the arena at the top of the stairs and tapped his fingers on the arm of the chair, admiring how lean his forearms were now that he'd dispensed of the extra weight he'd been carrying. Thankfully not all his body parts had shrunk like this. His cock was bigger than it'd ever been. He heard the way it made the Queen yelp with pleasure. Lucky bitch. She really should be more grateful.

Today was the day. He could wait no longer, no matter what his stupid whore of a wife thought. Her warnings were meaningless.

He had his son now. He didn't need the Queen anymore, except for his son to suckle on her tits. He would keep her, for now, but her days were numbered, just like his own mother's had been after he was born. Although, having a spare might come in handy, he supposed. Another son. Just in case. There was too much to think about right now.

Whether or not he let his wife live, his daughters were no longer of any use to him. His merciful years of letting them live were over. Young Prince Virtus would be the next ruler of Forte Cadence. Not

Rose or Eliza or Tash or … what was that young one's name again? Cara. That's right. Cara wouldn't rule either.

He'd laughed when he discovered his Queen had let his daughters escape, no doubt to her family in Aria Flats. Was she so stupid to think that he needed them in his palace to bring out their deaths? He could whisper for it from a million miles away and so it would be. He should probably wipe out his twin sister while he was at it, just in case.

He hated his twin almost more than he loved his son. It was just as well his father had had the sense to lie about their birth order or right now she'd be Queen and he'd be watching her as Prince Virtus. But nobody alive knew about that, except for him. His father had made sure of that, only telling Virtus himself about it on his deathbed. He wasn't even sure why he'd told him, although he supposed a King had a right to know about such things, even if they were no longer of any relevance. Just because his sister took her first breath a few minutes before him, didn't make her more worthy of the crown. Luckily his father had seen the crown between his legs and taken action to ensure the right person got the job.

His eldest daughter, Rose, had chosen not to run away with her sisters. She was probably too frightened to leave. Another foolish whore in the making. Not that she would live long enough to be a whore.

He thought back to the conversation he'd just had with the new Conductor, uncertain if he was up for the task. He was a strange young man, although he had potential. He had the sort of handsome face people respected. And being the Conductor was definitely the sort of responsibility that required respect. He'd need to put in some time with him, of course, to make sure he knew what was expected of him. He just needed to get the unpleasantness of disposing of his daughters out of the way first.

A smile spread across his face at the thought of the unpleasantness. A male heir at last. And what a strapping baby he was already. Strong arms and legs and quite a temper too. His daughters had never bellowed for their milk like that. Just more proof that men were superior to the weaker sex. They knew how to ensure their demands were met. Prince Virtus was an expert already. He'd make a fine King one day.

A guard approached.

"They're ready for you, Your Majesty," he said, bowing his head.

Excellent. Oh, how he loved a good Whispering. No doubt the foolish beetles would think his latest Whisper excessive, but what did they know? And who could they tell without the use of their voices?

He laughed as the door was opened for him and he stepped onto the balcony.

One thousand beetles, all lined up waiting for him. And the new Grand Beetle standing before them, holding the sword like it was going to take on a life of its own and run away from him if he loosened his grip.

He'd relax in time, when he came to realize how important his work was. How many lives he was saving by keeping Forte Cadence safe, even if a few lives had to be lost in the process.

"The Whisperers are whispering. The Whisperers are whispering. The Whisperers are whispering."

Excellent. It had begun.

The Conductor swept his sword across the arena, shaking slightly under the weight of it. Extra rations would need to be arranged to fatten this one up. Strength was needed to lead an army.

Rows of beetles fell silent and knelt on their mats with their heads bowed, waiting for their command. This was his favorite part. The waiting. Knowing he had all the power here.

The Conductor raised his sword above his head, then brought it down a little too quickly for King Virtus's liking. He'd need to speak to him about that. It was important to get all the small details of this ceremony exactly right for maximum effectiveness.

The Conductor looked to the balcony at the rear of the arena and nodded at him. Waiting. The Whisperers were ready. The Conductor was ready. Was he himself ready to do a job he should have arranged many years ago if his heart hadn't been so soft?

King Virtus nodded. Let it be done. He owed that to his son, just like his own father had owed it to him, taking care of his older sister well before he'd even been born, then swapping his birth order with Georgia to arrange the twins in the order they should have come into the world. Sometimes the universe made mistakes that needed correcting.

Hopefully, this new Conductor remembered his words precisely. The words were important. *The King's daughters are dead.* One letter could make all the difference here. If they were to whisper *daughter* in the singular, they'd need to do it all over again.

The Conductor cleared his throat in a way that was entirely unnecessary and appeared to take a deep breath before he let the fatal words fall from his lips.

"The King is dead."

It took King Virtus a few moments to understand what he'd just heard.

It wasn't until the Conductor said it again that he was able to react.

"How dare you!" he bellowed from the balcony, just as the first row of those traitorous beetles lifted their heads, removed their hoods and stood.

"Do not speak!" King Virtus shouted, clutching at the railing with both his hands.

"*The King is dead,*" they whispered.

"Anybody who says another word will be killed!"

It was a shame that he was going to have to kill more Whisperers, but this was unacceptable. Never had he witnessed such heresy!

The second row stood and King Virtus held his breath, waiting for the sweet sound of silence. It was okay. This could be undone. He would have them Whisper for his health and all would be fine.

"*The King is dead,*" the first two rows whispered together.

"No! Silence!"

Row after row joined in and the chant became louder, the arena filling with hushed voices, whispering in unison for his doom.

Sweat poured down his brow and his heart pumped at a rate he'd never experienced before. He had to do something! He had to stop this before it was too late.

"Guards," he said, spinning around to find he was alone on the balcony.

He went to the door and turned the handle to find it locked. How dare they! He was their King! Their ruler! They couldn't lock him in or out. If he wanted a door opened in his own palace, the door would open.

"Let me out!" His shouting was drowned out by the whispering, which had risen to a volume he'd never before heard in the arena. They weren't whispering at all, they were shouting, with joy in their voices.

His hands flew to his chest as he willed his heart to slow down. He wasn't going to die. He was the King. He decided when he died and now was not the time. This could be undone. His stupid wife could get another message from his ancestors to save him. This was ridiculous!

"The King is dead. The King is dead. The King is dead." Over and over those hideously evil words continued to hammer at his ears.

"Stop it! Stop it!" He returned to the balcony and leaned over the edge, calling out until his voice was hoarse and his breath was coming in gasps. "Stop it! We command you to stop!"

They would pay for this! Heads were going to roll.

"The King is dead. The King is dead."

He put his hands over his ears, unable to take it anymore. Those words! Those horrible words! They needed to stop. Why weren't they stopping?

He leaned over the railing to see the faces of these traitors. Let them look him in the eye as they chanted for his death.

"No!" He couldn't believe what he was seeing. Those disgusting beetles weren't chanting with their heads respectively bowed. They'd turned so their faces were pointing right at him. They had smiles on their disgusting mouths and their hands were outstretched, linked together like a chain of filth.

"The King is dead. The King is dead."

The Conductor had joined the beetles and was holding the hand of a young Whisperer who had the same eyes as him. There was no sign of his sword.

"Traitor!" the King yelled, removing his hands from his ears and grabbing hold of the railing in front of him once more and shaking it. "Traitor!"

The railing loosened and he shook it further, hoping it would crash down and knock some of those filthy traitors on the head. They'd pay for this.

"The King is dead. The King is dead."

Each word was like a knife in his chest. He could feel them stabbing at him, the pain so real he wasn't sure if perhaps he'd been attacked. He ran his hands over his chest, but it was fine. No, it wasn't fine. He *was* being attacked. Attacked with words and nobody knew better than him that words were a far more powerful weapon than any sword or fist. Words flew straight into the ears of the universe.

Then the pain became too great to bear and he clutched at his chest, crying out for help.

"Please!" he called, using this word for the first time in his life. "Please, help me! We won't hurt you! Things will be different. We promise. Please, just stop."

They didn't stop. His words stopped instead, and he stumbled, crashing toward the railing. It broke apart, swinging open like a gate, welcoming him to his final resting place.

The people below scurried for safety as the King fell to the floor. No longer Whisperers, they were now *people*. People who had hopes and dreams and names. People who no longer had a King.

Because the King was dead.

* * *

"Long live the Queen," said Jeremiah, leaning over the King's lifeless body.

"Long live the Queen," said Micah, nodding as she squeezed her brother's hand.

The people formed a circle around their dead King, and a new chant erupted and filled the arena.

"Long live the Queen! Long live the Queen!"

It took them a while to see her standing on the balcony, where only moments ago her father had taken his last breath.

A hush spread across the arena as they waited for her to speak.

"You are my people," she said. "I don't wish to speak to you from here because I am one of you. Not one who stands above you. I stand with you."

She stepped toward the part of the balcony where the railing had broken away.

"Will you catch me?" she asked.

The people below stretched out their arms and she let herself fall, trusting them like they had trusted her.

They caught her and set her on the floor and she took a few steps away from her father's crumpled body, smoothed her skirt and smiled.

"Freedom is no longer coming," she said, through her tears. "Freedom is here!"

AURELIA

THE NOW

*D*ead. Dead. Dead. Aurelia's husband was dead. Which meant her daughters would live. It also meant that, for the first time since her wedding day, she also was allowed to live.

It was easily the happiest day of Aurelia's life. Her husband's death was her birth.

The first thing she did was send Tryon to her sister to bring her daughters home. The second thing she did was search the palace until she found her beautiful Rose. Her daughter, the Queen.

Which made Aurelia the Queen Mother, a title she liked no more or less than the one she'd had before. She still preferred to be called Aurelia.

She found Rose in the garden, surrounded by Whisperers.

"Mother!" said Rose, walking over to her.

"My daughter," Aurelia said, pulling her into her arms and kissing her cheek.

"You've heard the news?" asked Rose.

"I have," Aurelia said. "The guards came to me immediately. I was a little…" she searched for the right word, "shocked."

Rose nodded.

"You are the Queen now," she said, aware she was stating what was obvious to all. "Should I dip my head and curtsy?"

"Don't you dare!" Rose laughed, her eyes crinkling, reminding Aurelia of how she'd giggled as a child. "I'm outlawing the curtsy immediately."

"You do realize the seriousness of the position you hold," Aurelia said, wondering if her daughter was ready for the task ahead.

Rose's face fell and her features smoothed out. "Of course I do, Mother. And I'll be needing your help."

Aurelia smiled. "Most definitely. And am I allowed to ask how you did it? Is it true you changed the Whisper?"

Rose smiled again. "I'll tell you everything later."

Aurelia nodded. "Just tell me one thing for now. Did he suffer?"

"Greatly." Rose studied her face for a reaction.

"Good." Aurelia felt a weight lift. Her husband had deserved no better.

"I'm glad you're here," said Rose. "There's something we need to do, and I wanted us to do it together."

Aurelia nodded, having a feeling she knew exactly what it was.

"What is it?" she asked her daughter, tucking a stray lock of hair behind her ear. She really was a beautiful girl. Aptly named after Aurelia's favorite flower.

"The dungeons. It's time to let all the people go free, not just the Whisperers. We'll open all their doors and send them home to their families."

This was what Aurelia had hoped Rose was going to say. There could be no celebration of freedom until everyone in the palace had that same right.

"Your first official act as Queen will be one of kindness," said Aurelia. "I'm proud of you."

"Gabrielle has waited long enough," said Rose.

Aurelia's hand fluttered to her mouth. "How do you know about Gabrielle?" She was sure she was the only person who knew Gabrielle's name.

"That's another long story," said Rose. "For later. The prisoners have waited long enough for their release."

This was true. Every minute in the dungeon must feel like a century.

"There are two people you need to meet," Rose said, turning to beckon to the group of Whisperers on the lawn. "Jeremiah! Micah!"

Two Whisperers approached. Aurelia studied their faces, recognizing one of them as the man who'd stolen her daughter's heart. The same man who'd brought her breakfast every day for many years. Had he played a part in what'd happened in the arena today?

"Mother, this is Jeremiah, and his sister, Micah." Rose stood between them, with an arm over each of their shoulders.

"Pleased to meet you," said Aurelia.

The Whisperers smiled at her.

"You've always been kind to me, Your Majesty," said the male Whisperer that Rose had called Jeremiah.

"Then please always be kind to my daughter," she said, already knowing this man had quite a different heart to the one that'd stopped beating inside the man she'd married.

"We have no time to waste," said Rose, taking a step toward the palace. "Let freedom truly be here."

Aurelia paused to burn the memory of this moment into her brain. The bad had become good. So good she could scarcely believe it. Gabrielle had been right. All she'd had to do was trust and wait. Her daughters were alive and her baby son now had a chance to grow into a good man, instead of the monster her husband would surely have raised him to be.

Together, the four of them made their way into the palace and down to the dungeon. Aurelia wasn't entirely certain why Jeremiah and Micah were with them, but it seemed to be important to Rose. There was someone down there, they said they needed to see.

The guard on duty greeted them with a bow. "Your Majesty," he said, directing his words to Rose. This was going to take some getting used to. Unless Rose outlawed the bow as well as the curtsy.

"We're releasing all the prisoners," said Rose. "Please open all their doors immediately."

The guard snapped to his full height once again, his eyes filling with fear.

"You're afraid they'll turn on you?" asked Aurelia.

The guard nodded. "My position at the palace hasn't been one of compassion, I'm afraid."

"Then return home to your family," said Rose. "We'll give you a few minutes as a head start. Tell the other guards."

The guard shuffled his feet.

"Your keys please," said Rose, stretching out her hand. "Quickly now."

The guard threw his keys at their feet and ran.

"Bloody women," he could be heard muttering under his breath, as he disappeared from sight.

Aurelia stifled a laugh. "I think the men in Forte Cadence have a little bit to get used to, don't you think."

"Not all of them," said Jeremiah, with an exaggerated look of offense on his face.

Aurelia laughed gently.

"It's true," Micah said to Aurelia. "My brother is the most honorable man you'll ever meet. I want you to know that."

"Of course." Aurelia nodded. It took a good man for his sister to speak up for him like this. It seemed her daughter had chosen well.

Rose stooped to pick up the keys. "Are you ready for this?" she asked them.

They all nodded.

"My people," said Rose, projecting her voice so it echoed off the stone walls of the dungeon. "King Virtus is dead."

"Good riddance!" one voice called.

"May he rot in hell!" called another.

Aurelia was surprised. She'd never heard the prisoners so vocal before.

"My name is Rose and I am your Queen," she continued. "I'm also your friend. I believe that respect goes both ways and I'm sorry for the way you've been treated. Some of you may be guilty of crimes worthy of punishment, but I believe you've already been punished. Others here are innocent. I have therefore decided to release you all. Every one of you will be free in just a moment. However, before I turn the key in your locks, I need you to do something for me."

"Anything!"

"Thank you, my Queen!"

"Please, let us go free!"

The voices of the prisoners were desperate yet filled with hope. This was a moment that surely they'd never forget.

Rose cleared her throat and Aurelia wondered what her one request would be. "I'd like you to leave in peace. Just as I'd like you to live the rest of your days in peace. If you have families to return to, then please go home to them. If you have nowhere to go, then I'll find you work in the palace. Work where you'll be treated with respect, fed, paid and given a warm bed to sleep in. Never again will you go hungry. Never again will you be kept hidden from the light. Do you understand?"

"Yes, my Queen!"

"Thank you, Your Grace!"

"God save the Queen!"

Rose looked at Jeremiah, as if needing his strength to continue. He smiled and nodded at her.

"Forte Cadence has been built with lies," Rose said. "Murder and evil have ruled this kingdom, but it will thrive on freedom, trust and respect. I apologize to each and every one of you for the crimes that were committed against you. If you do right by me, from this point on, then I will always do right by you."

Aurelia felt ashamed for having doubted her daughter. She was ready for this job. Far more ready than Aurelia had realized. She wasn't just going to be a good Queen. She was going to be a great one.

Rose went to each cell and turned the key in the lock.

"I'm sorry," she said, opening the door and bowing her head. "Go in peace."

Some prisoners scurried past before she changed her mind. Others took their time saying thank you and bowing before the woman who had their total love and respect.

They reached the cell of a woman with a birthmark on her face. Aurelia recognized her as the server from the royal dining hall.

"There she is," Micah said to Jeremiah.

He nodded.

Rose handed the key to Jeremiah and he put it in the lock.

"I'm sorry," he said to the prisoner. "Please, go home and find Samson."

"Don't be sorry," the prisoner said, clutching at Jeremiah's hand. "I'm sorry."

Micah stepped forward and the prisoner let go of Jeremiah to reach for her.

"Thank you for offering to take my place," she said.

"I hope your son is well," said Micah. "You're a good mother."

"May God forgive me," the woman said.

Aurelia wasn't sure what had taken place between them, but something powerful had obviously occurred. It made her wonder if instead of waiting for the bad to turn to good, she should've done more. Except Gabrielle had been clear with her. She'd needed to wait.

It was a surprise to see that the prisoner in the next cell was the other server from the royal dining hall. The male one. What on earth had happened while she'd been busy giving birth? Rose had a lot to fill her in on.

She watched her daughter turn the key in the lock and the prisoner stepped forward.

"I'm sorry it took so long," said Rose. "Please forgive me."

He knelt at her feet and looked up at her.

"My Queen," he said. "I was right to place my trust in you."

"You'll be rewarded for your part in our victory," she said, putting out her hand and urging him to his feet.

"Thank you, my Queen."

He took the hand of the Whisperer with the birthmark who was still standing in front of her cell.

"I've worked beside you for a year now," he said to her. "And I don't know your name."

"Jane," she said, shaking his hand.

"Dorian." He smiled at her, then looked toward Jeremiah and Micah, who approached and told them their names and shook their hands.

"Would you walk with them?" Rose asked. "I'd like to unlock this last cell with my mother alone, if you don't mind."

"Of course," said Jeremiah immediately.

Aurelia liked the way he was so quickly prepared to bend to Rose's wishes, trusting that she had her reasons for asking, without even knowing what they were.

Together, the four former Whisperers walked out of the dungeon. Four people who'd been stripped of their names but not of their will to survive. With their names and their freedom firmly back in place, they looked as if they'd grown two feet taller. Dignity was so important in life.

Aurelia tried to stop the feeling of shame washing over her. Had she been responsible for this? Sitting at the dining table each night, being served by two people who didn't even know each other's names. But she hadn't had a choice. To speak up would have only made things worse—for her and them. Gabrielle had been right. They'd needed to wait. Wait for her incredible daughter to grow old enough to turn the bad to good.

With the last of the prisoners released, there remained only one more cell. The cell at the end of the row. The cell without bars. The one that held the last prisoner to set free. This was the cell that held an angel who was perhaps the most important prisoner of all, for she'd been the one who'd saved them. If it weren't for her visions, none of this would have happened. The King would still be alive with his army of soldiers, and they'd all be trapped in his evil game, suffering and starving in their homes and watching their loved ones perish.

Rose handed the key to Aurelia. "This one's for you," she said.

Aurelia put the key in the lock and turned it, keen to see her friend, to tell her that they'd done it. All that waiting hadn't been for nothing. Gabrielle's suffering was over. It was time for her to be set free.

Only Gabrielle wasn't lying on her mattress like she normally was. Aurelia's heart sank. Was she too late? Had Gabrielle waited all this time, yet was unable to wait long enough?

"Gabrielle," Aurelia gasped, tears blinding her, as she scanned the darkness of the cell.

It couldn't be true. Her friend just couldn't be dead.

"Aurelia," came a voice from the darkness, as Gabrielle stepped toward Aurelia with arms outstretched. The cloud in her eyes had cleared, like a storm had passed, and she looked directly at Aurelia in a way she hadn't done since she'd come to the palace.

"The good is here," she said to Aurelia. "I told you the good would replace the bad."

"The good is here," repeated Aurelia, taking her friend in her arms and holding her close. She was so frail, surely she couldn't have lasted much longer. "I couldn't see you at first. I was afraid that…"

"I made it," said Gabrielle. "I made it."

"You made everything," said Aurelia, releasing her from her embrace, and wiping her eyes. "You made everything so much better."

Gabrielle shook her head. "Your daughter made it. And her friends here. And all the Whisperers together. And you. And me. We all made it. Together."

"Together," said Rose from the doorway. "Thank you, Gabrielle."

"You'll be the greatest ruler any land has ever seen," said Gabrielle, reaching out for Rose. "For you will rule with kindness and peace in your heart. The universe has heard us."

Rose took Gabrielle's hands in her own. "Will you sit by my side as an advisor?"

Aurelia smiled as she waited for Gabrielle's answer. Her husband had locked Gabrielle in a dungeon, afraid of her power. Her daughter wanted Gabrielle by her side, so she could make use of her gift.

"Of course, Your Grace," said Gabrielle. "But first could I trouble you for a hot meal and an even hotter bath?"

"Which would you like first?" Rose asked, laughing.

"Why not both at once?" Gabrielle winked. "I've waited a long time for today."

"I think we can arrange that," said Aurelia. "Let's get you out of here."

Aurelia wrapped one arm around Gabrielle and the other around her daughter, the other angel in her life.

And she knew for sure that not only was this the happiest day of her life, it was likely to be the happiest day of many, many other people's lives too.

MICAH

THE NOW

*M*icah stretched out on the soft grass and looked up at the sky. She'd forgotten how blue it was. And the air was so fresh.

She was with several other Whisperers, including Jeremiah, having watched Dorian and Jane walk out of the palace gates and begin their descent down Mount Allegro to the Valley of the Blessed, both keen to return to their families. Micah hoped that Jane's son was still alive. If he'd been unwell, his chance of survival was slim without his mother to fend for him. Samson. His name was Samson. Jane had been keen for them to know that and Micah was determined to think of him like this. Names had never been so important before.

The Whisperers they sat with now were those who were unsure about what to do next. Or rather where to go next. Although some Whisperers had marched directly out of the palace gates, just like Jane and Dorian, others had nowhere to go, so had remained behind to see if they could be of assistance to the Prin— the Queen. She'd told them that they would always have a home and a place inside the palace and as much as that'd once sounded like a terrible idea, right now it sounded quite appealing.

Micah thought about the Before and the After and realized that now she'd finally arrived at the Evernow—the life she'd live when she no longer pined for the Before or the After. A life when she was happy to live in the Now.

"How many of us do you think are left?" asked Jeremiah.

"Not sure," said Micah, turning to look at him. "Half maybe? However, more and more are leaving all the time."

"You do know that I'm staying, don't you?" His hand flew to his head and Micah remembered how he used to run his fingers through his hair when he was nervous.

"I know," she said. "There's nothing for us left in the valley now."

She realized this wasn't entirely true. Tallis was in the valley. And the longer she'd been away from him, the more she was starting to miss him.

"So, you'll stay with me?" Jeremiah's eyes were filled with a hope she was unwilling to dash.

"Of course," she said, not certain that was a promise she could keep. Maybe she could convince Tallis to come to her instead. Her feelings for him were so confusing. She'd felt them develop over the years, but was unsure how he felt about her. Did he still see her as his friend's little sister? Maybe he'd found himself a wife by now and all these confusing feelings were for nothing. This wasn't a thought she relished.

Queen Rose approached with her mother, both wearing broad smiles.

"I'd like to talk to you all," Queen Rose said, raising her voice. "Please gather and sit down so I can see you all."

The crowd came closer and tilted their heads to their new Queen.

"I want you to know that you're free to leave whenever you wish. You're no longer prisoners here, just as those trapped in the dungeon have also been freed. However, you're also free to stay. I need an army to protect Forte Cadence and ensure a peaceful life. I need you."

A murmur went through the crowd as people tried to imagine what that life might involve.

"Things will be different. You'll be well fed. You'll clothe yourself in whatever you desire and be permitted to grow your hair. You'll be called by your name and we'll build a new section of the palace to house you in privacy. You'll be able to visit your families. You'll be allowed to speak and your words will be heard. In other words, you won't be my slaves, you'll be my paid workers."

Micah noticed people were nodding and smiling.

"I've just been speaking with my advisor. A woman named Gabrielle. In time, I'd like all of you to meet her. She's strong. And she's kind. She was the one who dreamed of an army of Whisperers, although it was my father who built the rules around how you should live. Gabrielle has advised me that we've only just begun to tap into your power, for it's when you're happy and whispering with your hearts, as well as your words, that the true power is harnessed. We witnessed that in the arena today."

Micah smiled. The Queen was right. The power in the arena as they'd whispered for the King's death had been almost visible, it was so thick in the air. A happy and fulfilled army of Whisperers would truly be unbeatable.

"Who stands with me?" the Queen asked.

Jeremiah was the first to stand, raising his hand high in the air. "Long live the Queen," he called out.

He was quickly followed by several more Whisperers, who also stood and raised their hands, signaling their praise for their Queen.

It took only a few minutes more for the entire crowd gathered on the lawn to be standing, united, each and every one of them prepared to serve their Queen for the most important reason of all. Because it was their will.

Except for one person, who remained seated, unable to stand.

Micah.

She looked up at Jeremiah to see him staring down at her in confusion. He reached out his hand.

"Micah?"

A hush rippled across the crowd as they looked at her, waiting for her to join them.

"I can't join you," said Micah, standing to address them. "Not through lack of will, for I have plenty of that. But because I'm not like the rest of you. I'm different."

She drew in a deep breath as she tried to explain.

"I cheated on my Whisperers' test because I wanted to join my brother here. I knew what I had to say and I said it. I pretended to see things that I couldn't. I pretended not to see things that I could. Do you even know what it is that makes all of you special? The thing that you have in common that I don't possess? The reason I'm not one of you?"

People looked at each other, shrugging their shoulders and raising their eyebrows.

"You're color blind," said Micah. "A rare form of color blindness, where you see every color of the rainbow, apart from one. When we see the color orange, you see gray. The fruit that was used to lure you here was the King having a cruel joke. Those balls of fruit that you see as gray, the rest of us see as something bright and vibrant. Those paintings we looked at were simple color blindness tests. The last painting—the one of the bowl of oranges—was painted in color, with the oranges painted in gray. When you were asked what the difference was to the bowl on the table beside you, not one of you could say what it was. They looked the same to you."

She noticed the confused look on the people's faces and knew she was right. They'd had no idea what was so different about them.

"Then the cruelest joke of all," she continued. "These robes we wear. They're not gray, like you think they are. When you look across this crowd, you see a sea of drab misery, but I see the color of the burning sun."

People were looking down at their robes with furrowed brows, wondering if what she said could be true. She had no way to convince them.

"It's true," said the Queen Mother stepping forward. "What your eyes lack in their ability to see all the colors that we do, your voices have gained in their ability to reach distances as far as the stars. For some unknown reason, this is what gives you your power. The universe hears us all, but for some reason, it hears your voices the clearest of all."

"So, to answer your question, my Queen," said Micah to Rose. "I do stand with you. Not as a Whisperer, as I'm not gifted enough for that privilege, but as your servant. You saved my life and that of my brother and every person who stands here before you right now. I'm deeply grateful."

"You're not my servant, Micah," said the Queen, reaching out and placing a hand on her cheek. "You're my friend, and if your brother will have me, I'd like you to be Princess Micah, my sister."

"Sister?" Micah didn't understand, until she looked at Jeremiah and saw a soft blush spread across his cheeks. Her heart buoyed with happiness for him.

"Jeremiah," Queen Rose said, moving from Micah to go to her brother's side.

"Rose," he said, his eyes lighting in a way Micah had never seen before.

Rose took his hands and lowered her voice, so that only those closest to them could hear. "I'm afraid that I broke my promise to you. I promised to get you and Micah out and I asked to come with you. But it appears that instead of taking you to your freedom outside the palace, I'm asking you to find it here with me. Jeremiah, will you please stand by my side, not just as the Conductor of my willing army of voices, but as the Conductor of my heart?"

"Are you asking me to marry you?" The blush on Jeremiah's cheeks deepened to purple now.

"Yes, my Prince."

"Long live the Prince!" called someone from the front of the crowd. Laughter erupted, then cheering as people realized what'd happened and they whooped and whistled.

Micah doubted Jeremiah even heard them. He was too busy taking Queen Rose in his arms and placing the most tender kiss upon her lips.

Princess Micah. She turned the words over in her mind. How ironic that the one girl who never wanted to be a Princess was going to be exactly that. Although, her mother had told her she was better than a Princess. She supposed she was just going to have to reinvent the definition of Princess. Because if she was going to do this, she was going to do it her way.

ROSE

THE NOW

$\mathcal{R}$ose stood over her father's body, her mother on one side and her future husband on the other.

The King had been laid out on his bed and dressed in a white robe to symbolize purity in death. Was he pure in death? Perhaps everyone was. It wasn't very easy to sin when you were no longer alive. Did the sins of your lifetime cling to your body or did they fly free with your soul?

Rose reached out and touched her father's cold cheek. She didn't recall ever laying a finger on him when he was alive, not even as a young child. He always kept his distance from her. What was the point in getting attached to something you knew you weren't going to keep? She knew now that he'd never intended to let her live. He'd been planning her death since her birth, only somehow, she'd managed to kill him instead.

Had she killed him? Or had *they* killed him, for it was certainly a murder committed by many hands.

It was unclear if his death had been caused by his heart or his fall, but Rose didn't see that it mattered. He was dead. How he died didn't change that fact.

Her mother let out a sob and dabbed at her eyes with her fingertips.

"Are you sad, Mother?" asked Rose, a little surprised. Was there a small part of her that'd loved him just a little?

"No, my darling. I've never been happier." She smiled at Rose through her tears. "I never dreamed this day was possible."

"Do you think I'm like him at all?" Rose asked.

Her mother shook her head. "You know that you look like me. An exact copy of how I looked at your age."

In truth, her mother didn't look too many years older than she did. Rose suspected a Whispering had taken care of that at some stage.

"I didn't mean looks," said Rose, concerned about where her genetics had come from.

"Can I answer this one?" asked Jeremiah, leaning in closer to her.

"Of course," said Rose.

"Your father was evil. You have only goodness in your heart. You've had a more positive impact on Forte Cadence in the one day you've been Queen than this man did in his whole lifetime."

"It's true," said her mother. "I have so much hope for our future and the future of all the people in our kingdom. Your father's genes are clearly as weak as he was."

Rose looked back at her father with his thin frame and drawn face. How did one man manage to wreak so much havoc?

"I don't know if I'm up for the job," whispered Rose.

"Hush," her mother said. "Don't send those words to the universe. You'll make a fine Queen, the best ruler Forte Cadence has ever seen. Gabrielle said it herself. And you won't be alone. Your father thought he could rule the kingdom with his hand alone. You aren't that foolish."

"You're right," said Rose. "I didn't bring about this change on my own. It was the work of many. When we work together as a team we can achieve so much more than when we choose to work alone. I'd like to set up a panel of advisors to help me. With both of you, of course. And Gabrielle and Micah. Also, Dorian if I can convince him to return. I owe him so much. And my sisters and baby brother of course, as soon as they're old enough. Aunt Lily and Aunt Georgia too. I need a team to help me lead the way."

Jeremiah and her mother nodded their agreement.

"My father wanted Forte Cadence to be the most powerful kingdom in all the world. But not me. I just want it to be the most peaceful. My panel of advisors will be like a symphony, each playing a beautiful tune of their own, yet when we come together, the result will be stronger and impossibly more beautiful than we could ever play alone."

"The bad has turned to good," said her mother. "Gabrielle promised me it would. And it has. It really has. And now I have someone I want you to meet."

Rose's mother smiled and left the room. Rose suspected she knew exactly who her mother was talking about.

"Let's wait over here," said Jeremiah, leading her away from the bed to the other side of the spacious room.

"That's better," said Rose, glad to not be able to see her father's body anymore in this cavernous room.

"Rose," said Jeremiah, taking her hands in his. "I feel dreadful that I wasn't the one who asked you to marry me. I fear that you'll spend your whole life wondering if I would have."

"Hush," she said, pressing her fingers to his lips.

"Let me finish." He kissed her fingertips and moved them away. "I want you to know that the day I told you my name, I was binding myself to you. You're the only woman I've ever loved and the only woman I ever will love. Not because you were a Princess, but because you were Rose."

"I know," she said, drinking in his words, despite not needing to hear them. She knew exactly how he felt. She'd known it for the longest time. He'd spoken to her with his eyes long before he'd trusted her with his words. "And do you know what I used to call you before I knew your name?"

He shook his head.

"My Prince. You were always my Prince. And now you will be, for real. You're my dream come true." She brought her lips to his and kissed him.

"I love you," he said. "And I can't wait for you to be my wife."

"Shh." She kissed him harder, with more passion, and his words fell silent as she felt him lose himself in her. As much as she hated to steal his words from him, she didn't think she would ever get sick of doing this.

They broke away at the sound of a baby crying and Rose turned her head to see her mother holding her newborn brother in her arms.

It was the first time Rose had seen him and she rushed over, keen to look into his face and see the child who'd brought about such a revolution.

"May I hold him?" she asked her mother.

"Of course." Her mother placed him gently in her arms and he stopped crying, looking up at her in such a way it made her wonder how much this baby could see.

"Look at the way he's watching me." She laughed, drawing a line with her fingertip down his nose and resting it on his lips.

"He knows his Queen," said Jeremiah, coming over to meet him.

"I'm his sister first, and Queen second," she said. "Oh, Mother, he's beautiful."

"He really is," said Jeremiah. "I almost had a baby brother once."

Rose looked up at him, surprised. He hadn't told her much about his childhood before. He hadn't really had the chance. She'd never considered the possibility of him having a sibling apart from Micah.

"What happened?" asked her mother, saving her the question.

"My mother was pregnant when I... left for here. Micah tells me that she died before the baby was born."

"And you knew it was a boy?" asked Rose, wondering how this was possible.

Jeremiah shook his head. "Just a hunch."

"And your father?" her mother asked. "Is he still alive?"

Jeremiah shook his head once more. "Just me and Micah now."

"And me," said Rose.

"And me," her mother added. "And Eliza and Tash and Cara."

"And Virtus!" said Rose, jiggling her brother in her arms.

"Enver," said her mother, firmly. "His name is Enver."

"Since when?" asked Rose, surprised.

"Since right now. Let's not make this poor child share his father's name."

"Enver is a much nicer name," said Rose, laughing. "It's perfect. It reminds me of the words *ever* and *never*. And never, ever again will our kingdom go back to how it was. Enver's arrival has marked a new beginning."

"I have just one question," said Jeremiah, his face stern.

"What's that?" asked Rose, curious.

Jeremiah reached out and ran his fingertips through Enver's dark hair. "Does he have orange hair?"

Rose laughed. "No, Jeremiah. It's as black as night."

"Don't laugh," he said, breaking out in a smile of his own. "I only just found out that my sister is a redhead. I never knew!"

"Well from this day forward, I promise to point out to you every orange thing I ever see."

"Maybe we can add that to our wedding vows," said Jeremiah.

"Hand me Enver," her mother said, reaching out her arms. "It seems you two have a lot to talk about. I'm going to see if there's any word about your sisters."

Rose handed over her baby brother, giving him a quick kiss on his forehead before her mother left. They were lucky to have been blessed with such a healthy baby to love. How different his life could have turned out. However it turned out now, she'd make sure he was happy. She owed him that much and more.

"My family is your family now," said Rose, slipping her arms around Jeremiah. "And your family is mine. I'd like to go with you to the Valley of the Blessed and see where you grew up. Perhaps we can find where your parents were buried?"

He pulled her closer to him, enclosing her in his arms.

"I'd really like that."

"Me too."

It was strange, building a life with someone in the palace when she'd only ever imagined running far away. But just like the girl in the tower had restored the Prince's sight with her tears, it seemed her tears had restored her Prince's voice. And with it came more love and more happiness than she'd ever dared possible. It was her duty to each and every person who lived in Forte Cadence to make sure that this happiness spread to their hearts too. It didn't feel right to keep it all to herself. Besides, happiness was in infinite supply. All you had to do was release it.

JEREMIAH

THE NOW

*J*eremiah walked beside Rose on their way to the Valley of the Blessed. She refused to be taken by carriage, insisting that after being locked inside the palace for so long, her legs were desperate to walk.

The steep slope from the palace down to the valley wasn't easy to navigate and several times Rose stopped, claiming to be admiring the view, and Jeremiah pretended to believe her. She wasn't used to walking such distances. And there were no slopes, or rocky paths inside the palace.

His heart burst with love for Rose. To think he wasted all those years that she'd been talking to him without talking back. Although they weren't a complete waste, for with every word she'd spoken, she'd won a small piece of his heart. Eventually, she'd won enough of it that there was barely room left in it for anyone else.

He glanced at Micah and realized that wasn't true. He loved his sister, too.

They were accompanied on their journey by a large group of Whisperers and palace workers, who pushed carts loaded with fruit, vegetables and freshly-baked loaves of bread. Other carts were loaded with more luxury items like sweets, soaps, and brightly colored fabrics. They were all covered over with canvas, ready to be opened and handed out when they got to the town square.

Rose had overheard Jeremiah and Micah talking about Giving Day, with Micah explaining that in the five years since Jeremiah had left the Valley of the Blessed, the celebrations had dwindled even more. Rose decided it was time the people had a Giving Day they'd always remember. Life *was* a miracle worth celebrating. She didn't want them to lose hope like that.

She'd set about gathering gifts, stripping the palace pantry and storage rooms almost bare. It didn't feel right for them to have so much when the people had so little.

As Giving Day approached, the journey was planned and volunteers were called for, to help Rose with the carts. She tried to insist on pushing a cart herself, but Jeremiah wouldn't hear of it. She needed her strength to win over the people in the valley. Her gifts weren't a one-off. Their lives were about to change for the better. Permanently. Rose would need to work hard. Winning respect is so much more difficult than losing it.

He squeezed Rose's hand as they continued down Mount Allegro.

"I hope the people like my gifts," she said.

"They'll love them. Especially the surprise announcement."

She smiled. "There's no reason a female shouldn't be able to own property. Especially now that we have a female monarch. That law should've been changed years ago."

"That's where you're wrong," he said.

Rose let go of Jeremiah's hand and frowned.

"It should never have been a law in the first place." He grinned.

Rose clutched her chest and let out a laugh. "You had me worried for a moment there."

Eliza and Tash came skipping past them, flapping their arms, pretending they were butterflies. They reminded Jeremiah of Micah when she'd been that age, with more energy than such a small body knew what to do with. The girls had insisted on coming with them, keen to see more of the world than what was contained within the Palace walls.

Rose's mother and baby Enver had stayed behind at the palace with Gabrielle, who didn't have the strength yet for such a journey, despite growing stronger every day. Cara was with them too, having returned home with Eliza and Tash, in the arms of their doting Aunt Lily, who'd barely let go of them since setting foot in the palace. They'd developed a wonderful bond that Jeremiah had no doubt would continue well into the future. Lily had been invited to join the Symphony that Rose was putting together to help govern Forte Cadence. That was another word Rose had introduced. *Govern.* She insisted it sounded so much better than *rule.* She had no desire to rule over anybody, only to ensure that peace and harmony were maintained within the kingdom.

Rose's Aunt Georgia had arrived too, at the news of her twin brother's death. Rose had invited her to join her Symphony, asking her if she ever wished she were born first and had the chance to be Queen. Georgia had tipped back her head and laughed, saying that the last thing in the world she ever wanted was to be Queen. She was more than happy to serve as one of Rose's advisors.

Jeremiah glanced across at Micah again. She was being unusually quiet. Where had all the energy she'd had as a child gone? Had the palace sucked it out of her or had she just grown up? She'd turned into a beautiful young woman and his heart ached whenever he looked at her, to think of all she'd lost. Everything that King Virtus had stolen from her. Was it possible for her to get it back? Not all of it, that much was certain. There was no bringing back their parents or their baby sibling. But maybe some of her joy would return one day.

Returning to the valley wouldn't be easy for any of them, especially Micah. It was a place of memories of death and desperation. It was bad enough for him to return there knowing there'd be faces that were familiar and others that would've changed almost as much as he knew his own must have.

It'd been a shock to see himself in the mirror after so long. His face was thin and drawn and although his hair was growing back in tight curls, long gone was the mop he used to have to untangle before he left his house. His eyes were different too, as if the sorrow in his heart was leaching out of them. This was a common trait amongst the Whisperers. Just another way they all looked the same. Although, as their hair had begun to grow and their robes were replaced with ordinary clothes, their individuality was being restored. He'd made a point of learning all their names, replacing them in his mind with the names he'd previously given them. He kept those names to himself, of course, not sure what some of them would think of them. *Dancing Feet* may not be unhappy with hers, but *Long Nose* probably wouldn't be overly impressed.

They passed various people on their way to the valley, many of whom joined them on their walk, their numbers growing with each step they took. The people were curious, not only about what was loaded in the carts, but about their new Queen.

They approached a heartbreakingly familiar copse of trees. The very ones that Jeremiah had run to after his test for the Whisperers. The day he failed to receive an orange and instead received what was very nearly a death sentence.

There was a familiar figure standing under the largest of the trees, his arms dangling by his side, his tall, lanky frame reminding Jeremiah of his childhood. In the time that Micah called *the Before*.

Jeremiah squeezed Rose's hand, then let it go. "There's someone I need to say hello to."

"Who is it?" She followed his gaze to the trees.

"My friend," he said, quickening his pace, until he found himself running toward the figure, his arms open and a tear fighting its way from his eyes. He hadn't thought he had the capacity to cry anymore.

"Tallis!" he cried, throwing his arms around his friend, who embraced him in return.

"You're alive!" said Tallis, slapping him on the back. "You're alive!"

"Of course I'm alive," said Jeremiah. "You can't get rid of me so easily."

"I didn't dare believe you'd make it out."

Jeremiah let go of his friend so he could study his face. He'd grown from an adolescent to a man in the years that'd gone by, yet still he was the same. The same eyes, albeit missing some of their sparkle. The same face, underneath the hint of a beard. The same smile, that never failed to draw a smile from Jeremiah's own lips.

"How's your family?" asked Jeremiah.

"Still surviving." A sadness crossed Tallis's eyes.

"Things are going to get better from now," said Jeremiah.

Tallis nodded, cautiously. "That's what people are saying, but I don't dare believe it. Jeremiah…"

"Yes? What is it?" Jeremiah put a hand on his friend's shoulder. Tallis was struggling to find his words.

"Your family…" Tallis looked to the ground and kicked at a stone.

"I know," said Jeremiah, sadly. "My parents didn't make it. Nor did the baby."

"It's even worse than that, I'm afraid," said Tallis. "Micah is missing. Nobody's seen her for many months now. I used to see her at the markets, but she hasn't been there. Nor did she go to the orchards to pick berries this summer, like she usually does. I've been searching everywhere for her. At first, I thought maybe she'd fallen into the river where she'd go to wash. Then I came here and… I found this hanging in a tree."

He reached under his shirt and pulled out a leather cord.

"My lucky walnut!" Jeremiah broke into a smile and reached out a hand as Tallis removed it from his neck and handed it to him. Never did he think he'd see that walnut shell again. It seemed it'd brought Jeremiah luck after all. And Micah too.

"You don't understand." Tallis shook his head. "It's not good news. Micah never took that off. Never. Not since the day you left. She wouldn't leave it in a tree, unless … unless she walked into the forest with no intention of coming back."

Jeremiah looped the cord around his neck and put a hand on his friend's shoulder. "She's okay, Tallis. She didn't go to the forest with no intention of coming back. She went to the palace. Look. There she is. Micah!"

He saw his sister watching him from the group of people who'd stopped to wait for Jeremiah before they walked on. She looked unsure about approaching them, but at the sound of her name came skipping over. It seemed she hadn't grown out of her bursts of energy. The old Micah was slowly returning.

"Hi dragon," she said, grinning at Tallis.

"Micah! I thought you were dead."

"I left you the walnut so you'd know that I wasn't."

"Oh."

A moment of awkwardness hung in the air and Jeremiah stepped back, feeling that these two needed some space.

Tallis went to hug Micah and hesitated. Then clearly not being able to contain himself, he pulled her close and put his arms around her. Jeremiah smiled to see the tenderness of this embrace, compared to the backslapping hug he himself had just received. Was there more to their relationship than Micah had told him about? Perhaps there were feelings there that Micah hadn't realized. The deep flush on Tallis's face was evidence that he was more than aware of his feelings.

"Your hair," said Tallis, loosening the embrace and reaching out a hand.

"My hair will grow," said Micah, running a hand over the short spikes on her head.

"You still look beautiful," said Tallis, biting his lower lip.

Micah flushed a shade to match Tallis's face and shuffled her feet.

Right, so she was just as aware of what was happening between them as Tallis was.

Jeremiah was pleased. Who wouldn't want their best friend and their sister to fall in love. Especially when they'd all been surrounded by misery for so long.

"I want you to meet someone," said Jeremiah, smiling across at Rose and reaching out his hand to beckon her.

She returned his smile and walked over to them.

"Tallis, this is Rose," said Jeremiah. "We're to be married."

"I'm very pleased to meet you," said Tallis, putting out his hand for her to shake, making it clear he was completely unaware of who she was.

Rose took his hand. "Pleased to meet you, Tallis."

"Were you kept prisoner there too?" asked Tallis, tipping his head toward the palace. "If you don't mind me asking, why were you allowed to keep your hair?"

Rose smiled. "I was trapped there in a different way to Micah."

Tallis nodded, although clearly didn't understand. "Is the new Queen truly as good as everyone's saying? She can't be worse than her awful father, I suppose. Have any of you met her?"

"We have," said Jeremiah, laughing. "In fact, as of about a minute ago, you have too."

Tallis frowned, then gasped as the realization washed over him.

"Your Majesty?" he said, looking at Rose, and stooping to a bow. "Please forgive me for how I just spoke."

"Please, stand up tall and be proud of yourself, Tallis. My father *was* awful. You spoke the truth. I hope to be the sort of Queen who people talk about in the same way when I'm there as when I am not."

"Yes, my Queen." Tallis bowed his head as he spoke, then trailed his gaze to Jeremiah, his eyes widening as yet another realization washed over him. "Did you say that you're to be married?"

"That's right," said Jeremiah, taking Rose's hand in his.

Tallis pursed his lips as if to suppress a laugh and nodded.

"Tallis," said Rose, touching him gently on the arm. "I'm forming a Symphony to help me govern Forte Cadence and I'd like to have people with all different experiences sitting on it. Would you consider joining us? I need a representative from the Valley of the Blessed, to provide a voice for the people."

"But... you don't even know me, Your Majesty."

"Jeremiah and Micah clearly think highly of you. That's all I need to know. No need to answer me now. Why don't you accompany us today and you can give me your answer later?"

Tallis nodded. "I'm honored to be asked. And I don't need time to decide. Just as you trust the opinion of our friends here, so do I. I'll join your Sym... what was the word again? Forgive me."

"Symphony," said Micah. "We all use our individual voices and opinions to form a harmonious approach."

"Shall we continue on our journey?" asked Rose. "Our growing tribe is getting restless."

They rejoined the people. Tallis caught up to Jeremiah briefly to poke him in the ribs and hiss in his ear. "You're marrying the Queen!"

Jeremiah laughed. "I'm marrying Rose," he corrected.

Tallis clearly couldn't see the difference. But Jeremiah could, and that was all that mattered. He was marrying Rose the person, not Rose the Queen. A woman who was brave, fair and smart. A woman who made his heart race and had surprised him with her ideas, determination, and vision.

They set off once again, down the hill, toward the Valley of the Blessed. Only now it really was blessed, thought Jeremiah.

He leaned toward Rose as they walked, his lips brushing softly on her ear.

"I love you, Your Majesty," he said.

She smiled. "Please don't ever stop saying that. Although you can drop the Your Majesty bit. I keep thinking people are talking to my father."

"Well, I can promise you that I never said that to him."

"Jeremiah!" She laughed.

He sighed, letting out a deep breath. "And don't you ever stop saying that."

"What?" Her brow crinkled.

"My name."

She looped her arm through his and together they led the crowd of people toward their Evernow, no longer wishing for their past or their future, but happy to be exactly where they all found themselves right at this moment.

AFTER THE EVERNOW

"*The Whisperers are whispering. The Whisperers are whispering. The Whisperers are whispering.*"

Four hundred voices rose and swirled in the air, floating directly into the ears of the people gathered on the palace lawn outside the arena.

The doors had been thrown open, so the Whisperers' voices would carry, and the residents of the Valley of the Blessed had been invited to sit outside and listen, while they devoured baskets of food that lined the steps of the arena.

This was the first Whispering since King Virtus's death and the new Queen had made it clear that from now on these ceremonies were for all to enjoy. The balcony in the arena had been rebuilt and extended so that the people who didn't wish to sit on the lawn could come inside.

They waited, wondering what the Queen's first wish would be for.

"*The Whisperers are whispering. The Whisperers are whispering. The Whisperers are whispering.*"

Those who lined the balcony saw Jeremiah sweep his hand across the arena, satisfied his army's voices were warm. He smiled at them, his eyes alight with pride. They returned his smile with love in their eyes.

The first row of Whisperers fell into silence and knelt on their mats with their heads bowed. They wore clothing of all colors and their hair was growing in shades of brown, blonde and red.

Once in place, the second row followed, then the third. This continued until the final row of Whisperers were on their knees. An army of four hundred people, men and women alike, all waiting to hear the Queen's deepest wish.

Jeremiah raised his hand above his head, his eyes scanning his army, looking to make sure they were ready. The Whisperers kept their heads down, maintaining a respectful silence.

Satisfied once more, Jeremiah brought his hand down slowly, holding it at his side. He looked to the balcony at the rear of the arena where the Queen was standing with her people. He nodded at her. The Whisperers were ready.

The Queen blew him a kiss, then swept her hand across the arena to show her appreciation.

"The trees are bursting with fruit," Jeremiah whispered.

The first row of Whisperers lifted their heads, eyes and ears glued to their leader.

"The trees are bursting with fruit," Jeremiah repeated.

No noise could be heard as the first row of Whisperers rose to stand.

"The trees are bursting with fruit," they said. Not whispered. *Said.*

The second row lifted their heads and stood.

"The trees are bursting with fruit," the first two rows said together.

With each row that joined, the chant became louder, the arena filling with voices, calling out in unison, over and over, as they brought the Queen's wish to life.

Those people standing outside were certain they could see the trees around them bend forward in the gentle breeze as tiny buds formed on their branches. At last, a wish for the people. A wish that would fill their bellies and restore their health.

The Whisperers continued to send their words out to the sky and as they wished, their numbers grew, as the Whisperers who'd left for freedom, returned to join them and add their voices to the call.

The people watching were infected by the words, and unable to resist, they added their voices to the chorus.

Seeing this, Queen Rose, smiled and joined in.

"The trees are bursting with fruit!"

The Whisperers smiled as they sent their wish into the sky. Their purpose was to whisper. Their power was in their voices. They were individuals, with hopes and dreams and names, but together they could be more. They were part of a glorious army, granting wishes for their Queen. A Queen they trusted with their future.

There was one Whisperer who trusted her more than any other. He was the one who stood at the front, refusing to be called the Conductor.

His name was Jeremiah.

THE END

Ready to discover the next kingdom?

Check out Book 2, The Alchemists of Evernow!

http://mybook.to/hcalchemists

THE ALCHEMISTS OF EVERNOW

BOOK 2 THE KINGDOMS OF EVERNOW

Will she wake up in time to smell the evil,

or will the Alchemist conquer them all?

Trapped in the spell of an elixir made by an evil Alchemist, Jasmine is sleepwalking through life unaware that her mind isn't her own. Life around her is crumbling—men are dying, and women are falling victim to the Alchemist's cruel scent of magic, and nobody can see it.

When the Alchemist takes Jasmine's brother captive, she's woken from her dream and sees life for what it's become. But is she too late to save her brother and outsmart the Alchemist and his plans to control them all?

She seeks help from Ari, a stranger who sweeps into her life and sets all her true senses alight. Despite having a missing sister and secrets of his own, Ari decides to help Jasmine, believing that his problems are connected to hers. As they unravel the clues, they become convinced that the key to Jasmine's brother's disappearance is the same one that will unlock the mystery of where to find Ari's sister.

As love blooms in the Garden of Evernow, Jasmine and Ari fight against time to release the magic of the plants and create an elixir even more powerful than the Alchemist himself.

With twists and turns you won't see coming, the second book in the spellbinding *The Kingdoms of Evernow* series is a must-read by award-winning author, Heidi Catherine.

Grab your copy now!

http://mybook.to/hcalchemists

ALSO BY HEIDI CATHERINE

The Kingdoms of Evernow
Five kingdoms. Five senses.
One secret that will change them all.
The Kingdoms of Evernow (Prequel)
The Whisperers of Evernow
The Alchemists of Evernow
The Empress of Evernow
The Guardians of Evernow
The Angels of Evernow

The Soulweaver series
Two girls. Two lives. One soul.
The Soulweaver
The Truthseeker
The Shadowmaker

The Sovereign Code
Humans saved bees from extinction...
and created the deadliest threat we've seen yet
Harvest Day
Hive Mind
Queen Hunt
Venom Rising
Sting Wars

Elemental Games

Elemental powers. Deadly games. No escape.

Elemental Games

Elemental Uprising

Elemental Wars

Elemental Solution

The Thaw Chronicles

Four tests. Seven days. Nine teens.

Only the chosen shall breed.

Burning (Prequel)

Rising

Breaking

Falling

Reckoning

Extant

Exist

Exile

Expose

Tournaments of Thaw

Conquer the Thaw

The Oasis Trials

The Oasis Deception

The Last Oasis

WANT TO STAY IN TOUCH?

Heidi loves to connect with readers, so please say hello on social media, leave a review on Amazon or Goodreads, or visit her at www.heidicatherine.com

facebook.com/HeidiCatherineAuthor
instagram.com/HeidiCatherine
tiktok.com/@heidicatherineauthor
amazon.com/author/heidicatherine

ABOUT THE AUTHOR

Heidi writes fantasy and dystopian novels, which gives her a chance to escape into worlds vastly different to her own life in the burbs. While she quite enjoys killing her characters (especially the awful ones), she promises she's far better behaved in real life. Other than writing and reading, Heidi's current obsessions include watching far too much reality TV with the excuse that it's research for her books.

www.ingramcontent.com/pod-product-compliance
Lightning Source LLC
Chambersburg PA
CBHW031947240626
47153CB00003B/894